SHADOW OF THE JAGUAR

A LEINE BASSO THRILLER

D.V. BERKOM

ISBN: 978-1-7348599-0-4

1

Dr. Martin Stokes slammed his cup on the rough-hewn table, sloshing coca tea everywhere. The propane lamp danced, threatening to drop off the edge. Outside, a downpour pelted the palm-thatched roof of the mess area, obscuring the impenetrable jungle beyond.

"I said no." He raised his voice above the din and glared at his daughter, Nancy.

Nancy glared back, arms crossed. "I have as much right to the data as you do. Remember who secured the funding for this expedition."

"Just because you found the money doesn't give you the right to exploit the find." Martin closed his eyes and drew a deep breath, trying to tamp down his anger. He never should have allowed her to come along. Her driving need to bring something spectacular back to the university was overshadowing her usual common sense.

"I told you before and I'll tell you again. I am in no way going to exploit your—our find. I will deliberately obscure the location when I publish."

"What happens when the world demands proof of your

discovery?" Martin waited half a beat but didn't let her reply. "I'll tell you what. This spectacular, unspoiled area will be overrun by academics, followed by selfie-obsessed 'eco-tourists,' who will in turn be followed by greedy corporations searching for the next hot destination for the moneyed elite, all while ruining pristine jungle."

Nancy rolled her eyes. "Stop with your holier-than-thou conspiracy theories. Why keep fighting about the same thing? I won't let that happen."

"Did you not hear me? You can't stop it."

She spread her arms wide, encompassing the surrounding rainforest. "I love this place as much as you do. But the results from the LiDAR survey proves the ancient city identified in the conquistador's manuscript may be *nearby*. You can't keep that information to yourself."

Martin waved her comments away and returned to his field laptop. "Famous last words of someone who means well. I promised Taruca that I wouldn't do anything to endanger his tribe's way of life. Your plan will set events in motion that we can't control."

"But Dad—"

"I don't want to argue anymore. Pablo told me this morning the slashing and burning are getting closer. I will not allow your foolishness to destroy any more of this jungle."

"Who's doing the burning?" Nancy's alarmed reaction was too little, too late, as far as Martin was concerned.

"No one's certain. The government won't say, so I can only assume a lot of money has changed hands."

"But don't you see? That makes it even more imperative that we find the lost city." Nancy leaned toward him, both hands on the table. "Before the artifacts are destroyed completely."

"Of course you would think that." Martin shook his head in

disgust. "If you disagree with my stance on the subject, I suggest you go back to Iquitos and take it up with Austen."

"That would take days." Nancy's eyes widened. "You bastard. You'd search for the site without me, wouldn't you?"

Martin didn't respond. There was no point in continuing the conversation. Ever since the LiDAR-equipped drone revealed what appeared to be a large settlement perched high on a cliff with a secondary site partway below it, Nancy had campaigned heavily to go in search of the "lost city."

Austen Newell, the billionaire who was funding their expedition, insisted his intentions were pure. But Martin was all too familiar with the greed that could seize well-meaning philanthropists once they realized what kind of fame and fortune came with a find of this magnitude.

Along with his interest in discovering a lost city, Austen had also told Martin privately that he wanted him to search for what could be the cure for a specific kind of paralysis documented in the 500-year-old manuscript. The billionaire had offered a hefty finder's fee for any information that could lead to a confirmation.

Martin slipped his hand in his pocket and worried the smooth stone of the tiny jaguar statue Taruca had given him. The elder had implored Martin to keep his tribe safe from outside influence and Martin had agreed, even though it directly opposed his mission.

He'd have to persuade his daughter to back away from the discovery, or risk breaking his promise to Taruca.

Nancy let out a frustrated sigh and turned her back to him. It was difficult to make a grand exit during a downpour. There was really nowhere to go except the sleeping platform or the makeshift privy, and getting there was a wet undertaking at the moment. Martin reveled in the isolation of being deep in the Amazon basin.

His daughter, not so much.

He'd been so proud of her when she'd graduated *summa cum laude* with a doctorate in ethnopharmacology. He wished her mother would have been there to witness their little love-bug walking across that stage in all her glory, and again when she won the coveted professorship.

But now Nancy was a creature of academia—that strange, insulated animal that was the bane of Martin's way of thinking. "Publish or perish" wasn't just an old adage. It was an absolute and tended to warp those caught up in the academic system. Sadly, it appeared that his beloved daughter had drunk the Kool-Aid.

The elder's secret changed everything. Martin would search the city, when and if they found it. If what the old man had told him was true, Martin would bring back whatever he could for Austen...

...and destroy the data pointing to the location.

That way he'd keep his promise to Taruca and complete his contract with Newell.

The downpour ended as quickly as it started, leaving in its wake shining wet leaves dripping with runoff. Mud puddles dotted the walkways, the ultimate breeding ground for mosquitos. Martin grabbed the ever-present can of insect repellant off the table and sprayed himself down for the third time that day.

Not that it would help.

He'd never sweated so much as when he was in the jungle. The stifling heat and humidity that gave rise to the number of biting, stinging, and sucking insects impervious to DEET was astounding. Even so, Martin loved everything about the Amazon. The immense diversity nearly stole his breath. Besides, there were always mosquito nets for when it got too bad.

Roughly the size of the contiguous United States and bordered by nine countries, the Amazon basin stretched across a full two-thirds of Peru. The rainforest manufactured twenty percent of the planet's oxygen using barely six percent of land-mass, earning it the nickname "The Lungs of the Planet." The Amazon River was 6400 kilometers long and connected diverse populations despite having few bridges along its entire length.

The lifeblood of a continent.

Unfortunately, the unprecedented rate of destruction perpetuated by foreign and domestic interests endangered everything Martin was there to achieve. Smoke from the fires raging across the basin permeated the air. Some days were so bad, Martin and camp personnel would limit their activity to less physical pursuits. Allowed to remain unchecked, all manner of species, discovered and undiscovered, unknown cures for modern-day maladies, not to mention the very air humankind took for granted, would be destroyed.

Humanity's breathtaking short-sightedness.

Trained as an ethnobotanist, Martin felt it was his responsibility to protect the natural world and indigenous medicinal culture, but he was between a rock and a hard place. Part of him was excited to discover what could be a new civilization and with it the possibility of fulfilling his ultimate promise to Austen. Another part dreaded the outcome. The lost city could hold the answers to so many questions. Answers his daughter Nancy would be more than happy to provide, and for which Austen Newell would pay. Her name and Austen's would become synonymous with the discovery.

Heady stuff.

Nancy left the protection of the mess area and headed for the sleeping platform. At the same time, Mateo materialized from the jungle with a bunch of bananas on his back and headed their direction. He carried a woven bag filled with what Martin assumed were mangoes.

A good haul.

Martin checked his wristwatch. Three o'clock. Time for their daily dose of electricity and a cocktail. Darkness fell early in the jungle. They ran the generator long enough to recharge the laptop and the satellite phone, as well as several lanterns. They'd been using solar panels in a clearing for a portion of their needs and a gas-powered generator for the rest. The gas was running low, making the monthly supply delivery imperative.

Refrigeration was too much of a power drain and he'd switched from his favorite beer to rum. Nancy liked adding fresh mango to her drinks, insisting she didn't miss ice.

Mateo tossed her a freshly picked banana and continued toward the mess area.

"Thanks, Mateo." Nancy shoved the fruit in her pocket as she climbed the ladder to the platform.

Mateo set the bananas on the table and walked over to the generator to start the engine. The rumble of the motor fissured the peaceful setting, reminding Martin why he'd left Los Angeles. True, he missed his brother, Lou, and Lou's wife, Nita, but the thought of going back to the madness of the US left him cold.

Life was so much better here. More alive. More real.

More *vital*.

Martin didn't see, as much as felt, a shift in the surrounding energy. Puzzled, he glanced over his reading glasses at Mateo. The man's body had gone rigid, and a wary look creased his features.

"What's wrong?" Martin asked.

Mateo nodded toward the center of the camp. "We've got company."

Martin pivoted on his stool to see what he was talking about. Several men dressed in camouflage emerged from the jungle and strode to the middle of the encampment. Their faces had been painted black and green to match their clothes. All of them carried automatic rifles.

Commandos? In this part of Peru? Martin hadn't heard of any paramilitary forces nearby. Herberto, Austen's contact in Iquitos, had assured them they wouldn't have any problems.

Apparently Herberto had been wrong.

Martin closed his laptop and walked out to greet them. One man, taller than the rest, strode to the front.

"*Hola, amigos.* What can I do for you gentlemen?" Martin smiled, unsure if they meant them harm. His tiny jungle camp was woefully unprepared for an armed insurrection. They had three machetes, a 9mm pistol, a hunting rifle, and a couple of cleavers.

Not much of a defense.

The tall one smiled, his dark eyes cold in the waning light. "I am here for the treasure," the man said in Spanish.

A wave of alarm swept through Martin. "I'm afraid I don't know what you're talking about."

No one knew about the elder's wild claims except Martin. Taruca had waved off Mateo and two other camp personnel so he could speak with Martin alone. It was then that the elder had told him the miraculous story of the lost city.

"Oh, I think you do." The taller man wagged his finger at Martin.

Martin shook his head. "No, I'm afraid I don't. If you could explain, maybe I could help you. My name is Martin. And you are?"

"I am Dario. And these"—Dario swept his arm in a wide circle, encompassing his men—"are my compadres. I call them *Los Asesinos*—The Killers." Dario grinned again, aiming his rifle at Martin's chest.

Sweat rolled down the sides of Martin's face and his stomach roiled. This was too early in the expedition to have drawn the attention of organized criminals. *How did they find out about our camp?*

"Why don't we sit down, have a cup of tea, and talk about it?" Martin made to move toward the propane stove, intending to put some water on to boil. Five of the six gunmen raised their rifles in unison, aiming their barrels directly at Martin. He froze.

"I am not here for tea."

"I don't want to cause any trouble." Martin raised his hands, his mind scrambling for a way to defuse the situation. He glanced at the sleeping platform but realized too late his mistake.

Dario followed his glance and grinned even wider. "Hello. Who are you?" He walked toward the platform. Eyes wide with fear, Nancy shrank back from the edge, moving out of sight.

Martin stepped forward. "Leave her out of this. She doesn't know anything."

Dario paused, turned back to Martin. "Doesn't know anything about what?"

"You said you were looking for treasure. She doesn't know anything about any treasure."

"But you do?"

Martin tried to swallow but his throat wouldn't comply. "There is no treasure."

"That's not what I heard." Dario moved closer, his hand resting casually on his gun. "I heard that you found something. Something big."

Martin spread his hands wide. "As you see, we have very little. Take what you want and leave."

Dario's eyes flashed in anger. "Enough. Tell me where to find the city. Now."

Had someone in the camp accessed the report? The data on his laptop was password-protected, but he would often leave the program running while he attended to something else.

Martin nervously eyed the rifles pointed at him. "I told you. I don't know what you're talking about."

Dario nodded at his men. "Take the woman."

"No—" Martin stepped toward Dario. Mateo was right behind him.

Dario fired a round into the dirt near Martin's feet. Martin jumped.

"One more step and I won't miss."

"Let. Me. Go." Her panic obvious, Nancy reached for Martin. "Daddy?"

The pleading in her voice speared Martin's heart. He took another step toward her but Mateo grabbed his arm.

"We are outgunned," he said, his voice low.

Martin stood down at the urgency in his voice. He watched helplessly as Dario's men dragged his daughter from the sleeping platform.

Scrambling for something to delay the inevitable, he blurted, "I—I don't have the information right now, but I can get it for you."

Dario smiled. "Then this will help you to get it more quickly." He gestured to his men, who dragged Nancy across camp and melted into the dense foliage.

"What are you doing?" Alarmed, Martin started after the disappearing group.

Dario barred his way forward with the barrel of his gun.

Martin froze. "I just said that I would get you the information."

"So?" Dario cocked his head.

"So let my daughter go."

Dario broke into another grin. "I don't think so. I think that keeping your daughter with us will make you work harder."

"I'll need time."

"You have ten days." Gun raised, Dario walked backward until he reached the edge of the jungle, then disappeared.

Martin's shoulders slumped forward. Mateo was at his side in an instant.

"Are you all right?" he asked.

Martin shook his head. "I let them take her."

"You had no choice."

"But I could have made up something."

Mateo shrugged. "Then they would have found out the truth and become even angrier. I think maybe it's good that you didn't have anything to give them. They would not have left anyone alive."

"What will they do to her?" Martin squeezed his eyes shut as horrific visions of torture filled his mind.

"I don't know," Mateo said. "He gave us ten days. We must come up with a plan."

Martin moved back into the mess area and picked up the satellite phone.

"What are you doing?" Mateo asked.

"Calling for help."

2

The first stanza of *The Godfather* theme played from somewhere underneath the pile of Leine Basso's clothes. She rolled onto her side, taking the bedsheet with her, and scanned the floor.

There. She grabbed the phone peeking out from under her discarded shirt and checked the screen.

Lou.

"Leine here." Her bedmate's hand moved enticingly up her thigh, headed for trouble. She captured his errant fingers and squeezed, hard.

"Leine. It's Lou. I've got a problem. Can you come into the office?"

"Sure." She glanced at the time. "I can be there in half an hour."

"Good. See you then."

Leine ended the call and began to gather her clothes.

"Leaving so soon?"

She turned to look at Santa and her breath caught. The sheet barely covered his hips, exposing muscular shoulders, washboard abs, and a line of curly black hair headed south.

Damn. He still affected her like he did when they first met. Shaking it off, she nodded. "Lou needs me."

Santa leaned back against the pillow and pulled off the sheet. His dark eyes pierced her with a look that melted her to her toes. "I need you, too."

She shrugged on her shirt and the rest of her clothes, then readjusted the knife in her ankle sheath. The shoulder holster went on last, the 9mm Sig nestled snugly against her left armpit.

A girl needed to accessorize.

Leine sighed. "You know this was a mistake, right?"

"What? Last night? Or this morning?"

She paused for a moment as she zipped her slacks. Her mouth was as dry as a pile of fallen leaves. "Definitely the tequila. But yeah, this." She gestured at both of them. "We made a pact. No more hooking up."

Santiago "Santa" Jensen was lead detective for the Robbery Homicide Division of the Los Angeles Police Department and the love of Leine's life. Unfortunately, the LAPD tended to frown on its homicide detectives fraternizing with former off-book assassins. It didn't help that Santa disagreed with Leine's tendency to go vigilante on the scumbags that trafficked young men and women.

Go figure.

Santa rolled onto his side, grabbed a pack of cigarettes, and shook one out.

"I wish you wouldn't do that." Leine hated that he'd started smoking. He took it up after they broke it off the first time. Apparently he'd been a smoker several years ago but quit before they met.

"You just told me what we did was wrong. Now you want to tell me what to do?" He lit up and exhaled a cloud of blue smoke.

Leine waved at the air as she grabbed her handbag. "Fine. Do what you want. Just don't kiss me with that mouth."

"I can do all kinds of things with my mouth."

"And I expect that to continue."

Santa grinned. "I thought we had a pact."

Leine returned the smile. "Pacts are made to be broken."

LEINE WALKED THROUGH THE DOUBLE GLASS DOORS INTO THE SHEN reception area and waved at the woman sitting behind the front desk. SHEN stood for Stop Human Enslavement Now, the organization Leine worked with to help bring justice to the victims of human trafficking.

"Hey, Brigitte."

Brigitte smiled and waved back. "He's waiting for you in room three."

"Thanks." Leine proceeded down the long hallway past interview rooms one and two, stopping at room three. Lou stood in front of the large monitor, which projected the live image of a man who looked vaguely familiar.

"Here she is," Lou said. "Leine Basso, this is Austen Newell—I'm sure you've heard of him."

Leine nodded at Austen and set her bag on the table. "I have, yes. Good to meet you."

"Likewise."

A wealthy financier from New York, Austen Newell had gotten his start at his father's private equity company. At the age of twenty-seven he'd been christened Wall Street's wunderkind for his uncanny ability to read the market and soon became the head of one of the largest hedge funds in the world. At the age of thirty-five he'd cashed in and traveled, searching for places and industries to invest in and leaving death-defying stories of derring-do in his wake. While trekking through South America five years ago, he'd contracted a rare form of paralysis and was unable to continue his adventures. Frustrated, he began funding expeditions to remote areas, living vicariously through the men and women he supported.

Austen's intense expression reminded Leine of her old boss, Eric. His smooth complexion and lack of wrinkles belied his middle age, as did his reddish-blond hair. Lou, on the other hand, didn't look well. The bags under his eyes and the gray cast to his face screamed of a sleepless night.

"What can I do for you gentlemen?" she asked.

Lou leaned forward and put his hands on the conference table. "My niece has been abducted."

"Nancy?" Leine had met Nancy and her father, Martin, several times before at various get-togethers—the Stokes family was close. "Where did it happen?"

"My brother's camp in the Amazon."

Leine turned toward the screen. Austen's face loomed large on the screen. "How do you know Martin and Nancy?"

"I'm financing Martin's expedition in the Amazon basin. Nancy was adamant about joining him there. I should never have agreed."

"Had there been threats against them prior to the start of the expedition?"

Austen shook his head. "That's why this is so bizarre. The area where the camp is based is considered among some of the least dangerous in terms of criminal activity. Obviously, the jungle itself isn't a walk in the park. Nancy said she was comfortable with the risks."

"Do we know who took her? Have they made their demands?" Leine looked from Austen to Lou.

"Martin said the head kidnapper's name is Dario," Lou said.

"He gave Martin ten days to find the location of some mythical lost city."

"So I'm going to ask the obvious question here. Does Martin know what the guy's talking about?"

Lou glanced at Austen. "He says he doesn't have a clue. Austen thinks differently."

Austen shifted in his chair. "The expedition came across a tribe of natives that had rarely been in contact with the modern world. The elder, or chieftain I guess you'd call him, mentioned a mythical place not far from their encampment. A lost city. Martin dismissed the man's story as myth. I don't."

"How did this Dario find out about their conversation?" Leine asked.

"It's possible someone in the group managed to contact Dario and tell him what they'd heard," Austen offered. "Otherwise we don't know."

"Is there a way to find out if the city exists?"

Austen nodded. "The expedition is equipped with a LiDAR-capable drone. But even if the tech came back with no evidence of this lost city, I doubt it would deter these thugs."

"I've heard of LiDAR," Leine said, "but I have to confess I don't know much about the technology."

"It uses a combination of laser light pulses to penetrate and map densely forested areas. It's a game-changer when it comes to charting inhospitable areas."

"So either way, if Martin were to use this drone to find or not find what the chieftain mentioned, Nancy's life is in danger."

"Exactly," Lou replied.

"What would you like me to do?"

"I need you to go to South America." Lou typed something into his laptop and turned the computer toward her. The screen displayed a satellite image of dense jungle surrounding what appeared to be a rustic camp. "And find Nancy."

Austen added, "Lou tells me you're the best at locating people. Spare no expense. Take whatever you need. I've arranged for your transportation to the camp. You can leave tomorrow."

"Any backup?" Although used to doing things on her own, a jungle op with trained professionals would be preferable.

"I called in a marker or two," Lou answered. "There's a team of six on their way to the camp as we speak."

"Anybody I know?"

Lou shook his head. "Not on short notice. I ended up putting together a team from scratch. They all come highly recommended."

"That works. Can you have the doc call in a prescription for antimalarial meds?" Leine picked up her handbag and prepared to leave.

Lou handed her a thumb drive. "Here's all the information."

"Thanks."

"There's one last thing."

"What's that?"

The door opened and April walked in. She smiled at the men and nodded at Leine. "Hey, Mom."

"Hey, kiddo."

In her mid-twenties, April had gone from world vagabond to aspiring novelist to one of the best mentors at the new SHEN academy—she currently taught self-defense to new recruits. Leine always marveled at how her daughter seemed to have inherited the best of both her mother and father: she was tall and athletic and had dark, flowing auburn hair and green eyes like her mother. She also tempered the optimism of youth with her mother's pragmatic outlook. Coupled with her father's razor-sharp ability to analyze people and situations, she was a force to be reckoned with.

"I'd like you to take April along," Lou said. "She needs to get out of LA, experience something other than bad traffic and smog."

"I've worked jobs in Greece, Scotland, England, and France. What the hell is wrong with sending her to any one of those places?"

"C'mon, Mom. It's the *Amazon*."

"You know what it's like there, right?" Leine asked her. "Hot and humid, with bugs the size of Volkswagens?" Not to mention dangerous gunmen who'd kidnapped a university professor.

April rolled her eyes. "Yes, of course I know. Martin's a friend of mine too, and so is Nancy. I want to help find her."

Leine studied her. "There's something else at work here."

"Well, there is the whole Amazon thing," April replied, her excitement obvious. "Being able to see one of the most magnificent places on earth before it's destroyed by human activity is the chance of a lifetime. Besides," she smiled at Leine, "I get to spend more time with you."

Leine smiled back. Quite a change from all those years before when she and April had been estranged. "It's going to be dangerous. I'm not just talking about poisonous snakes and spiders. Those men were armed. And you'll need to get shots— yellow fever, Hep A and B, typhoid..."

April crossed her arms. "Really? You're going to play the 'dangerous' card? I'm as trained as you were when Eric sent you on your first assignment. I'm also years older." Eric had been Leine's boss at the Agency—an off-book government-sanctioned group of elite assassins. He'd discovered Leine as a teenager at a firing range in Southern California shortly after her father died, learning to shoot every weapon she could get her hands on.

Suffice it to say, she'd had some anger issues. Eric identified and used that anger and trained her to become an elite assassin. He was also April's father.

Which April didn't know.

"And I've already had my shots." April grinned at Lou.

Leine was about to protest when she caught Lou's eye. She knew by his look that he was going to send someone with her, whether it was her daughter or another operative. Leine didn't have the heart to argue with him—Martin was his family. She would have liked to break April in on a less dangerous op, but she realized this was a gift. She'd be able to watch April, make sure she followed instructions, help season her. If not, she could always send her back. Harsh, maybe, but if her daughter didn't toe the line, she could put them both in danger. Leine treated all operatives the same—family or not. Her first job was to keep both herself and the team alive to do what was required.

"Are you all right with that, Austen?" Leine asked.

"Absolutely," Austen replied. "I've already taken care of her travel arrangements. You'll both be on the same flight."

Leine nodded. "Be sure to pack light. Add some netting and plenty of DEET. I'll take care of the rest."

The excitement on April's face was a reward Leine hadn't anticipated. She hoped the trip would be a good experience.

Jungle operations rarely were.

A pril pressed her face to the window of the airplane and pointed at the brown river snaking through dense jungle below them.

"Is that the Amazon?" she asked, the excitement in her voice palpable.

Leine glanced out the same window. "That's it."

"Cool."

They were about to land in Iquitos, Peru. The two-hour flight from Lima had been uneventful, and Leine had enjoyed April's running commentary on the scenery below them.

Truth be told, Leine wasn't looking forward to the intense heat and humidity of the jungle. Exhaustion, heatstroke, and dehydration were real dangers, especially when they were required to hike through mud, rain, and dense forest.

Austen Newell had arranged for his business partner, Herberto Rodriguez, to meet them at the airport and shuttle them both to the hotel. They'd spend the night then take a fast boat to where Martin's employee, Mateo, would be waiting. From there, he would take them by motorized canoe down a lesser-known tributary farther into the basin, where they'd disembark and hike several miles through the rainforest to Martin's camp.

Leine and April had packed waterproof hiking boots and extra socks, a UV water purifier, mosquito netting, bungee cords, ponchos that could be used as impromptu shelters, and enough insect repellant to handle a cockroach apocalypse. Sunscreen and other necessities, like malaria pills and a first aid kit, took up precious room in their carry-on baggage at the expense of other comforts. Leine wasn't concerned with looking stylish or being comfortable.

She was concerned with survival.

The plane landed and Leine and April filed out with the other passengers. Leine took in a breath of hot, humid air.

Ahh. There's nothing quite like the jungle.

"Holy crap." April's eyes widened in alarm. "I can...hardly breathe."

"You'll get used to it."

They walked through the airport and out the front doors. A slender dark-haired man wearing a white baseball cap and holding a placard that read "Basso" stood out in the stream of tourists.

The two women walked over to him. Leine held out her hand. "I'm Leine Basso."

The man, who looked to be in his late twenties or early thirties, lowered the placard. He bowed and shook her hand. "*Mucho gusto,* Leine Basso. I am Juan. Mr. Rodriguez sent me to take you to your hotel." Juan gestured to their bags. "With your permission, I will take your luggage to the car."

"That won't be necessary," Leine said.

"Very well. Follow me, please." Tucking the placard under his arm, he headed into the scorching midday sun. Leine and April shouldered their backpacks and followed him to a white SUV.

"You must be tired, yes? I will take you to the hotel where you can refresh yourselves and rest. Mr. Rodriguez would like you both to join him later this evening for dinner."

"We'd be happy to. When does Mr. Rodriguez normally eat?" A late *cena* would give her plenty of time to do what she needed in town.

"He will call for you at eight thirty."

"Perfect."

Leine took the passenger seat, and April sat in the back. Juan raced past lush green palms, colorfully painted buildings, fast-moving motorbikes and tuk tuks—motorized rickshaws that wove in and out of traffic with death-defying ease—reminding Leine of the drivers in Thailand and India. The air conditioning in the car was a welcome respite from the intense humidity outside.

They arrived at the hotel half an hour later. Leine checked them in, and they went up to their room. Their footsteps on the tiled floors echoed along the empty hallway.

April dropped her things on the bed closest to the window and sprawled across the mattress.

"I'm beat. I think I'll clean up and take a short nap."

"Sounds good," Leine said, putting her bag on the chair. "I've got a couple of errands to run."

April sat up. "Do you want me to come along?"

"Relax. There'll be time to see Iquitos later when we're through with the op."

"Okay." She dropped back onto the mattress with a sigh. "I think the heat really took it out of me."

Leine grabbed her backpack and left.

Forty-five minutes later, the tuk tuk pulled up next to a two-story colonial building with a rusted metal roof.

"Can you wait?" she asked in Spanish. The driver nodded.

Leine exited the motorized rickshaw and walked to the front door. Her knock brought an older woman dressed in brightly colored traditional Peruvian clothing. She wore her gray hair pulled back in a tight bun.

"I'm here to see Nestor. My name is Leine Basso."

The older woman nodded and motioned for Leine to enter.

Inside was cool and dark, benefitting from thick plaster walls and tall windows shuttered against the afternoon sun.

"Come."

The woman led Leine down a narrow hallway through a courtyard with a nonfunctioning fountain, to a large room near the back.

"Wait here."

The woman disappeared. Leine set her pack down on a nearby chair and studied the room. Ancient wood furniture dominated the furnishings along with a plastic table and chairs. Chipped green and yellow paint flecked the walls, mirroring the cracked tile floor. The scent of mildew clung to the air, a token of the ever-present damp in the tropics. Movement caught her eye as a large black beetle scurried along the crack between the floor and the wall.

A moment later a man with salt-and-pepper hair walked into the room. He wiped his hands on a towel, which he draped over the back of a plastic chair.

"May I help you?" he asked.

"Nestor?"

The man nodded.

"I'm Leine Basso. Lou Stokes contacted you regarding a package for me?"

Nestor lifted his chin in acknowledgement. "How is Lou? It's been a long time since I heard from him. I was led to believe he retired years ago."

His friendly, seemingly innocuous question was actually the first half of a pre-arranged code to ensure each person was the intended participant. She responded with the equally innocuous, "It's been over ten years since he left. He's head of an anti-trafficking organization in the States."

"Ah. And this is why you are in Peru?"

"Not exactly. But it's related."

Nestor nodded. "Your order is ready. I'll be back in a moment. Please, make yourself at home."

Nestor vanished into the back, and Leine sat down to wait. The woman from the front door returned, carrying a tray with a glass of *limonada*. Leine thanked her and took the drink. The woman disappeared down a hallway, leaving Leine alone with her thoughts.

Back in the day, Leine had run several ops for the Agency throughout Central and South America. Criminals and terrorists would be sorely tempted to find a more fertile playground. Latin America boasted a seemingly infinite coastline, densely forested mountains, hidden airstrips, and loosely patrolled borders. Widespread government corruption fueled powerful narco-traffickers and terrorist organizations like Hezbollah, all of which contributed to the illicit flow of weapons, drugs, and people.

Not exactly a vacation paradise. But Leine was jaded. She'd had the veil of innocence ripped away at an early age. The world was a scary place.

Sometimes she really missed that veil.

A short time later, Nestor returned carrying a large duffle bag and set it on the floor in front of her. Leine leaned over, unzipped the bag, and peered inside. The contents were as requested: fragmentation grenades, a mini Uzi, a combat knife, two 9mm pistols, extra mags and ammunition, two pairs of night vision goggles, binoculars, plastic zip ties, a radio antenna, and two radios with ear mics. Along with the satellite phone and first aid kit she'd brought with her, she and April would be well-equipped.

"This will do nicely. Thank you, Nestor. I trust Lou made the necessary financial arrangements?"

Nestor nodded. "The wire came just this morning." He paused for a moment. "If I may make a friendly suggestion?"

"Of course."

"I do not know why you are here, but I do know that when Herberto Rodriguez is involved, one needs to be careful."

"Could you be more specific?" She hadn't said anything about Herberto to Nestor. Lou had either mentioned something to him, or Nestor had an effective spy network. Most likely the latter.

"He is a very powerful man. Someone who is connected in many ways to both good and bad actors. People go to him when they have problems that are difficult to fix."

"What makes you think Rodriguez is involved?"

"I make it my business to know everything that goes on in Iquitos." Nestor shrugged. "I deal with many different people. Preparedness is one of the staples of my business. My survival depends on it."

"Thank you for the warning." Leine picked up her pack and the duffel bag. "And for your services."

Nestor showed her through the courtyard and the front of the house to the tuk tuk waiting outside. She climbed in and Nestor leaned through the opening.

"Be very careful."

"I will, Nestor. *Muchas gracias* for the warning."

Nestor stepped back from the tuk tuk, and the driver pulled away from the curb. Leine settled back in her seat, pondering

Nestor's words. Two warnings in the same meeting. Not something a man like Nestor would waste time with unless he had a good reason.

Herberto Rodriguez was far more than just a friendly acquaintance of Austen Newell's.

4

Austen Newell studied the scanned document on his computer screen for what he calculated to be the hundredth time. No matter how many passes he made over the manuscript, he came up with the same questions.

His fluency in Spanish notwithstanding, the conquistador's cryptic remarks hinted at a discovery never seen before or since.

Was it merely wishful thinking?

Austen shifted in his state-of-the-art wheelchair. If what the Spaniard wrote was true, if Martin's expedition had actually found the lost city cited in the manuscript, then he was that much closer to a cure.

He returned to the passage that had the more compelling of the two descriptions detailing Fernando Valenzuela Hidalgo III's encounter with the mysterious people of the City of Clouds.

"Several of the inhabitants crowded round me as I lay among them, touching my clothes and armor. Their fascination with my facial hair would have been amusing, were it not for my current state. It was as if I were the miracle, not they. How could I express my amazement at what my guide had told me transpired in this singular

city of lost souls? The residents of this mysterious City of Clouds were hale and hearty, with no visible afflictions.

"But my guide insisted every last one had been seized with the same maleficent infirmity as what had also laid me low, that which brought me to them now, in my darkest hour."

Austen closed his eyes, imagining the proud conquistador, afflicted by the same disease as the one ravaging Austen Newell's body, leaving him weaker than a newborn from the waist down.

Dozens of tests and operations later, and still the doctors couldn't agree on what caused Austen's deteriorating condition. He'd been close, he thought, when he'd gone for a consultation in Lima with an expert in South American jungle diseases. The physician explained that Austen had most likely contracted a parasite while traveling through the Amazon. But this particular parasite was a master of disguise and would hide within Austen's own cells, mimicking his DNA, tricking the drugs and other medical protocols into seeing healthy DNA, destroying all hope of finding a cure.

Austen clicked on the next page and continued reading.

"After giving me a cup of an unpleasant mixture of herbs to drink, they took me to a room lined with amazing stones—some blue as the sky, others deep green like the surrounding forest, still more with streaks as black as night. Sunlight shone through them, their hue lending the room a most calming demeanor. I imagined Christ's own angels coming down from on high to inhabit the place.

"Peculiar carvings on the walls were of the natural world, with snakes, and frogs, and ants being in the majority. The animals had eyes of precious stones, all of differing fineness. The value of the room itself would be priceless if ever this city is found again, once I am gone."

The manuscript went on to describe a strange ritual performed in that room by what Hidalgo had been assured was a shaman of some renown. The details were sparse, with Hidalgo himself apologizing for his lapse in memory:

"My misfortune is such that I cannot remember the words or incantations, nor the type of herbs used in the ceremony. My guide complained of a deleterious effect on his memory throughout the ceremony, described as that of a mist enshrouding his mind. Although, once the ritual was concluded, both he and I regained our normal clear thinking, and I the miraculous use of my legs."

Austen sighed. No matter how many times he read Hidalgo's words, he couldn't parse their meaning into anything remotely relevant to a cure for his disease.

Was the stone room the key to his miraculous recovery? Or the drink given to Hidalgo prior to the ceremony? Perhaps the herbs used in combination with the liquid given to him plus the magnetic vibration of the stones and Hidalgo's heartfelt belief in the efficacy of the ritual were what cured him.

Frustrated, Austen wheeled away from his desk, the weight of the unknown heavy in his heart. Up to now, the paralysis had been arrested at his lower spine, but recent tests concluded this wasn't the case anymore. Austen's mobility had eroded, due to the incessant weakness marching up his vertebrae. The doctors had given him a prognosis of little more than six months.

Could his paralysis be neurological in nature? Could a belief in healing be enough to move his body to overcome the debilitating weakness? Part of him yearned for a simple explanation, wanted to believe mind over matter to be true. The other, more pragmatic part of him had decided that he would exhaust all avenues to find the cure, no matter the cost or the effort required. The irony of being one of the world's wealthiest people unable to buy time or health wasn't lost on him.

Austen rolled over to a lighted case on a stand near the center of the room. There, in the spotlight of the temperature-

and humidity-controlled box, lay Hidalgo's actual manuscript, open to the page describing the ritual. He stared at the yellowed pages and the small, neatly drawn handwriting of the conquistador, willing its secrets to reveal themselves to him.

Martin had to find the lost city—or Austen would die.

———

5

April and Leine were waiting for Juan in the lobby of their hotel when Herberto's SUV arrived to pick them up. Juan exited the vehicle and opened the rear passenger doors for them.

"Where's Mr. Rodriguez?" Leine asked.

"He sends his apologies. He has been delayed, but will meet you both at the restaurant."

Leine gave April a look as they climbed inside. She'd relayed Nestor's warning and given her daughter one of the 9mm pistols with two full magazines. She armed herself with the same, in addition to the combat knife.

Juan pulled away from the hotel and merged into evening traffic. Leine surreptitiously checked the side mirror as April played tourist and looked out the back and side windows, adding a running commentary. It was a good ruse, allowing her to check for surveillance without giving Juan cause for concern.

"How far is the restaurant?" April asked him.

"Not far. Maybe ten minutes."

There didn't appear to be anyone following them, but Herberto knew where they were headed and could have someone waiting. Her senses on edge, Nestor's warning replayed in her mind.

They arrived without incident. A white-coated maître d' ushered Leine and April into the elegant dining room and past several white linen-covered tables and well-heeled diners to a four-top at the back. The stocky man seated at the table rose at their approach, his face beaming.

"It is good to finally meet you," he gushed, bowing first over April's hand and then Leine's. "I am Herberto Rodriguez." He gestured for them to sit. "I am so sorry for my inexcusable absence." A great sigh emanated from him and he shook his head. "Business. There is always something that must be attended to, yes?"

Leine smiled. "I hope we aren't keeping you from anything."

"Of course not. How could I not enjoy hosting two beautiful women for dinner?"

A waiter appeared at the table. Herberto murmured something to him. The waiter nodded and left.

"I hope you don't mind, but I took the liberty of ordering the wine." He leaned over and added, "Good wines can be hit or miss in Iquitos." He shrugged. "Part of the challenge of being a city accessible only by air or water."

A few moments later the waiter arrived with the wine—a lovely Malbec. Herberto guided them through the menu, offering suggestions and laughing at April's remarks. Leine studied him closely, searching for signs of nervousness or deception, but he was either being genuine or he was a very good actor.

After what Nestor told her, she assumed the latter.

The meal was better than Leine had anticipated having in such an isolated city, and Herberto proved to be an amiable and astute dinner companion. Leine could tell April was charmed, which was likely what he'd intended. It wasn't until dessert had been served that the conversation came around to the reason Leine and April were in Iquitos.

Herberto's expression became grave. "I do not know who it is that has captured Martin's daughter, but there are many lawless bandits who operate in the rainforest. Smugglers have their own routes through which they move their products, be it guns, drugs, or human beings. I fear Martin has disrupted one of these routes with the location of his camp, and in doing so has awakened a hornet's nest."

"This is disappointing," Leine replied. "I was hoping you might have an idea of who these people are. Your reputation in Iquitos is well known."

Herberto shrugged and spread his hands. "Normally, I would be able to find out something that would be helpful. Iquitos is a small community. But the *pendejos* who took the professor are not known to me or my associates. I'm sorry I cannot help you."

The waiter stopped at the table and asked if they would like some espresso. Leine and April declined. Herberto accepted a demitasse.

There was a loud crash near the entrance. Leine tensed and reached for her sidearm. Three masked gunmen swarmed through the front door.

"On the floor!" one of the gunmen yelled, sweeping the barrel of his assault rifle over the room. A woman screamed but abruptly stopped when a second gunman aimed his weapon at her. She dropped to the floor next to her companion, weeping softly.

"We must do as he says," Herberto hissed and slid off his chair onto the floor. Leine signaled for April to take cover behind a support column to their left, while she sprinted for one on the right, behind a large potted palm.

Clearly alarmed, Herberto mouthed, "What are you doing?" at Leine. She put her finger to her lips and turned her attention to the gunmen. Her back to Herberto, she slid the 9mm free of its holster and waited. April did the same.

Two of the gunmen split up, and each took a side of the restaurant, going table to table, demanding wallets, purses, and other valuables. The third gunman remained at the door as overwatch.

The gunman closest to their table barked orders at patrons, each of whom filled a bag with valuables. Leine waited until both she and April had a bead on both gunmen before she gave her daughter a slight nod. The two women opened fire, dropping both masked men simultaneously. Screams erupted from the frightened diners. Panicked, several people sprang to their feet and ran. Pandemonium spread as more diners did the same. The third gunman dove for cover behind a giant potted palm.

Taking advantage of the confusion, Leine moved along the perimeter, headed for the maître d's station. As she rounded the pillar near the reception area, the third gunman popped up, aimed his rifle directly at Herberto's table, but hesitated. Leine fired, hitting him in the head. He crumpled to the floor, his rifle still in his hand.

Leine shot him twice more, ensuring he was dead. The maître d's eyes widened in fear and he held up his hands.

"Please, *senora*, I have a family."

"Are there more gunmen?" Leine asked, ignoring his pleas.

"More? No. I have not seen anyone other than these three...men."

Leine gave him a curt nod. Adrenaline raced through her veins. "Make sure everyone gets out safely. And call the police," she added, heading back to where Herberto had climbed onto his chair. He appeared stunned. April joined them, her gun no longer visible.

"We could have died." He glanced at both Leine and April. "I am grateful to you. I had no idea you were armed. How did you come by your weapons?"

Leine ignored his question. "We should probably leave before the police get here."

Herberto nodded as he stood. "There is a back door."

Juan raced through the front doors and hustled to his boss's side. "Are you all right, *jefe*?"

Herberto frowned and pushed him away. "Yes, yes. I'm fine. I would not be if it wasn't for these two ladies." He waved at Leine and April. "Thank goodness they were armed." A look passed between the two men, but it was too brief for Leine to decode.

Was it anger? Frustration? At whom? Her and April? At Juan for not being present when the gunmen showed up?

He and Juan led the way through the kitchen, past the sous chefs and other staff. Leine trailed behind, wary of trusting Herberto. Had he staged the robbery? He hadn't seemed very happy about Leine and April having pistols, even though they'd neutralized the gunmen. Yes, his reaction could be attributed to garden-variety Latin American chauvinism rearing its ugly head, but Leine didn't think so. She was pretty sure he'd been trying to kill them.

The only question was why.

6

Early the next morning, Leine and April were packed and waiting outside the lobby of their hotel. They discarded the idea of changing their room to a different floor. If Herberto was as connected as Nestor suggested, the room change would most likely have been reported, signaling to the fixer that Leine had suspicions. Leine and April had taken turns keeping watch—four hours on and four off—in case Herberto decided to try again.

Luckily, he had no idea Leine had procured additional firepower, giving him even more reason to underestimate them. Still, she'd have to remain vigilant. The initial boat ride to the rendezvous point with Austen's man, Mateo, would be rife with opportunities to kill them both—with few witnesses. She'd called Lou, and he secured another boat leaving much earlier than the one Herberto had hired.

Their tuk tuk arrived and parked curbside. Leine and April climbed in the back with their bags. A short time later, they arrived at the normally bustling market. Stall owners were just setting up for the day as they walked past to the debarkation area. Several two- and three-story boats stood side by side, with smaller motorized riverboats interspersed between them.

Leine and April walked to one of the smaller vessels with the name *Amazonia II* emblazoned in chipped paint across its bow. The mate stowed their bags as Leine and April climbed aboard and took seats underneath the palm-thatched roof. A few other passengers boarded, and the captain got underway.

If Herberto had been trying to kill them, she didn't think he'd stop with the robbery at the restaurant. She assumed Juan would alert him to their non-appearance that morning, so she'd have to keep watch for a tail.

The million-dollar question now was why did he want them dead? According to Lou and Austen, he was Austen's man on the ground in Peru. Leine glanced at April, who hadn't mentioned anything about the man she'd killed at the restaurant the night before.

People reacted in different ways to traumatic events. She'd have to keep an eye on her.

The heat rose with the sun, but the slight breeze off the river cooled temperatures to a manageable level. April dozed in the shade, while Leine flipped through her daughter's field guide with chapters devoted to medicinal plants of the Amazon.

The trip itself would take the better part of a day. Their first stop would be near a tributary at a wide spot in the jungle with a long wooden dock its only claim to fame. There, Leine and April would meet up with Martin's assistant, Mateo, who would take them along the tributary farther into the jungle to another spot where the main trail began. They'd make camp there then begin their hike into the jungle early the next morning. With good weather, they'd be at Martin's camp in three days. That left little time to find Nancy before the kidnapper's deadline.

Austen had suggested they fly part of the way in, but the recent heavy rains made landing a helicopter difficult at best, if they could even find a clearing large enough. Although they could fast-rope down once they reached the main objective, the noise factor would pre-announce their arrival for miles. That didn't, however, preclude Herberto hiring one to find them, or possibly sending another boat to the rendezvous point.

The duffel bag of weapons at Leine's feet gave her some peace of mind.

A few hours into their journey, one of the other passengers pointed toward the horizon. Something was coming toward them. Moments later, a half-dozen pink dolphins sliced through the water next to them. They played at the bow for a while, diving under and racing the boat, before peeling away and heading off in another direction. April had roused from her nap in time to see them, and she laughed delightedly with the rest of the passengers.

A short time later, the unmistakable *thwap* of a helicopter echoed through the air. Leine swiveled in her seat and scanned the horizon behind them.

The black spot of the chopper grew larger, obviously headed their way. She leaned closer to April and said, "Put on your hat." They already wore sunglasses. Leine rummaged inside her pack and pulled out a long-sleeved shirt, which she shrugged on. April did the same. "I'm going to sit up near the bow. If it's Herberto, he's looking for two women together."

"We could hide."

Leine shook her head. "The other passengers would be suspicious. Just act like everyone else. Don't shy away, but keep your face turned."

April nodded and pulled her hat low. The oversized shirt and sunglasses disguised her well.

Leine tucked her hair underneath her hat, picked up the duffel bag, and moved to a vacant spot at the front of the boat. Moments later, the helicopter roared past, then looped back and circled the boat, low and slow. She shaded her eyes against the gleam of the cockpit's glass, trying to make out the man flying the aircraft. The pilot didn't look familiar, but the glimpse she got of the passenger next to him bore a resemblance to Herberto's guy, Juan.

The chopper made a second circuit, kicking up spray. The captain eased back on the throttle, slowing their progress, and waited for them to leave. Leine turned away at the last minute and mimicked the other passengers in the boat, expressing surprise to her seatmates. April followed her lead and acted like a curious onlooker.

The downdraft from the helicopter's blades made controlling the boat difficult. The captain yelled at the aircraft and attempted to wave them off. Leine inched the duffel bag closer.

The aircraft pivoted and roared upriver.

Leine waited until they were out of range before she made her way back to her daughter.

"Did you see who it was?" April asked.

"Pretty sure Juan was in the passenger seat." She set the duffel bag on the floor.

"So Herberto is looking for us."

Leine nodded.

"Do they know where we're headed?"

"In a general sense, yes. But not the exact rendezvous point." Thankfully, Lou had followed operational protocol, keeping those in the loop to a bare minimum.

They'd still need to stay vigilant.

The sun had just begun to sink below the trees when the riverboat glided up to the dilapidated wooden dock, pulling in next to an even more dilapidated-looking motorized canoe. There were no other boats nearby. Bats swooped and dove over the surface of the river hunting insects as a chorus of frogs croaked their discordant song.

The only person in sight, an attractive younger man with dark hair, assisted the crew in docking the riverboat. He smiled and helped April and Leine from the vessel, then took their bags as the captain handed them off.

"I am Mateo." Mateo carried himself with the ease of the young and good-looking. He shook hands with them both before transferring their backpacks and duffel bag to the other boat.

"How far is it to the next stop?" Leine asked.

"A few hours."

"It's going to be dark soon."

Mateo smiled. "The river is beautiful at night."

April gave Leine a look that said she didn't exactly trust him to get them to their destination. Leine shrugged. Her analytical daughter would have to get used to winging it if she wanted to be in the field. Adapting to conditions on the ground was one of the aspects of fieldwork that Leine enjoyed most. Nothing got her blood pumping more than being able to solve operational puzzles in time to move on to the next.

Mateo handed them each a canteen, then helmed the outboard motor, steering them along the narrowing river past few other watercraft. At first, clusters of elevated huts could be seen through the trees, but those thinned out the farther into the Amazon they traveled.

The time just before sunset is that magical moment when normally shy animals come out to feed. Clouds of mosquitos danced over the calm water as snowy egrets launched into the air, startled by the boat's passing. Countless insects buzzed as frogs chirped and sang along with macaws and a cacophony of other birds, filling the air with sound. The sky turned a brilliant orange-red, deepening to indigo. Mateo steered into a smaller tributary, slowing the boat as he did.

"April, could you operate the spotlight on the bow?" Mateo asked.

"Sure. Where do you want me to direct the beam?"

"Make a sweep of the area in front and to the sides, and watch for any debris that could damage the boat, like floating logs."

"Aye-aye, captain." April saluted and made her way to the bow, where she flicked on the gimbaled light, casting a wide, bright beam across the deceptively calm water. Several minutes later, the last of the sunlight faded.

The temperature dropped a bit, but the humidity remained. Leine joined her daughter at the bow.

"What is that?" April asked, swinging the light toward two small bright spots near the river bank. The bright spots belonged to the eyes of a black caiman, an ancient resident of the Amazon. The alligator-like reptile submerged into the watery depths as they sped by.

"That was so cool." April swung the light slowly back and forth across the front of the bow, lingering on the riverbank.

"Maybe you will see a jaguar." Mateo smiled, his teeth visible in the darkness.

"Won't the motor scare them away?" April asked.

"Would you like me to turn it off?"

"Are you certain it will start again?" April asked.

Leine smiled. She got the sense her daughter was only half teasing.

Mateo laughed. "Maybe you're right. I will keep it on. For now."

They saw several more caimans and a family of capybaras— a large, rodent-like animal.

"The capybara is a relative of the guinea pig, and a particular favorite of the jaguar," Mateo said.

"So wherever you see a capybara, a jaguar might not be far behind?" April asked.

"Yes. This is possible. They are quite good to eat."

"Aww. They're so cute. How could you eat one?"

Leine touched her daughter on the arm. "Want to take a break?"

"Sure. I'm going to go back and talk to Mateo for a bit."

"Have fun. But keep your eyes open."

April nodded. "I will."

Leine swept the light back and forth, checking the murky river for floating logs and anything else that might put a hole in their canoe. She didn't relish the idea of swimming for shore in a river full of caimans and poisonous snakes. Above them, brilliant stars twinkled against an inky backdrop. Leine never grew tired of the night sky in areas far from the light pollution of the city—and missed it terribly when she was in LA. The thought of relocating crossed her mind, and not for the first time.

A few hours later, Mateo instructed Leine to direct the light to the bank on their left. A sandy shoreline with a gap in the forest materialized. He throttled back and cut the engine as they drifted onto the sand. Leine leapt from the boat with the bowline in hand, and April handed her their packs.

Mateo threw the last of the cargo onto the riverbank and jumped out of the boat. He helped Leine pull the canoe farther up onto shore, where he tied the line to a tree.

"We will hike for a bit and then make camp. We leave at first light."

"Sounds good," Leine said. She and April shouldered their packs.

Mateo slipped behind a palm tree and reemerged with walking sticks he'd obviously stashed. He then reached inside his gear for three headlamps, two of which he offered to Leine and April.

"Thanks, but we brought our own." Leine opened the duffel bag to retrieve the night vision goggles and handed April a pair. They both slid them on.

With a nod, he donned the headlamp, then hoisted the massive pack before striking off into the jungle at a brisk pace.

The pungent smell of damp earth and greenery accompanied them along the rough-cut trail. Animal sounds echoed through the impossibly dark night, serenading them as they walked. Mateo led, with April in the middle, while Leine brought up the rear. The going was slow. Eerie sounds filled the air, and April kept her head on a swivel, obviously nervous. Mateo warned them to beware of the roots and other obstacles in their path. Humidity and sucking mud dogged their every step. A couple of hours in, Leine could see that April was struggling.

"How much farther, Mateo?" Leine called.

"Not much longer," he said over his shoulder.

The rumble of thunder in the distance and the scent of ozone told Leine they were about to get very wet. She stopped and fished out her poncho. April and Mateo did the same.

"Cover your packs," Mateo suggested.

They pulled their ponchos over their heads, making sure to cover their backpacks with the waterproof fabric.

A moment later, there was a loud *crack*, followed by a drenching downpour. In no time the trail transformed into a river of mud, making walking even more difficult. April struggled to keep her balance on the slick ground and grabbed onto a nearby tree trunk more than once.

"Use your walking stick, April," Leine warned.

"What's wrong with using the trees?"

Mateo pointed to a vine snaking up along a nearby tree trunk. "You must be careful of where you put your hands. There are poisonous vines that can make you very sick."

"You also need to watch out for snakes," Leine added. "They can look like vines."

"Okay. Got it."

Eventually, Mateo veered off the main trail into a clearing. The NVGs illuminated a raised platform with a thatch roof and a ladder.

"Home sweet home," Mateo joked.

In Leine's opinion, five-star accommodations wouldn't have been more welcome.

Ten minutes later, the small party and their packs were safely tucked away on the semi-dry sleeping platform, far from the mud-slicked jungle floor, and far enough above any predators that might lurk below. There were four hammocks, all outfitted with mosquito netting, and a low table with reed mats for seating.

Mateo unhooked an electric lantern hanging from his pack and set it on the table. He turned it on, then pulled out several containers, providing them with a simple meal of dried fish and mango.

"I don't think I've ever enjoyed a meal as much as right now," April exclaimed. She sat cross-legged on one of the mats, next to her pack. Leine used her own pack as a backrest, as did Mateo.

"I couldn't agree more," Leine said. Escaping the torrential downpour made a world of difference to their moods. True, the rain would bring even more cloying humidity, but that was to be expected in the jungle. As long as the snakes and poisonous spiders left them alone for the night, Leine couldn't be happier.

LEINE WOKE THE NEXT MORNING TO THE SOUND OF RAUCOUS birdcall. Her sleep had been intermittent—the storm and jungle sounds often woke her—but she'd managed to rest. The morning sky dawned a vibrant orange-pink. Scarlet macaws flew from tree to tree, squawking at each other in a riot of sound. Capuchin monkeys chased each other through the branches, chattering and screeching. The temperature had spiked, warning of a searing-hot day ahead.

She lay in her hammock for a few moments, immersing herself in the sounds of the morning. Then she swung her legs over the side and sat up.

She pushed the mosquito netting aside and jostled April awake. April rubbed the sleep from her eyes and raised her head.

"Where's Mateo?"

Their tour guide was nowhere in sight. One of his packs was gone.

"Not sure. I just woke up myself." Leine grabbed her boots from the hammock and put them on. She had a stiff back but otherwise felt good. After a quick stretch, she walked to the edge of the platform and scanned the clearing, then checked what she could see of the jungle. Although the ground was still damp, most of the rain had soaked into the earth or evaporated in the heat. A rock-lined fire pit stood in the center of the clearing. Several muddy footprints at the base of the ladder marked their arrival the night before. She couldn't tell which were Mateo's— not from the height of the platform.

Leine took a swig of water from her canteen. "He's probably out looking for breakfast."

"I wonder what he'll bring back?"

"Capybara?"

April made a face. "An adorable rodent for breakfast?"

Leine chuckled. "You're going to have to get used to eating bush meat if you want to keep doing fieldwork. There will be times when food will be hard to come by."

April rolled her eyes. "I suppose you're going to tell me you've eaten insects or something, right?"

"Hey—don't knock it until you've tried it. Fried maggots are especially tasty."

April made a retching sound. Leine smiled and shook her head. Her daughter had a lot to learn. It was going to be fun to watch.

Two saplings shuddered at the edge of the clearing heralding Mateo's arrival. A bundle of branches hung down his back in a kind of loose carrier that he'd strapped to his forehead, and he carried a dead animal. He walked over to the ring of stones and placed the carcass on the ground, then removed the bundle of branches and set them inside the circle.

April leaned over and grabbed her hiking boots.

"Make sure to shake those out," Leine warned, "or you might get a nasty surprise."

April froze before slowly turning first one boot and then the other upside down. "What am I hoping I don't find?"

"Spiders or scorpions, possibly a snake."

April shuddered and finished putting on her boots. "Welcome to the jungle."

"I'd suggest keeping them in your hammock at night."

She gave Leine a look. "Now you tell me."

The two women joined Mateo by the fire pit as he stoked the branches into a roaring fire.

"I thought I would give you a taste of what the jaguars prize." He grinned at April and gestured toward what Leine could now see was indeed a capybara.

"Yum," April said, without enthusiasm.

Mateo smiled. "You'll see."

He was right. The capybara was delicious. April even agreed.

"As long as I don't tell myself that I'm eating a humongous rat, it's surprisingly good."

Mateo beamed as he finished off his last bite. "Told you."

April smiled back and fluttered her eyelashes.

Hmm. Was her daughter flirting? Leine would watch them to see where it might lead. But she wasn't about to let down her guard. Had Herberto suggested hiring him to Martin or had Martin hired him without Herberto's help? If he was one of Herberto's men, he might be trying to lull them into a false sense of safety. Her gut said he was safe, but she'd been wrong before.

And this time, if she was wrong her daughter would pay.

7

"Both she and her daughter had guns." Herberto paced the marble floor of his office, cellphone to his ear. "And now they have gone. I checked with the tuk tuk driver. He said he dropped them off at the market early this morning. He did not stay to see which boat they boarded. I hired a helicopter to find them, but we failed. It seems they believe I was somehow responsible for last night's...event."

"What happened to the first group you sent to kill them?"

The caller's voice grated on Herberto's nerves. In all the years Herberto had known the man, he'd never expressed anything akin to strong emotion. Even his anger was controlled. To a man like Herberto, this was incomprehensible. What kind of life would it be if there were no dramatic highs or crushing lows? Herberto thrived on drama, intrigue.

"Dead."

"I trust events have been set in motion?"

Herberto winced. He didn't want to anger him. He would have to couch his words. *El Jefe's* anger rarely missed its mark, and Herberto preferred to keep his comfortable lifestyle—and his life.

He took a deep breath and said, "They have, yes. But I would counsel patience. My men know little of that section of the Amazon."

El Jefe sighed. "Well, then, we'll go with plan B."

Herberto wanted to laugh. *El Jefe* had more plans than an architect. Plan B effectively took the assassination operation out of Herberto's hands and placed it in someone else's. He wanted to feel relief, but that emotion didn't come. He now had no control over the outcome, and he didn't like it.

"But he already has his hands full, *jefe*. Do you think it wise to entrust with him such an important task?"

"I thought you trusted him. You *did* recommend him for the other job."

"And he and his men performed admirably. The daughter has been taken to a secret location, to be held until Martin agrees to lead him to the lost city." Herberto paused, searching for the right words. "But expecting him to eliminate the two women in addition to holding another hostage, well, I'm afraid he might not be the best person for the job."

"And why is that?"

Herberto closed his eyes. He wasn't going to tell him that Dario would resort to extortion, especially if murder was required. Making the request could get Herberto killed. Dario had assumed Herberto was the originator of the kidnapping request, and he didn't disabuse him of the notion. If he found out that Herberto wasn't the top man, it would put Herberto in the unfortunate position of being irrelevant—a loose end.

Dario had a habit of tying up loose ends.

"Trust me. You do not want him to commit murder on your behalf."

"It wouldn't be on my behalf. It would be on yours. Or have you breached our agreement and revealed my identity?"

"Of course not, *jefe*. I only meant that the cost of hiring Dario to take care of the two women would be too great."

"Don't worry. I have another option."

"I'm afraid I don't understand."

"It would be best if you didn't. You just implied that you don't want to be involved. So I will ensure that you're not."

The line went dead. Herberto wiped at the perspiration coursing down his face as he set the phone down.

He'd have to double his security.

8

"How much farther?" April stopped to take a drink of water from her canteen. Circles of sweat stained her shirt.

Mateo squinted into the sun. "Two days, maybe more, depending on the weather."

April raised her eyebrows at Leine. "Seriously? How isolated is this camp?"

"Isolated. But don't worry," Mateo added. "As long as you stay with me, you will be safe."

"I wasn't—" April started to say, but Leine interrupted.

"We're grateful for your expertise, Mateo. Thank you." Leine drank from her canteen and screwed the cap back on. Later, she'd explain to April the finer points of keeping on the good side of local guides. Leine was all for cultivating Mateo's solicitous nature.

Like Leine, her daughter was used to doing things for herself. Unlike Leine, she hadn't experienced much Male-as-Protector behavior from her peers and tended to bristle when men deployed that particular arrow from their arsenal. In this part of the world, a woman got a lot further when she took cultural differences into consideration.

The three set out along the sometimes nonexistent trail through the dense jungle, stopping at intervals to allow Mateo to whack a path through the foliage with his machete. He'd explained that when he first came through on his way to meet them, he hadn't cleared the trail, as he normally reserved that activity for the return trip. Often, he didn't know how long retrieving supplies or people would take him, and the jungle had a tendency to grow over his clearing attempts. Besides, hacking through the jungle was hard work. Why do it twice?

"So what you're saying is to always keep you in our sights?" April asked, her tone playful.

Mateo sobered immediately. "You must never allow me to get too far ahead. Losing your way in the jungle is easy to do, and more difficult to correct."

His answer notwithstanding, Leine had the coordinates for Martin's camp and the GPS on the sat phone, so if anything did happen to Mateo, she was reasonably confident they'd be able to reach camp, eventually.

It was the length of "eventually" that could be a problem.

About midday, they reached a clearing and decided to stop. Water splashed nearby.

"That sounds like a whole bunch of awesome," April commented as she allowed her pack to slide to the ground.

"Follow me." Mateo's mysterious expression intrigued Leine.

"You don't have to ask me twice," April said.

"You can leave your packs here if you like. I'll be back soon to watch them." Mateo nodded at the ground.

"Thanks, anyway." Leine smiled. "But I'd feel better keeping them with us."

He shrugged and disappeared through the foliage. Packs in hand, the two women followed.

The game trail opened onto a hidden valley that could have

been a movie set for *Jurassic Park*. A gushing waterfall splashed into a deep green pool below, surrounded by huge boulders and enormous plants. A couple of ceiba trees towered over the scene. April dropped her bags and started to unbutton her long-sleeved shirt.

"Now *that's* what I'm talking about. Is it safe?" she asked Mateo.

"Yes." Mateo beamed as though he himself had created the lovely spot just for them. "I will prepare our meal while you swim."

He disappeared the way they'd come while April shed the long-sleeved shirt and started on her T-shirt.

"Yeah, I wouldn't do that if I were you," Leine said.

"Why not? It looks so refreshing."

"It's up to you, but fresh water isn't always fresh."

"What do you mean?"

"Parasites, mostly."

"Ew. Really?" She looked longingly at the water. "Crap. I was really looking forward to a swim."

"Like I said, it's your choice. It may be absolutely fine. I'll keep watch." She didn't want to be too far from her pistol or the weapons cache. Too many things could go wrong.

And she wasn't sure she could trust Mateo. Yet.

"No, I'll stay here with you." April slid her T-shirt back on. "I sure as heck don't want to contract a parasite. I've read those little buggers are hard to get rid of."

"Great. Why don't you get some rest? I'm going to check on our guide and then I'll be back."

Leine quietly followed Mateo through the undergrowth. Just before she got to the clearing, she paused in the shadow of a palm and peered through the fronds. Mateo busied himself setting up a makeshift cutting board and getting everything ready for their lunch. Leine melted back into the jungle and returned to her daughter.

April leaned against her pack with her earphones in and her eyes closed, head bobbing as she listened to music. Leine walked over to their things and unzipped the duffel bag containing the mini Uzi, the frag grenades, and the rest of their supplies, and double-checked the extra magazines. April opened one eye to see what she was doing, then closed it again.

Satisfied everything was how she wanted it in case either of them needed quick access, Leine sat back against the base of a palm. A giant blue butterfly floated past and kissed the rock face of the waterfall. It then hovered over the small pool, remaining in place for several seconds. Leine nudged April and nodded toward the airborne insect.

"Blue Morpho," Leine said.

April smiled. "It's gorgeous."

As they watched, two others joined it, then several more. A moment later, the fluttering group floated off into the jungle.

"That was awesome." April leaned back and replaced her earphones. Leine took a deep breath and closed her eyes.

The heat was manageable in the shade. She allowed the mesmerizing sound of falling water and buzzing insects to lull her into a semi-relaxed state.

"Think lunch is ready?"

At the sound of April's voice, Leine snapped back to the present. Her daughter climbed to her feet and dusted off her cargo pants.

Leine checked her watch. Half an hour had gone by. She'd have to be more careful. "Did Mateo come back?"

"Uh-uh. Not yet."

Leine stood and picked up her pack and the duffel bag. "We

should probably go help him. I don't want the poor guy to think he's got to do everything."

"Lead the way."

The two women headed back along the game trail to the first clearing. Leine expected to see Mateo and lunch.

She didn't.

9

"Maybe we didn't go far enough," April said.

"No, this is it." Leine walked over to a set of footprints in the mud near the center of the clearing. Alongside them were depressions in the dirt where Mateo had set his packs down.

"Where do you think he went?"

"I don't know." She didn't want to alarm her daughter. Yet. But a bad feeling about their guide gnawed at her gut. She followed their footprints back to the main trail, but there was no evidence that he'd continued in the same direction they'd been hiking. She searched, and found, a set of footprints heading back the way they'd come.

April walked up behind her. "Think he abandoned us?"

"Too early to tell."

"What if someone grabbed him?"

Leine shook her head. "No signs of a struggle."

April sighed. "So he was just *acting* nice. Do you think he's actually Martin's guy from camp?"

"Remember—he identified himself using the phrase we agreed on. And I've asked him several identifying questions.

Mateo knows Martin, so yes, I believe he's who he says he is. Maybe Herberto got to Mateo."

"You mean Herberto hired Mateo to kill us?"

"He could have blackmailed him."

"But how? It's not like Herberto could just call the guy and threaten to kill him or his family."

"No, but the weapons guy in Iquitos suggested Herberto had a vast network of spies in the area. It wouldn't take much to get someone to relay the message to Mateo. The real question is why does Herberto want us dead?"

"Why didn't Mateo try to kill us earlier? He had plenty of opportunities."

Leine was glad to see her daughter's analytical mind had kicked in. Instead of freaking out about being left alone in the middle of the jungle without food, April was reasoning through Mateo's motivation.

She might just make a good field operative yet.

"If he was going to try to kill us while we slept, there'd be evidence. Who wants to get rid of two bodies in this heat? Losing us in the jungle makes the most sense. There's a lot of poisonous stuff out here, and we don't have many supplies." Water wouldn't be a problem. Leine had brought purification tablets.

"What about the boat? He could have swamped us, or hit something in the river."

"But then he'd have been in trouble, too."

"Yeah."

April's shoulders sagged.

Leine studied her daughter. "You like him, don't you?"

She nodded. "He seemed nice. And interesting. I guess I can't trust my instincts yet."

During one of the modules at the SHEN academy, Leine had led the discussion in a class titled *Just the Facts, Ma'am,* on knowing when to trust your instincts, when to go with solid, known facts, and when to combine the two. She'd argued that the more experience a person had, the more that person could trust his or her gut—to a point. There was always the danger of disregarding new data—whether feelings or actual cold, hard facts—and failing because of previous bias. Just because something worked before didn't mean that would be true for a different situation. And learning to read people took practice.

So much practice.

"Don't feel bad. I still get it wrong sometimes. People are complex. That's what makes them so fascinating—and challenging. To do well in this kind of business you have to become a lifelong observer of your fellow human beings."

"Did you trust him?"

Leine shrugged. "I hadn't made up my mind."

"Do we have to go back the way we came? It's going to blow our timeline for getting to Martin's camp."

"Not necessarily." Leine dug inside her pack for the topographic map of the jungle Lou had provided. The satellite wouldn't be in position for several hours, so no GPS—they'd have to old-school it.

She checked the route they'd traveled, comparing it to the compass readings she'd taken. "According to my calculations, the camp's twenty-five kilometers south-southeast of our current position." She checked her watch. They'd covered six kilometers so far that day, which translated to approximately one kilometer an hour, due to hacking their way through the jungle with a machete.

But they didn't have a machete. They'd have to go back the way they'd come. The return trip wouldn't take as long, but it was still a delay.

"Looks like Mateo took us out of the way several kilometers," she said to April. "We have to retrace our steps to the main trail."

"Then we'd better get going. I want to find it before dark."

Leine studied her daughter. A flash of déjà vu came and went. Like she was seeing herself, years before.

"Have I told you how much I love you?" Leine gave her a hug.

Maybe the apple didn't fall too far from the tree, after all.

———

TWO HOURS INTO THE HIKE BACK TO THE MAIN TRAIL, LEINE stopped.

"What?" April asked.

"Hear that?" she asked. A branch snapped. Leine eased her bags to the ground and drew her weapon. April did the same.

"What is it?" April whispered.

Leine shook her head. Jaguars and anacondas were the only large predators they needed to worry about. Smaller stuff was a concern—poisonous spiders, snakes, and fire ants, not to mention parasites, infection, and poisonous plants—but they wouldn't make that kind of noise.

Another branch cracked. Closer this time.

Leine pivoted toward the sound.

Her breathing ratcheted up, anticipating an attack.

"Wait until I say fire," Leine said in a low voice. She moved so that she and April were an arm's length apart, and waited.

The sounds grew louder, coming at them through the dense underbrush.

Leine tensed, waiting.

The leaves of a nearby palm shook.

She curled her finger around the trigger and exhaled.

"Don't shoot!" Mateo stumbled out of the bushes onto the trail.

"What the fuck, Mateo?" April exclaimed as she lowered her pistol. Leine continued to aim hers at their guide.

"Where have you been?" Leine asked. She'd be damned if

she'd allow Mateo to draw on her or her daughter. She'd rather kill the man and be left to their own devices.

Mateo froze, his gaze riveted to Leine's gun. "Wait. Please. I have been looking for you."

"Sure you have," Leine answered. "Allow me to repeat the question. Where have you been?"

Mateo started to lower his hands, but April raised her gun and he froze again. "When I came back to the waterfall," he said to her, "you were not there. Why did you leave?"

"Because you left."

Mateo shook his head, an exasperated look on his face. "You should never go off on your own in the jungle unless you know where you are. I am so happy to find you."

Leine lifted her chin. "You haven't answered my question, Mateo."

"May I?" he asked, nodding toward his hands.

"Keep your hands where I can see them." Leine kept her gun trained on him.

Mateo nodded and lowered his arms. "I went in search of banana and mango for our meal."

"You took everything with you," April said. "What were we supposed to think?"

Mateo looked from Leine to April back to Leine. "You think I would leave you out in the jungle alone? What kind of guide do you think I am?"

"You said you went in search of bananas," Leine said. "Did you find any?"

"Yes." Mateo lowered his pack, unzipped the top, and dug inside. He pulled out three bananas and a mango to show her. "I took my pack with me so that none of the animals would get into it."

She lowered her gun a fraction. "Okay. But how do I know

you didn't just grab those as a cover story when you figured out we were heading back to the main trail?"

"I believe him." April lowered her gun and slid it back into her holster. A look of relief crossed Mateo's face. He glanced at Leine with a hopeful expression.

"Open your pack."

"C'mon, Mom. He's fine."

Leine stared at Mateo. Finally, he relented.

"Look—there is nothing to be concerned about." He pulled out food containers and a medical kit so she could see to the bottom.

She relaxed her grip on the gun and straightened. "I'll give you the benefit of the doubt. For now."

Mateo nodded and handed each of the women a banana. "I thought you might be hungry."

April peeled the fruit and took a bite. "Delicious."

Leine slid hers into her backpack. "How about next time you let us know when you're heading out? That way there's no confusion."

"Of course. I didn't think to tell you."

"So are the birds around here aggressive?" April asked, looking pointedly at his pack.

Mateo nodded toward the tree canopy. "The monkeys are the smartest. They can find a way into almost anything within minutes." He opened one of the plastic containers he'd removed, which he offered to Leine. "Please. Help yourself."

Inside were large pieces of dried jerky. Leine picked out a chunk and nibbled on it as he offered the container to April, who did the same.

"According to my reckoning, we were about six kilometers off the main route to the camp. Why?" Leine took a sip of water from her canteen.

"There is another path through the jungle, but not many people know of it. It shortens the hike by several kilometers."

"Would it still be worthwhile, now that we're more than halfway to the main trail?" April asked.

Mateo shrugged. "I think it would be the same distance. But I see that your mother is not comfortable going the other way, so I will take you back to the main trail and we can continue from there."

"I'd feel much better if we did," Leine said. Especially if he left them again. She still wasn't sure she could trust him. She and April would have a much better chance of making it to Martin's camp if they stayed on the main trail. Worse yet, what if one of them got hurt? Yes, the change of plans might add a few hours of walking, but Leine felt infinitely better knowing they were going to resume their hike through the jungle on better-known trails.

Rescue would be easier, as well. Lou had a handle on where they were headed. If they left the main trail again, he might have a hard time finding them if they needed to be extracted.

After lunch, they hoisted their packs and resumed their trek to the main trail. Raucous birds and screaming howler monkeys serenaded them through the steamy jungle, and they fell into an easy rhythm. Occasionally, Mateo would point out this or that plant and its traditional uses. Leine memorized each one in case they found themselves at the mercy of their environment. She'd done a bit of research during the two flights to Iquitos, but there were so many medicinal plants in the Amazon, she doubted she'd even scratched the surface. April appeared to be enjoying Mateo's narration, a lot, reminding Leine that her daughter was most likely interested in their guide.

Something to monitor. Closely.

Leine and April were having a discussion about the relative merits of hollow-point bullets when Mateo stopped suddenly.

The two women did the same. The long shadows of late afternoon stretched across their path.

"What is it?" Leine asked.

Mateo put his finger to his lips. The bird and monkey chatter had ceased, creating an eerie silence. A chill skittered along Leine's spine and the little hairs on the back of her neck stood on end.

Leaves rustled to their left, followed by a low cough. April froze, her eyes widening. Leine and April drew their pistols at the same time. Mateo unsheathed the machete and dropped to a defensive stance.

A deep-throated roar shattered the calm.

10

Mateo roared back and raised his machete with both hands. April gripped her 9mm and aimed toward the sound, chin tucked in determination.

With a snarl, a jaguar exploded through the underbrush, a blur of black and fur and orange and teeth, headed straight for Mateo. Leine fired over the big cat's head. The sound fractured the air. Startled, the jaguar twisted mid-stride and scrambled for purchase. The razor-sharp claws dug into the earth, and the animal loped away, vanishing into the dense forest.

"Oh. My. God," April breathed, lowering her gun.

Mateo exhaled. "That was lucky." He shook his head in wonderment.

"Luck had nothing to do with it." Leine re-holstered her gun. "The gunshot scared him off."

"Not the gunfire, although that was certainly effective," Mateo said. "I meant the presence of a jaguar on our path. This is very lucky."

April let out a nervous laugh. "Yeah. Not exactly what I'd call it."

Mateo sheathed the machete and picked up his pack. "There

are men who live their entire lives in the jungle and never see a jaguar. He is a solitary hunter and a master tracker, and has surely been following us for some time. He could have easily attacked any of us without notice, yet he roared to let us know he was there. He was warning us away from his territory."

"Or looking for a quick meal," April added.

"Whatever he intended, I am thankful he has gone." Mateo made the sign of the cross and shouldered his pack. "It is getting late. We should continue."

———

THAT NIGHT THEY BUILT A TEMPORARY STRUCTURE WITH SAPLINGS and ponchos and draped the mosquito netting over the top. After waking throughout the night, completely alert and tracking noises from the jungle, Leine relieved Mateo early on in his watch. By the sound of her breathing, April slept soundly.

Leine walked outside. A blue-white moon illuminated the surrounding jungle, creating dark shadows that stretched across the small clearing. She took a sip of water from her canteen and surveyed the area. The lack of sleep didn't surprise or bother her —she was used to going without when she was in operational mode.

In her line of work, awareness meant survival.

She walked to a fallen tree at the edge of the clearing. After making sure there wasn't anything living in or on it that could give her a nasty surprise, she sat down. Closing her eyes, she soaked in the intermittent birdcalls and sounds of nearby wildlife, sensing rather than feeling the movement of animals and insects. A slight breeze ruffled her hair. The deep, earthy scent of decayed plant matter rose from the ground, filling her mind.

Sensory data came at her from everywhere, and she deepened her breathing, allowing her body and mind to relax into a receptive state. Some would refer to her actions as meditative. Leine preferred the term situational awareness. No matter what anyone called it, the ability to absorb her surroundings gave her a competitive edge.

The sound of leaves rustling behind her directed her focus and she opened her eyes. A guttural cough echoed nearby. Senses on a knife's edge, Leine slid her pistol free and stood.

She turned toward the threat, certain the jaguar had returned. This time, she would shoot to kill, not just scare it off.

Peering through the inky shadows, she listened intently for the telltale movement indicating the big cat's location.

Another deep huff, this time to her left. She tracked the sound, aiming her weapon toward the invisible adversary. She took a deep breath and let it go as she narrowed her eyes, concentrating on the area where she heard the noise.

A low, menacing growl emanated from the palm fronds directly in front of her. Her heart beat triple time. Perspiration beaded between her shoulder blades and slid down her spine, pooling at the small of her back. Leine stood her ground with both hands on her pistol, her finger firmly on the trigger.

If you leave now we'll both walk away from this, able to fight another day.

The thought came and went as she continued to aim at the same spot. Moments later, the energy in the clearing shifted. The awareness she'd felt when the jaguar was near had vanished.

Like the jaguar.

Leine lowered her weapon, not entirely convinced the big cat was gone. Scuffling sounded behind her, and she turned as Mateo emerged from the lean-to.

"Did you hear something?" he asked, nodding toward the gun in her hand.

Leine slid the pistol back into her holster. "I thought the jaguar was back, but if it was, it's gone now."

"Perhaps it is tracking us, waiting for the best time to attack."

"It may well have been." Leine stared into the darkness. "I have a feeling he won't bother us anymore tonight."

Mateo gave her an odd look. "Let's hope you are right."

11

The following day, Leine, April, and Mateo reached a narrow tributary surrounded on each side by tall cliffs. Moss and ferns dotted the rock walls. Towering trees draped in green bracketed the swiftly moving river. Colorful birds swooped and plunged over the water and congregated *en masse* on a far cliff, as monkeys chattered among themselves high in the canopy. Mateo peeled off the main path and paralleled the river via a steep path hugging the cliff.

"Why do the parrots group together?" April asked.

"The cliff is made of clay. They are eating it."

She studied the brightly colored birds. "Why clay?"

"Scientists say there are two possibilities. Either the birds are eating it to neutralize toxins in the plants they eat, or they are trying to get more sodium in their diet."

"Salt must be hard to come by in this area," Leine said.

Mateo nodded. "Yes. We are a long way from the ocean. With all the rain, any salt that might be in the ground is washed away."

They continued past the raucous birds.

"That's a long way down," April commented when they'd reached a particularly precarious section of the trail.

"This trail has been in use for centuries." Mateo pointed out designs scratched in the rock. "It is a major trade route between tribes."

April averted her eyes from the rocky crevasse below her and mumbled, "They couldn't cut through the jungle?"

As the day wore on, the sun steadily rose to its highest point and with it the temperature. Mateo stopped at a wide spot on the trail near a waterfall to prepare lunch. April immediately removed her boots and socks and plunged her feet in the pool at the base of the falls. Leine shrugged off her pack and sat on a nearby boulder. She balled up her bandana and tossed it to April.

"Get that wet for me, will you?"

April obliged and tossed it back. Leine mopped her face and then wrapped it around her neck, sighing with relief.

"Are we close?" April asked.

"Very close." Mateo refilled his canteen from the waterfall and then motioned for theirs. He filled both and handed them back to the women. "We should be at the camp by nightfall."

"Oh, good," April said, smiling. "I'm ready for a little civilization."

Mateo gave Leine a look that said, *are you going to tell her or should I?*

Leine pulled her sweaty shirt away from her body, trying to get a breeze going. "I wouldn't exactly call Martin's camp civilized. You do realize there's no plumbing, right?"

"I know, Mom. I meant seeing other people and an end to this grueling hike."

"Seeing other people, yes. I'm afraid this is just the beginning of what may be more grueling hikes. We still have to locate Nancy."

"Oh, never mind." April took out her earbuds and shoved them in her ears.

Leine studied her daughter. She'd been quite the trooper, never complaining about the heat or humidity, or the huge, itchy welts from mosquitos the size of aircraft carriers, or the snakes and scorpions and poisonous plants she learned to avoid. Or the mud, or the close encounter with a jaguar, or the isolation of being in the middle of the Amazon rainforest with only her mother and a guide who might have left them to fend for themselves.

Quite a trial by fire.

Even though Leine didn't choose this op for her daughter, it was surely going to make a mark. And that might turn out to be a good thing.

As long as Leine got her home alive.

After a lunch of mango, salt pills, and smoked fish, they set out with renewed vigor to make up for lost time. Leine centered herself and worked to hone her awareness in an effort to ignore the stifling heat.

April glanced over her shoulder at her mother. "How do you do it? You're so calm and serene."

"Mind over matter."

April chuckled. "If you don't mind, it doesn't matter."

"Yup." Leine smiled. It was a favorite saying they'd used over the years.

April turned back but miscalculated the path's location and slipped. Her ankle twisted and she lost her balance. She wind-milled her arms as Leine lunged for her.

"Mom!"

Mateo managed to latch on to one of the straps of her pack, arresting her fall. Leine grabbed Mateo to help anchor him and pull her back, but April's tenuous foothold failed and she slid off the muddy trail with a scream. Mateo and Leine fell, dragged to their knees by the combined weight of April and the pack. April's legs dangled in mid-air, searching for solid footing.

She didn't find any.

Heart in her throat, Leine yelled, "Hold on." With a nod from Mateo, Leine let go of him and dropped, stretching flat on her belly. "Give me your hand." She strained for April's slender fingers as her daughter reached for hers.

The gap between them narrowed to centimeters and the tips of their fingers brushed.

Mateo grunted from the effort to keep her from falling. He eased her closer to Leine.

"I've almost got her," Leine said, struggling to grasp her fingers. "Another inch."

Mateo nodded. Sweat poured down his face. The two women touched. Leine wrapped her hand around April's wrist.

"Got you—" Leine pulled in tandem with Mateo.

The strap slipped through Mateo's fingers, and he fell back onto the muddy trail.

April shrieked.

Leine slid toward the edge, her daughter's weight dragging her toward the abyss. At the last minute she hooked her arm around a shallow tree root to stop the slide. The muscles in her shoulders screamed.

"Mateo—" she gasped.

Mateo didn't move.

What the hell? "Mateo," she shouted again. *"We're going to die—"*

One end of the root let loose from the ground, dropping the two women a foot. Dirt and mud showered April and she screamed again. Leine's grip on her hand was slick with sweat. She tightened her hold, but April inched from her grasp.

I am not going to let my daughter die in the Amazon, dammit. With her eye on the tree root she took a deep breath and pulled.

The root gave way another inch, but Leine kept pulling. A moment later, April's hand slipped from her grasp.

No!

Leine's hand hit air. Mateo lunged for April, breaking her fall with both hands on the strap. Leine scrambled toward them and grabbed her daughter's outstretched hand. Together, they hauled April back onto the trail.

"Oh my God, honey, are you all right?" Tears of relief burned in Leine's eyes as she checked April for injury.

April nodded, still overcome with fright. Tears streaked her face.

Leine helped her remove her pack and smoothed her hair from her face. Other than a few scrapes, and the aftereffects of an adrenaline surge, she appeared to be all right.

"What the hell happened?" Leine turned on Mateo, concern for her daughter exploding into anger.

Still breathing heavily from the effort, he shook his head. "I —I don't know. I couldn't move." He lowered his gaze. "I am not worthy to be your guide."

Leine took a deep breath and let it go, the tension waning. The shame on his face told her he would be harder on himself than she ever could.

"Don't be too tough on yourself," she said. "Anyone can freeze up at a crucial time." When it came to controlling a person's own autonomic response, it took several years of training and even then it often didn't work. "I'm just relieved you came through."

"You would have been able to pull her to safety on your own."

"Maybe." Normally, Leine wouldn't doubt it, adrenaline being what it was. Stories abounded of feats of human strength due to hormones dumped into the body by the adrenal glands— people lifting cars or continuing to fight long after being fatally wounded. Plus, her daughter was in trouble—a mother's protection couldn't be underestimated.

But it could have easily gone the other way.

Best not to think about that.

What she did need to think about was why Mateo let go and what happened afterward. Yes, it could have been what he said, but her trust in him had waned. Had he seen an opportunity to let them both plunge to their deaths?

His actions weren't enough to outright accuse him of nefarious intent, but they were enough to keep her on edge.

12

Once April recovered, they resumed their trek to the camp. April hugged the rock face, well away from the edge of the cliff. Soon, the trail branched off and led them into the jungle.

Mateo had been correct on timing, and they arrived at Martin's camp as the shadows lengthened into early evening.

A tall, lanky man turned at their approach and strode toward them, arms outstretched. Minus the full white beard, Martin was the spitting image of his older brother, Lou. A nasty red welt peeked out from a bandage covering the left side of his forehead.

"God, it's good to see you." Martin wrapped Leine and April in a bear hug and stepped back. "Glad to see Mateo brought you here in one piece." He gave Mateo a grateful look. "It's not an easy trek."

"You can say that again," April said.

"What happened to your head?" Leine nodded at the bandage.

"It's nothing." Martin waved away Leine's concern. "A scratch. Come on and make yourselves at home."

Martin led them to the palm-thatched mess area.

"Hugo," he said to a burly man sharpening a machete next to the generator, "would you mind taking our guest's things and stowing them up on the platform?"

"Of course." Hugo stopped what he was doing and took April's pack. Leine detached the duffel bag and handed him her backpack.

At his quizzical look, she told him, "I'd like to keep this one handy."

With a nod, he shouldered the bags and set out across the clearing toward the platform.

Martin turned to the newcomers and said, "I'd offer you your choice of drink, but we're woefully understocked in the alcohol department. It's rum or nothing, I'm afraid."

"I'd like mine sans alcohol," Leine said.

"Certainly."

After he'd made them each a drink with fresh mango juice and half a mashed banana, he opened his laptop and booted it up. They all took a seat around the table.

"I'm sorry to get right to business, but we don't have long."

"Not a problem," Leine said.

"I've heard nothing from Nancy or her captor." Martin's pallor seemed to drain even more as he spoke. The bags under his eyes and the pained look on his face spoke of sleepless nights and high stress. "We have only days to come up with the information he wants."

"Something about a lost city, right?" April asked.

Martin nodded. "He's operating on the assumption that I have the coordinates."

"Do you?" Leine asked.

"Not exactly, no. What I do have is a promising LiDAR report and information from an elder tribesman."

"May I see the report?" Leine nodded at the laptop. Martin slid it toward her.

"The LiDAR picked up images under the vegetation that appear to be manmade. The square shapes are most likely dwellings or some other kinds of structures. That doesn't mean there's gold or treasure there."

"What about these?" Using the tip of her finger, Leine traced a series of straight lines radiating outward from the main site like spokes on a wheel.

"I believe those represent a raised roadway, similar to what the Mayans created in parts of Mexico and Central America."

Leine leaned closer. "It looks like the main site is on a steep ridge. How do you plan to get there?"

"We'll have to hike in. I've got enough climbing gear for three."

"Have you tried to find it?" Leine asked.

"Foolishly, yes." He touched the wound on his face, wincing as he did. "Hugo and I made an attempt right after Nancy was taken. You have to understand—my daughter—" He blinked several times and cleared his throat. "My daughter is an only child. I wasn't thinking clearly." He took a deep breath. "I'm sure you understand."

"I do," Leine replied. "That's where you got the cut?"

Martin nodded. "It happened early on, thankfully. At that point I realized I shouldn't have left the camp in case Dario or his men came back. We're understaffed at the moment. Once the supply team returns, we'll have more personnel to keep things running."

"Did Lou tell you about the team headed here from Colombia?" Leine took a sip of her drink.

"I just got word from him. Apparently, the helicopter they used to ferry the group to the deployment zone brought unwanted attention from a local group of insurgents. They're taking fire and don't know when they'll be able to resume the operation."

"So we're on our own." That changed things. Leine would have to rethink her initial plan. Hopefully the team would finish the insurgents off quickly, but she couldn't count on it. "When is the supply team due to arrive?"

Martin glanced at Mateo. "They should have been here two days ago. I haven't heard from them."

"How many people are here right now?"

"Other than the four of us, there's Hugo, Gunnar, our cook Renata and her husband Pablo, and Renata's assistant, Esme. Two other workers, Ignacio and Noah, are on the supply run."

"What are their roles?" Leine asked.

"Hugo oversees the technical aspects of the expedition— solar panels, the generator, and the drone. Gunnar is on loan from the Peruvian government, and is an expert in ancient languages. Ignacio has the most experience trekking through the jungle." Martin nodded at Mateo. "Not that Mateo isn't well equipped as a guide, but Ignacio has more practical experience, especially in this section of the Amazon. He's a member of the local tribe and grew up in the jungle."

"What about Noah and Pablo?"

"Pablo is responsible for hunting and fishing, and making sure the camp has sufficient clean water. He helps out where needed. Noah doubles as security and muscle—he's good with a machete."

"You don't have a designated medic?"

"Mateo's been trained in sourcing medicinal plants, as well as first aid. His father's a shaman."

April cocked her head and looked at Mateo. "Really?"

Mateo grimaced. "My father is a disgrace."

"I don't see how you can say that, Mateo," Martin chided. "The man prefers to live alone. You can't fault him for that."

"I don't want to talk about it." Mateo stood abruptly. "If you will excuse me."

Leine watched him stride purposefully across the clearing toward a smaller structure she guessed was a storage shed. April watched him leave, a concerned expression on her face. Leine turned back to Martin. "What's his story?"

"He and his father had a falling out a while back. Something about following in his father's footsteps."

"Becoming a shaman can't be a walk in the park."

Martin nodded. "That isn't all that's bothering Mateo. His family's been through a lot. He lost his mother and sister to drug traffickers—Mateo was away attending school at the time. His father never forgave himself or Mateo for not being there."

"Where was his father?" April asked.

"Deployed with the Counterterrorism Detachment of the Brazilian Army's First Special Forces Battalion."

Leine whistled. "That's quite a life change to go from the equivalent of a Delta Force operative to a medicine man living in the jungle."

"After the death of his wife and daughter he vowed to never again be an instrument of war."

"He didn't want to avenge his family's death?" April asked, glancing at Leine.

Martin shrugged. "Death affects people differently."

"I'll say." April gave her mother a pointed look.

"We should decide on a plan to rescue Nancy," Leine said, changing the subject.

"We searched the jungle." Martin shook his head. "No luck locating Dario's camp. It's like looking for a needle in a haystack."

"Well, now you have help," Leine said. "What would you like us to do?" She nodded at April. "We can help search for Nancy, or we can attempt to find the lost city. Both April and I are experienced climbers."

"I don't have experience specific to the jungle, but Mom does," April added. "And I'm a fast learner."

Martin drained his drink and set it down. "I'd like to try to make it to the city, but I'm not sure how long it will take to get there. It looks like a couple of days would do it, but distances in the jungle are deceiving. What appears to be a short trek becomes a days-long slog, depending on the terrain. I also need to be here when Dario comes back. If I'm not, I'm afraid he'll kill Nancy."

"April and I could try to locate the city, but we'd need someone to guide us, which would leave you down a man. Or, we could try to locate Nancy. If I were Dario, I wouldn't keep my base of operations too far from here. April and I could work that on our own. There are drawbacks to both, though."

"What's that?"

"If Dario has this camp under surveillance, then he'll know we're looking for him, which could put Nancy in even more danger."

Martin nodded. "And he'll know we're searching for the lost city,"

"Exactly. What's to stop him from following us, then killing everyone when and if we find it?" Leine thought for a moment. "Unless...how many gunmen were here the day they took Nancy?"

"Six, including Dario. Definitely paramilitary types—they wore camo and body armor, and carried assault rifles."

"Okay. I'll operate off the assumption that he brought a majority of his crew as a show of force to your first meeting. He doesn't know where the site is, so what if April and I act as decoys? He'll need a minimum of one gunman to guard Nancy, leaving five. You, Gunnar, and Hugo use the coordinates to try and locate the lost city. Dario will most likely send at least one gunman to follow your group."

"Then what?" Martin asked. "What if Dario finds out what we're doing? You still don't know where he's holding Nancy."

"We'll have to eliminate the gunmen before they have a chance to check in. Dario would need a hell of an antenna to reach his men by radio, but even then contact isn't assured. He'll eventually figure it out when his men don't return, but that should give us enough time to take out the rest. Then April and I can search for Dario's camp." Leine paused for a moment. "There is one other consideration."

"What?"

"We still haven't answered the question of how Dario found out about your discovery in the first place."

Martin rubbed his eyes and nodded. "I know. I've been wracking my brain, trying to figure out who would have leaked the information."

"Who knew about your conversation with the tribal elder?"

"Mateo, Hugo, Ignacio, Gunnar, and Nancy are aware that I spoke with him in private."

Leine glanced at Martin. "And you trust them?"

"With my life." He gave her a tired smile. "Mateo's been with me since the beginning, and Ignacio is well-known and respected in these parts. I've never heard a bad word said about either man. Hugo, either."

"That may be true, but you and I know things often happen that change a person's loyalties. What about Gunnar?"

Martin shrugged. "I don't know him well, but from what I've observed he's a dedicated professional deeply interested in advancing the study of ancient Peru."

"Who knows what's in the LiDAR report?"

"Only myself and Nancy. I've kept it from everyone else."

"Which tells me you don't trust your crew as much as you profess."

"Don't put words in my mouth. Of course I trust them. But

the less they know the better."

Martin's annoyance told Leine she'd struck a nerve. She decided to strike an even deeper one. "What about Nancy?"

Martin frowned. "You think she had something to do with any of this?"

"We have to look at everything."

"You didn't see her." Martin shook his head at the memory. "She was terrified. If she knew what was coming, I doubt she'd be able to feign that kind of emotion. Meryl Streep she isn't."

"Fair enough," Leine said. "I say we go with the plan I just outlined."

"But that leaves Renata, Esme, and Pablo by themselves. What if Dario returns and I'm not here?"

"We'll make sure you're back in camp with time to spare. If he's watching you, which I assume he is, then he'll know you're looking for the city. It's in his best interest to let you look."

"As long as I can be back in time, I'll do it."

"There's going to be significant risk, whichever plan we agree on." Leine sighed. "You have topographic maps covering the surrounding area?"

Martin nodded. "I do. I just wish Ignacio and Noah were here. I would prefer not to have you two and Mateo go into the jungle by yourselves."

"You sent Mateo alone to guide us back to camp."

"Yes, but he's traveled that route many times. It's easy for even a seasoned veteran to become lost in the Amazon."

April climbed to her feet. "Speaking of Mateo. Someone should see how he's doing." She left to make her way toward the shed where Mateo had gone. Martin watched her, a knowing look in his eye.

"Do we have a budding romance?" he asked. "I noticed them stealing glances with each other."

"That appears to be the case, yes."

"He's a good man. Your daughter could do worse."

"I'm sure she could. And just so you know, I'm not a mother who meddles. I assume April's got a brain and can make an informed decision about her own love life. Besides, we've got bigger fish to fry." Leine took a moment to run through other scenarios in her mind but couldn't come up with a better plan. "So what are your thoughts? If you can think of another idea, I'm happy to look at it."

Martin sighed. "I'm so worried about my daughter I couldn't think strategically if my life depended on it. How do you want to coordinate this?"

"Make sure our stories are straight in case one of your workers is the leak. I have two sets of night vision goggles and a few weapons, as well as radios and a jungle antenna. I'd like to rig up the antenna, see if we can get some coms working, although," she glanced at the towering trees surrounding them, "it's not looking too good. Do you have someone who's comfortable with heights?"

"Pablo. Go ahead and tell him what you need."

"Great. We'll leave before dawn to get into position. With any luck, the first gunman will walk right into our trap."

"What will you do with him?"

"Depends on how things go. We'll try to extract Nancy's location. If the plan goes sideways or takes too long, we'll eliminate him and try to live capture the next thug we come across."

Martin winced. "You speak easily of murder."

"Sometimes it's necessary." Leine studied Martin. "Lou told me you two used to go hunting together when you were younger. He also told me about your time in Iraq."

Martin gave her a dark look. "My deployment is a time I'd rather forget, but yes, if you're asking me have I killed someone, I have." He shook his head. "Not my finest hour."

"Look, Martin, these men won't hesitate to torture Nancy to

get what they want—and you can't rule out murder, either. You're going to have to act like the soldier you once were. If you see one of Dario's thugs, shoot him."

"Shouldn't I try to get information from him first?"

"How are you with a pistol?"

"Moderately accurate."

"Unless you can detain him without serious harm to yourself or someone else, shoot to kill. April and I will work the intelligence angle. They're wearing body armor, so center mass won't cut it. If something goes wrong and Dario gets wind of it, tell him you mistook his guy for a jaguar and you acted instinctively."

"You have it all figured out, don't you?" Martin studied Leine. "I'd hate to have your dreams."

Leine tamped down the sarcastic reply that sprang to mind. *He's not trying to bait you—he's just coming at it from a different place than you are.* "It's what I'm good at." She leaned forward, capturing his gaze with her own. "I'm exactly who you want on your side, Martin. Why do you think Lou sent me?"

"You're right. I'm sorry. I haven't been myself lately."

She reached across the table and covered his hand with her own. "Your daughter's in danger. There are a lot of unknowns." She checked her watch—the one her first love, Carlos, had given her as a gift. The device was a watch, heart monitor, clinometer, altimeter, distance calculator, and compass all rolled into one. "It's getting late. If it's all right with you, I'd like to turn in soon. We'll leave before dawn."

"Of course. You and April must be hungry. We usually run the generator about now. Renata and Pablo will prepare the fish Pablo caught earlier today for this evening's meal. I'll have Hugo set up some extra hammocks."

"Thanks, Martin." She rose from the table and paused. Their eyes locked. "We're going to get her back."

13

Mateo waited until April had gone back to help Renata prepare the evening meal before he sought out Hugo near the supply shed. He wasn't sure what to tell him. He'd failed in his task, which didn't bode well for him. He'd wracked his brain trying to come up with something that sounded good, but each time he tested his story, he was able to blow holes in it.

Ever since Dario had approached him in Iquitos, he'd had to carry this leaden weight on his shoulders. But what could he do? If Mateo confessed to Martin, Martin would never trust him again and would most certainly banish Mateo from camp. That couldn't happen—Mateo was the only one who could keep April and her mother safe. He refused to put her in danger. Besides, he thought April felt the same way he did—if he told her what he'd been tasked to do, she'd never trust him again.

He couldn't bring himself to kill her, or her mother.

Hugo was in the middle of putting away the tools he'd cleaned and sharpened when Mateo tapped him on the shoulder. Hugo wiped his hands on a rag and gave him a look.

"The fuck, Mateo?" Hugo's eyes practically snapped with fury.

Mateo put his hand up to ward off the other man's anger. "I —I tried," he whispered, checking behind him for anyone listening nearby. "It isn't that easy. They're both trained."

Hugo scoffed. "Bullshit. You had the element of surprise. You know what I think?"

"What?"

"I think you're falling for the girl, and you couldn't bring yourself to do your job." Hugo studied the younger man. "I'm right, aren't I?"

Mateo worked to slow his galloping heart. "She's the one with feelings. I'm working her, trying to fool her. Her mother's the one to be careful of."

Hugo scowled. "I told Dario you wouldn't be able to do it. I'm going to have to take care of it myself."

"No." Mateo's heart leapt. He couldn't allow Hugo to kill the women. He'd have to convince him he was still on board. Otherwise, both Leine and April would be in mortal danger, and he wouldn't be able to stop it. Not only that, but Hugo and the other thugs employed by the boss would go after Mateo's father, as well as Mateo himself. He couldn't put his only surviving family in danger. He may not be on speaking terms with his father, but that didn't mean Mateo wanted him dead.

Hugo leaned against the tool shed and crossed his arms. "Well?"

"Well what?"

"How are you going to do it? What's your plan?"

Mateo forced himself to look Hugo in the eyes. "I will let you know."

Hugo scoffed. "Yeah. You let me know." Mateo turned to leave. Then he added, "Remember what is at stake, Mateo. We know how to get to your father."

Mateo nodded and started back for the mess area, his mind working feverishly for an answer to his predicament. How could he kill April? Her eyes, the scent of her skin, her quick smile—all filled his heart. He'd never before been in love, but he thought that now he was.

It was horrible.

He doubted he could even get near Leine. His attempt to lose them in the jungle hadn't come close to working. Then, when April slipped off the path and almost fell to her death, Mateo had forced himself to hold back, assuming fate had taken care of his problem. But when it looked like Leine was going to lose her grip, Mateo couldn't help himself and sprang into action.

Mateo doubted he'd be able to outright kill either of them, anyway. He'd never killed anyone. Years ago his father had warned him of the psychological impact of murdering someone. Mateo had taken his warning to heart.

He could attempt to stop Hugo somehow, but the larger man would be on guard. Mateo didn't know which way to turn, but it was becoming clear to him that he would have to commit murder, one way or the other.

He would become the hunter or he and his father would die.

14

The night sounds of the jungle spurred her on, and she sifted through the different scents wafting past her as she prowled quietly through the forest. Her keen eyesight registered every movement as she assessed their cause, instinctively knowing she was at the top of her game and instilled terror in all that shared her turf.

There. Movement caught her eye and she slowed, savoring the hunt, the chase. She stopped, muscles tense and quivering, tail swatting the air like a sword, waiting for the perfect moment to spring...

Leine's eyes snapped open. Something had woken her, but she wasn't sure what. She eased her pistol from its holster and waited. Quiet snores floated toward her across the platform.

The dream flitted through her consciousness, the edges out of reach. She'd been running through the jungle, hunting something or someone.

No. That wasn't it, exactly.

A faint crackling sound reached her, and she eased her legs over the side of the hammock. Shaking off the dream, she slipped through the netting and crossed to the edge of the platform.

The mess area was an inferno. Flames writhed along the supports of the wooden structure, consuming them. Just then, a section of thatch caught and the fire raced across the roof.

"Fire!"

Everyone leapt from their hammocks and scrambled for the ladder. Leine's gaze locked on April's. Her daughter quickly shook out her boots and threw them on before joining the others.

Something landed on Leine's neck, and she brushed it away in annoyance. Some insect. A bat darted toward her and veered off. In the firelight, the silhouette of a man could be seen running from the structure. He melted into the dark jungle.

Leine raced down the ladder and sprinted toward the fire, Martin close on her heels.

"The equipment," he yelled, racing past her toward the blaze. He tossed her a key ring as he ran. "I'll deal with the fire."

Leine headed for the cupboard where Martin kept the field laptop. The fire was close. The heat hit her full force, stealing her breath. She covered her nose with her shirt as she bent over the padlock.

The metal was warm to the touch, but still workable. She unlocked the door and pulled out a large rubber container. Prying off the lid she reached inside, finding the computer.

"April!"

April appeared at her side. Leine handed the computer and the satellite phone to her daughter, then turned back for the drone. The device sat on a lower shelf next to the plastic tub containing the other electronics. She carefully slid it from the cupboard, the digital camera still attached.

"Here." Leine handed the drone to April, who'd already returned. A piece of burning thatch fell from the roof and landed on Leine's arm, singeing her shirtsleeve. She batted the flames out and kept searching.

The fire changed course and latched on to the cupboards, devouring the rest of the structure.

"Martin—the generator," Leine yelled. Martin threw a bucket of water onto the roof and handed the empty container off to Hugo before he turned toward Leine.

The gas tank ignited.

The explosion threw Martin to his hands and knees. Heart racing, Leine rushed to help him up, while she furiously scanned the camp for April. She'd been over by the platform, well away from the blast.

"Are you all right?"

Martin nodded and climbed unsteadily to his feet. "Did you save the laptop and the drone?"

"Yes. And the phone. Did we miss anything?"

By the look on his face, they had.

The fire's reflection flickered orange and yellow in the lenses of his eyeglasses as he stared at the inferno. "My notes were inside the drawer." He indicated the wooden table, now engulfed in flames. His chest rose and fell with the effort of watching his work go up in smoke.

"How did this happen?" he said out loud. "We're in a rainforest, for God's sake."

"I saw someone running away from camp as the fire broke out," Leine said. "I didn't recognize him, though."

"Why would anyone do this? Dario wouldn't have destroyed my work. He's betting on me finding the city. Destroying my notes and equipment will only cause a delay." He paused. "He's going to kill Nancy, isn't he?" She barely heard him—his voice came out in a whisper.

"Not if I can help it, no." Leine led Martin away from the fire and lowered him onto a plastic chair next to the sleeping platform. "Play for time. Explain to Dario that the data was destroyed in the fire. Ask him if he has any idea why someone would do this."

"Ask for an extension?" Martin shook his head. "I doubt we'll get any sympathy from that man."

It was a long shot. She glanced at the pile of equipment they'd saved. She motioned for April to join them.

"I'm so sorry, Martin," April said when she reached them.

Martin stared stoically at the blackened remnants of the mess area. "Thank you for your help, April."

"Where'd you put the laptop?" Leine asked her.

April nodded toward the sleeping platform. "Up there."

"Good. Can you make sure it's hidden? Put it inside my hammock or somewhere no one will look."

"Will do." April scrambled up the ladder and disappeared over the edge.

Leine turned to Martin. "We need to act as though the laptop is lost. Apparently there's a leak in camp."

"Are you sure nobody saw her put it up there?"

"I doubt anyone noticed in the chaos. If someone says something, April can deny it."

"What about when the embers cool and there's no melted laptop?"

"Then the man who started the fire has it." Leine shrugged. "Simple."

Martin stared at the conflagration, despair plain on his face. "Yeah. Simple."

ONCE THE FIRE HAD BEEN CONTAINED, MARTIN CALLED A MEETING. He told everyone he had decided to stay to clean up and wait for the supply party that was now several days late. He also insisted he needed to remain in camp in case Dario returned.

Leine briefed Mateo, Gunnar, and Hugo, explaining how to

search in a grid pattern to find the city. She handed out topo maps and made sure all three had a compass. Gunnar joined Hugo, while Mateo went solo. Pablo would remain in camp with Renata, Esme, and Martin.

At the edge of camp, Leine paused at the base of a tall tree and leaned her head back. Pablo had rigged the jungle antenna high up in the branches. Long wires dangled from the equipment, but they were out of reach.

"Looks like I'm going to have to climb." She set her pack down and pulled out the gear Pablo used. Earlier, she'd transferred what weapons and equipment she thought she'd need from the duffel bag to a larger pack for ease of travel.

"Let me." April held out her hand for the harness and rope. "I'm more agile."

Leine arched her eyebrow. "Oh?"

April rolled her eyes. "Really? We're going to do that? You're older, Mom. Deal."

"Okay, smartass." Leine handed her the gear. "Go for it."

April buckled herself into the harness while Leine ran the securing line around the tree and fastened it. April put on the foot gaffs last.

"Ready?"

April nodded.

"Just go to the first branch. You should be able to grab hold of the wires from there."

"Got it." She tested her weight, secured the line around the back of the tree, and walked up the trunk, digging the metal gaffs attached to her feet into the bark. She made it to the first branch and yanked on the line, allowing the length to snake down. Leine caught it and pulled, then waved April down.

Once Leine had connected the components and tested the radios, they packed up and headed out. The antenna would give them some range, although with such heavy tree canopy it would be sketchy, at best.

Travel was slow going at first. Leine used one of the camp's machetes to hack through the underbrush. Soon enough, the understory thinned due to lack of sunlight, leaving the forest floor easier to maneuver. Streaks of light speared the ground, illuminating plants fighting for sun.

A few hours later the two women stopped for a break. They hadn't found evidence of Dario's camp, and Leine hadn't detected a tail. After a light meal of dried fruit and fish, they resumed their search.

"Think we're close?" April asked.

Leine had cautioned at the start of the hike that their conversation might be overheard if one of Dario's men was following them, so everything needed to be said as though they were searching for the lost city rather than Nancy.

Leine checked their map and shaded in where they'd already been. "According to Martin's calculations, the LiDAR report showed evidence of two possible sites, one on top of the other. Keep your eyes peeled for anything out of the ordinary. Especially straight lines and planes. Nature rarely follows a straight line." She folded the map and put it away. "Check your coms. I want to make sure they're still working."

April keyed her mic. "One-two. Testing, one-two."

Leine gave her a thumbs-up.

They walked deeper into the jungle, avoiding tree roots and poisonous vines, and followed a stream of leafcutter ants along a game path. The tiny insects carried cargo several times their size, reminding Leine of the fully loaded motorbikes and tuk tuks that were ubiquitous in South America and Southeast Asia.

The hairs on Leine's neck prickled, and she scanned the jungle. She caught something in her periphery but kept walking as though she hadn't seen it.

They'd picked up a tail.

"Two o'clock," she said in a low voice. April kept her eyes straight ahead but gave a brief nod, letting her know she understood.

The two women came abreast of a massive ceiba, putting the thick tree trunk between them and the interloper. Leine gestured for April to continue while she stayed back. She slid her gun from its holster and eased around the base of the tree.

April had gone approximately ten yards when the man following them broke cover. His black and green face paint and jungle camo had done a good job of concealing his location, as did the vegetation attached to his headgear. Leine raised her weapon and took aim, waiting to see what his next move would be. Killing him outright wouldn't help—she needed him alive.

He swiveled his head, tracking April, but at the same time was obviously searching for Leine.

His movements told her he was comfortable in a jungle setting. Leine tracked him around the tree. A second later, he dropped out of visual range.

Shit. Leine skirted the ceiba and crouched low, keeping a bushy tree between her current location and his last. She scanned the jungle for her daughter and found her near the top of a slight rise. Leine keyed the mic on her radio twice, their agreed-upon signal for *stop*. April bent over as though checking her shoe. Good. They weren't out of range.

There was movement to Leine's right, near the side of the rise. She blinked to clear her vision and raised the binoculars, dialing in his position.

He was well versed at blending into the jungle. If she looked away for an instant, he disappeared. She tailed him, keeping an element of cover between her and her quarry, and silently closed the distance.

She was ten feet from him when her foot hit a twig with a loud *snap*. He froze.

"Hands on your head," she demanded in Spanish, aiming her pistol at the back of his head. Slowly, he straightened. "*Pronto.*" She keyed her mic several times, indicating she had things under control. April didn't confirm.

The man's shoulders lowered a fraction as his right arm moved.

A loud *pop* cracked through the air. The gunman's head snapped back and he collapsed to the forest floor. A group of parrots flushed from the surrounding trees, and howler monkeys screeched in protest. April sprinted toward Leine, her eyes wide.

"He was going to shoot you," she said, breathless from running. Her face pale, she stared at the now-dead gunman. "Oh my God. I killed him, didn't I?"

"Yes." Leine holstered her pistol and leaned down to relieve him of his sidearm. She tucked the gun into her pack, then slid the man's assault rifle from his shoulder. "I'm shocked. An AK-47. Weapon of choice for discerning criminals everywhere." She handed April the rifle and the additional magazine the gunman carried.

April stared at her mother as she took the weapon. "Aren't you going to say anything?"

Leine removed the gun strapped to the man's ankle before she straightened and studied her daughter. "What do you want me to say? You'll get over it? You won't. If you're anything like me, it'll stay with you a long time—probably the rest of your life."

"But you were going to interrogate him, right? Isn't that why you didn't kill him right away?"

"There's not a lot we can do about that now."

"I'm sorry. He looked like he was going to kill you. I—I should have waited."

Leine shook her head. "I tried to signal you, but I think we've moved out of range. Don't worry. Your instincts are good, just like they were with Azazel." Out for revenge, Azazel had been a twisted serial killer and the son of an early target of Leine's. April had shot him while he'd tortured Leine. His death marked the beginning of a thaw in Leine and April's relationship. "You saw a threat and acted. I didn't see what you saw. I might have done the same."

April let out a breath. "Really?" Her hand started to shake and tears welled in her eyes. "Shit. I'm going to fucking cry now?"

"It's from the adrenaline dump." Leine led her to a downed tree and sat next to her, relieved that April was showing some kind of reaction. Bottling up her emotions wouldn't do a lot of good. "Remember when you shot Azazel? Go ahead and cry if it helps." She resisted the urge to wrap her arm around her daughter. If April was going to do the kind of work being a field operative entailed, she would undoubtedly go through this scenario again. Leine wouldn't be there for her every time. Probably not even the next time.

"How did you deal with the first one?" April asked.

"The same, except I had to wait until I was safe before reacting." She sighed and stared into the distance as memories flooded back.

She'd been nineteen. Eric had sent her along with one of his best operatives on a job to assassinate an international arms trafficker who was providing Russian-made weapons to an enemy of the United States. Back then the targets were bad actors that threatened the country, not the hit-for-hire jobs Eric turned to before Leine left the Agency.

Leine had been bait, playing on the trafficker's voracious

sexual appetite, and was supposed to drug him, which would allow the experienced operative to deliver the *coup de grace*. Instead, Leine seized the chance and garroted the arms dealer while he slept. She'd cleaned off his blood, quickly gotten dressed, and escaped into the stairwell where the other operative was waiting. He'd been about to say something but stopped when their eyes met.

The adrenaline caught up with her—her heart raced and her knees shook—as she descended several flights. Acting normally when she reached the lobby had been a massive exercise in self-control, and set the bar for subsequent jobs. It was only later that evening on a return flight back to the US that she'd gone into the lavatory and thrown up.

After that, she learned to compartmentalize.

Leine handed April a tissue. She blew her nose and took a deep breath.

"Do you ever get used to this?"

"It's best if you don't." Leine tucked a strand of hair behind her daughter's ear—the only display of affection she allowed herself. "Killing someone isn't normal—it should always affect you." *Hopefully in a different way than it does me,* she thought. "Let's hope you aren't in this kind of situation again. I know plenty of folks in law enforcement who made it through their entire careers without shooting anyone."

April shook her head. "I don't know how you handle it, Mom. If I had to do what you did for that many years, I'd be a total whack job." She studied Leine. "You don't act screwed up."

"You can't always see what's inside people." Memories of the Kill Wall, an encrypted file on Leine's laptop showcasing dozens of photographs of recent targets, slipped unbidden into her mind. "Be glad of that, April."

They covered the dead man's body with leaves and branches before resuming their hike. This time they changed course and followed the map to the quadrant of the jungle Mateo was searching.

Two hours later as they topped a ridge shown on the topo map, April spotted movement below them on the forest floor. It was Mateo.

But he wasn't alone.

Leine got down low and gestured for April to do the same. Using the binoculars, Leine focused on the man with Mateo. He carried an AK and dressed similarly to the gunman April had just killed. A full head taller than Mateo, he had a stockier build. He gestured angrily at Mateo, as though giving him orders. Mateo, for his part, remained calm with arms crossed and answered the man when he could get in a word.

"What's he doing with that guy?" April asked.

"Looks like Mateo knows one of Dario's gunmen."

April glanced at Leine in alarm. "As in, he's working for Dario?"

She handed the binoculars to April. "You tell me."

April watched Mateo through the glasses for a moment. Leine could tell by the set of her jaw that she was angry.

"That asshole." She gave back the binoculars. "He was trying to kill us."

"But he didn't."

"So?"

"So he had plenty of opportunity and didn't go through with it. I think something else is at play here."

"Like what? I thought you didn't trust him?"

"I don't. But look at the interplay between these two. Dario's guy is angry. Mateo's staying calm. Dario's man wouldn't be angry if Mateo was doing what he was supposed to. That tells me Mateo's going against orders."

April grabbed the field glasses and looked through them

again. "You might be right." She watched a second longer, then lowered the glasses. "What do you want to do?"

"Let's watch them for a bit—see what happens. When and if they split up, we follow the gunman."

"What about Mateo?"

"We already know what he's doing."

"You think the gunman will lead us to Dario's camp."

"Or he'll track Gunnar and Hugo. Either way, it works for us to follow him. If he heads back to camp, we could find Nancy. If he tracks Hugo and Gunnar, we might find another gunman and then neutralize them both."

"Why wouldn't this guy try to find out where you and I went? Mateo thinks we're looking for the lost city too."

"Dario already put someone on our tail. No one knows that guy is dead—yet. Besides, we're two women searching the jungle. I doubt Dario believes we're much of a threat."

April smiled for the first time since killing the gunman. "I love it when people underestimate me."

Leine returned the smile. *Yep. The kid is a chip off the old block.*

15

T he gunman who'd been arguing with Mateo peeled off and started trekking through the forest, moving quickly and confidently through the jungle. By the time he stopped to rest, Leine and April were both breathing heavily. Sweat streamed down Leine's face and neck.

"Oh, thank God." April leaned over to catch her breath while Leine watched their quarry.

"Tracking someone who knows the jungle is a bitch." Leine took a swig of water from her bottle.

April scrubbed her cheek and glanced at her hand. She turned it toward Leine to show her the dead mosquito.

"That's a big one," Leine remarked, keeping her voice low. She rummaged in her pocket for a travel-size bottle of DEET and tossed it to her. "Here. You've probably sweated off the first coat."

April opened the cap and squeezed a dollop onto her hand. "You say that like it works."

Leine chuckled. "It's better than nothing." She returned to watching her quarry. "Just think. We'll be pounds lighter when we get back home. Jungle trekking makes a gym membership unnecessary."

"Especially true if we contract a parasite or five."

The gunman pulled out a bandana and wiped his face and neck. He took a drink from his water bottle and poured some on the bandana, which he tied around his neck. Then he unfolded a piece of paper and studied it for a moment. Afterward, he screwed the cap back on his bottle and stood.

Leine groaned. "Here we go again."

April stared at Leine. "Already? Shit." She shoved her canteen into her pack and stood.

The gunman took off at a brisk pace. Leine and April had to hustle to keep up. He continued through the jungle like he'd lived there all his life.

An hour later, he slowed and ducked down, melting into the understory.

"Heads up," Leine murmured to April. "Looks like we've arrived."

The two women took cover behind a dense thicket of gigantic ferns. Leine aimed the binoculars where the gunman was looking and caught a glimpse of Gunnar and Hugo. The two men sat on a large rock, their packs beside them. A nearby waterfall splashed into a pool next to a wide overhang.

The gunman they'd been following swiveled his head. Leine scanned the surrounding jungle but didn't see a second gunman near Gunnar and Hugo.

"I'll take this one. Keep your eyes peeled for another guy tracking them."

"Think you can get something out of him?" April asked.

"I'm going to try."

They circled behind their quarry. He crouched near a low-growing bush, his assault rifle aimed at Hugo and Gunnar.

Leine waited until April was in position before giving her the signal to go. April raised her weapon, and at the same time Leine stepped behind the gunman.

"Give me your gun," Leine ordered in Spanish.

The gunman glanced over his shoulder with an annoyed look on his face. His expression changed when he saw Leine and the gun. He stood slowly and raised his hands. Keeping her weapon trained on him, Leine took his rifle and slung it over her shoulder.

"Hands on your head. Now."

Slowly, he moved his hands and clasped them on the back of his head.

She pulled out a plastic zip tie. "Give me your right hand."

He did as instructed, and she lassoed his wrist. "Now the left." She cinched the tie tightly around both wrists and stepped back.

"Turn around."

The man rotated to face Leine. His eyes narrowed as he took in the two women.

"Who the fuck are you?" he asked, his lip curling up in a snarl.

"You aren't really in a position to ask." Leine raised her gun to emphasize her point. "Who are you?"

The man looked away, hostility plain on his face.

"Suit yourself."

Leine grabbed him by the elbow and shoved him toward Hugo and Gunnar.

Gunnar glanced up from his meal and his eyes widened. He nudged Hugo with his elbow and nodded toward the threesome headed their way. Hugo froze, his sandwich halfway to his lips. He dropped his sandwich and slid off the rock. Gunnar put his lunch down and did the same.

"What are you doing here?" Gunnar asked, eyeing the gunman. He and Hugo drew closer.

Leine pulled her prisoner up short and said, "On your knees." When the gunman didn't comply, she kicked the back of his legs behind his knees and he collapsed. April joined them.

Hugo reached behind his back and pulled out a forty-five.

"Don't shoot this *pendejo* just yet," Leine said. "I want to pry some information out of him first."

"Oh, I won't," Hugo said. He brought his hand to his mouth and whistled.

The other gunman Leine had been looking for stepped from behind the rock near the waterfall. A musclebound sparkplug of a man, he grabbed Gunnar and shoved a pistol in his side. Leine pivoted and aimed at Sparkplug. He kept his head behind Gunnar's, making a head shot a no-go.

Alarmed, Leine glanced at Hugo, then April. Hugo had an opening to take him down. *Why the hell isn't he taking the shot?*

"Take him," she said to Hugo, nodding at Sparkplug.

Hugo grabbed April from behind and shoved the forty-five against her temple. "Drop your weapon or she dies in front of you."

Leine's breath caught.

Hugo's the leak. Was he acting alone?

"You work for Dario?" She calculated the distance to the two gunmen, searching for an opening. If she tried for Hugo, Sparkplug would most likely shoot Gunnar or attempt to shoot her. Trying for Gunnar's captor would put April in more danger.

Ignoring the question, Hugo shoved his face closer to April's hair and inhaled. "Mm, tasty." He glared at Leine. "Put down your gun, now, or you'll be watching me fuck a corpse."

Sweat rolled down Gunnar's face. "*Madre de Dios*, Hugo. What are you doing?"

"Shut up," Hugo warned. He nodded at Leine. "The gun. Now."

April locked eyes with Leine and gave her an almost imperceptible nod, acknowledging what they both knew—never surrender a weapon.

A gunshot cracked through the air. A flock of scarlet macaws squawked and took flight. Howler monkeys screeched in alarm. Sparkplug grunted and slumped to the ground, releasing Gunnar.

Hugo swiveled, bringing April with him, and fired at the unseen gunman. April grabbed Hugo's arm with both hands and dropped like a dead weight, forcing him over. Leine squeezed off three rounds, hitting Hugo in the neck and shoulder, before taking cover. April launched herself at Gunnar and shoved him to the ground. Hands still cuffed behind his back, Leine and April's prisoner bent over and ran. He'd only made it a few feet before he tripped and fell on his face. He stayed down.

Leine swiveled toward the source of the gunshot and scanned the jungle.

"Don't shoot!" Rifle held aloft, Mateo emerged from behind a ceiba tree. "It's me."

Leine let out a breath, but didn't show herself.

Mateo continued toward them, hands up. "I promise I won't shoot—"

Three loud *pops* split the air in rapid succession, scattering what was left of the birds and monkeys. Leine pivoted in time to see Hugo lower his arm, the forty-five in his hand. Blood soaked his neck and half his shirt.

"No," April screamed. She sprang to her feet and ran to Mateo.

Leine fired at Hugo until her gun locked, riddling his body with bullets. She released the magazine and slammed in a fresh one.

Wary, she walked over to Hugo to make sure he was dead. Blood saturated his head and upper torso. She checked him for a pulse. There was none. She pulled the forty-five from his grip and slid it into her waistband.

April called out, "Mateo's been shot." Panic filled her voice.

"Bad?"

"Bad enough."

Leine sprinted to her pack. "I'll get the kit."

She searched the pack and found the first aid kit, then hurried to where Mateo lay on the ground. Gunnar cradled his head.

Movement caught Leine's eye. Their prisoner staggered from the scene, but his bound hands messed with his balance and he lurched forward onto his knees. Blood stained his shoulder.

Must have gotten shot in the crossfire.

He struggled to his feet and resumed his odd getaway. Leine glanced at April, crouched next to Mateo. She'd been trained in field triage so would know what needed to be done.

Leine slung the AK across her back and trotted after the bound gunman.

"I DON'T KNOW WHAT YOU'RE TALKING ABOUT." THE GUNMAN, WHO went by the name of Bobo, spit a gob of blood onto the ground, barely missing Leine's boot. She hadn't been able to break him —yet. She'd tried everything from threats to pain to psychological torment, and still he hadn't talked. Her attempts hadn't been in vain—his reactions told her that he feared his boss, Dario, more than he did Leine. Bobo had grown weak from blood loss. The gunshot wound to his shoulder told Leine everything she needed to know about Hugo—a loyal soldier, he'd known he was a dead man and had tried to take out both their prisoner and Mateo to keep Dario's operation secret.

Such dedication.

Leine decided to crank things up a notch.

She walked past April and Gunnar tending to Mateo. Mercifully, Mateo had passed out from the pain. Although the wound was bad, in normal circumstances he'd have a fair chance of survival. But the jungle wasn't any kind of normal. Infection, parasites, or any number of complications could arise. Gunnar and April were doing what they could.

A few minutes later, she found what she was looking for. Distinctive-looking reddish-brown ants streamed along the trunk of a flowering tree buttressed by wide, shallow roots. Using a plastic pill container from the first aid kit, and careful not to let any of them hitch a ride on her hand, she captured several of the ants and quickly closed the lid, trapping them inside.

When she returned, Bobo appeared to have drifted off to sleep. Leine kicked his foot to wake him and his eyes snapped open. She bent down to show him the ants.

"You know what these are, right?" she asked.

Bobo's eyes saucered. His gaze shifted from the container to Leine's face, then back to the ants.

"*Sí.* Bullet ants." He visibly swallowed.

Leine straightened. "Yep. From what I understand, their sting is the gift that keeps on giving." A bite from just one of the ants was often described as a deep, throbbing ache that intensified over the course of twenty-four hours, mimicking the pain of a gunshot wound. Leine held up the container to get a good look at them. "I think this many should do the trick, don't you?" She smiled at Bobo, whose face had turned an even lighter shade of gray. Beads of sweat formed on his upper lip.

"You ready to talk?" She loosened the lid but held it closed. The ants swarmed to the top of the container. "Or do we see what happens when I drop them down your shirt near the gunshot wound?" She pulled his collar away from his neck and tipped the container forward.

"*Aiyeeee,*" he shrieked and tried to squirm away.

Leine paused. "That's a no?"

Bobo closed his eyes. After a few moments, he pulled in a ragged breath and let it go. When he opened them, she could tell he was ready to talk.

16

L eine walked over to join April and Gunnar to see how Mateo was doing. April had just changed his bandage. She glanced at her mother with a worried expression.

"We need to get him back to camp. Martin has better medical supplies."

"There is only so much we can do out here," agreed Gunnar.

The round had traveled through his torso, just below his ribs, exiting his back. Whether the bullet had damaged any internal organs remained to be seen. April had given him what antibiotics they had, but if he was going to survive, they needed more.

"The trip back will take several hours over rough terrain. Are you sure he can handle the journey?"

April shrugged. "I can't guarantee he'll survive if we stay. Besides, he's not conscious right now. He won't notice."

"Okay. Let's do it. We need to put together a travois so we can take turns pulling him. We can use the ponchos."

"Did you get Bobo to talk?"

Leine nodded. "I have a rough idea where Dario's camp is, although he couldn't give me specific coordinates. He's not in any shape to guide us there. He's lost a lot of blood. I doubt he'll last much longer."

"Then we should get moving." April opened her pack and pulled out her poncho and a length of rope. "We can use the rope to lash the poles together—"

Mateo stirred. A groan escaped his lips.

April froze. "That's the first time he's moved since he was shot."

Leine crouched near him. "Mateo. Can you hear me?"

April leaned down and brushed his hair from his forehead. "Mateo. It's me, April."

Restless, Mateo shifted his legs and moved his head from side to side. He groaned again, then opened his eyes and looked at April.

"Welcome back." April smiled.

Mateo struggled to sit up.

"Hold on, hold on. You need to stay quiet," Leine said, as she and April held him by his shoulders. "You've been seriously wounded."

Mateo stopped struggling and looked down at his torso. "What happened? Where's Hugo?" Obviously alarmed, he tried to sit up again, but the two women gently restrained him.

"Hugo's dead," Leine assured him.

"And the others?" Mateo sank back onto Gunnar's lap.

"You killed the gunman who was holding Gunnar," April said.

"Leine's been questioning the other man," Gunnar added.

"What did he tell you?"

"He gave me a general description of where Dario's camp is," Leine said, "but I'm not sure if I can find it without him. But first things first—we need to get you back to camp."

Mateo shook his head. "My father."

Leine gave him a sharp look. "What about your father?"

"Find him. He will help me."

"I think we should still take him back to camp," April said. "We can look for his father later, once we've given him fluids and more antibiotics."

"No. Find my father. It will be too difficult to move me. Besides, I'll slow you down. We will never make Martin's camp by nightfall."

The three exchanged looks. Gunnar shrugged.

Leine turned to Gunnar. "Do you feel comfortable heading back to camp on your own to pick up more supplies? You can let Martin know what happened."

"Yes. I'm certain I can find my way back."

"Great. April—you stay here with Mateo. Keep him company, change his dressings when he needs it." She nodded at the overhang near the waterfall. "Let's get you two under that overhang. You'll be safer there."

Gunnar and Leine helped Mateo stand and then carried him to the overhang. There was plenty of clearance for April to sit up with her back against the rock wall. Gunnar positioned Mateo at an angle with his head on top of April's pack.

Leine dug into her bag for extra magazines and handed two to April. "Keep these handy." Then she pulled out her rain gear and draped it over the two of them. "Attach my poncho to yours with duct tape. That should be enough to keep you both dry in case it rains."

"What will you do?" April asked.

"Tell me where to find your father," Leine said to Mateo. "If it's on the way, I'll keep an eye out for Dario's camp. If not, I'll resume my search after I find him."

"What about him?" Gunnar glanced back at the half-dead gunman Leine had tied to a tree. "Are you going to just leave him here?"

"No." Leine stood. "I'll take care of him. You should go, Gunnar."

April looked away.

Gunnar glanced at both Leine and April. "You mean kill him?"

"You need to go now, Gunnar." April's firm tone left no question.

Gunnar avoided both women's eyes as he picked up his pack. He paused for a moment. "I want you to know I will never speak of this again." Then he set off through the jungle toward Martin's camp.

Leine sighed as she watched him leave. She pulled out the topo map and spread it near Mateo. "Where should I look for your father?"

ONCE APRIL AND MATEO WERE SITUATED WITH PLENTY OF ammunition and water, Leine struck out, following the route Mateo had indicated would take her to his father's home.

Bobo had drawn his last breath sometime during Mateo and April's move to the overhang, eliminating the need to kill him. Leine covered his body with leaves and did the same for the other two gunmen after dragging them near Bobo. The jungle would reclaim them soon enough, attracting predators and scavengers alike.

She'd have preferred to bury the bodies, but there was no time. April and Mateo were far enough away and had plenty of ammunition in case predators smelled the blood and came looking for dessert. She pushed the worry for both her daughter and Mateo to the back of her mind and continued on.

"He is an expert at camouflage, so you will need to present

yourself at the great ceiba tree in the middle of a certain clearing," Mateo had said, pointing to the area on the map. He then drew a symbol on Leine's hand—a half circle with two lines emanating straight up that connected with two points. "He told me to carve this into the trunk of the tree should I ever need his help."

"How will I know it's the right one?" Leine had asked.

"It's the largest tree in the clearing. Look for a similar mark," he'd replied, "approximately one meter from the forest floor on the north side."

Leine moved swiftly through the jungle, making her way toward the area Mateo indicated on the map. She scanned the forest, alert for other gunmen Dario might have dispatched to follow Hugo and Gunnar. She hoped Gunnar made it to and from Martin's camp without picking up another tail.

The faster she found Mateo's father, the sooner she'd be able to search for Dario's camp, find Nancy, and eliminate the remaining gunmen. Mateo's survival now hinged on jungle medicine, of which Leine had precious little knowledge.

Not that she didn't believe in local cures. Years before when she'd run operations in South America, she'd seen some amazing shit she couldn't explain—but she knew what she was dealing with when it came to Western medicine. A gunshot wound required a specific medical protocol. She doubted leaves and sap and chanting would be enough to keep Mateo alive, but he'd been adamant about finding his father.

Hours later, when the sun had sunk below the trees, casting long shadows, she crested a ridge and found a clearing with an immense ceiba tree at its center. Ribbon-like buttress roots as tall as Leine flowed close to sixty feet from its base, the bark resembling the rough hide of an elephant. She glanced upward, guessing the giant's height to be somewhere around two hundred feet. Moving to the north side, she scanned the tree and found a faint symbol weathered with age, just as Mateo had described.

Leine unsheathed her knife, preparing to carve the symbol into the bark.

"Sorry, buddy," she said and raised the blade.

"Stop."

Leine froze, the tip of the knife touching the tree. She lowered her hand and slowly turned. A wiry man with long dark hair and red markings on his face stood several feet from her, a spear in his hand. Barefoot, he wore a long-sleeved shirt, a pair of filthy khakis, and a dozen necklaces made of what might have been seeds. A headband sporting bright red and yellow feathers completed the ensemble. His alert brown eyes reminded her of a raptor's gaze.

"You must not disturb this tree." His Spanish was good, if a bit rusty, telling her he might be Mateo's father. There was a certain family resemblance, although it was hard to see through the tangled dreadlocks.

Leine relaxed her arms to her sides to show him she meant no harm. "Mateo sent me."

Recognition sparked his eyes. "What were you about to carve into this tree?"

She showed him her palm with the drawing of the symbol.

He lowered his spear. "Why has he sent you?"

"He's been seriously wounded. He asked me to find you and bring you to him."

"How far?"

"Several hours to the east. Near a waterfall under a large rock overhang. My daughter is with him."

"We must go." He abruptly turned and headed back the way Leine had come. Leine followed.

Not much of a conversationalist.

He covered large swaths of jungle like the resident he was,

never stopping or slowing his stride. For someone who had to be at least mid-forties, he was in amazing shape. She stepped where he stepped and was able to close the distance between them.

"What's your name?" she asked, her breath coming fast from the effort of hiking at the increased pace. *Damned humidity*.

"Zolin," he said over his shoulder.

"I'm Leine."

"Yes."

"Do you know where we're going?"

Zolin stopped abruptly. "To the waterfall with the over-hanging rock to the east, correct?"

"Well, yes, but—"

Zolin resumed his rugged pace. Leine ran to catch up.

"You know *which* waterfall?"

"The spirits will show me."

"Wait a minute. The spirits?" Leine bent over and put her hands on her knees to catch her breath.

Zolin turned. The expression on his face spoke to his impatience at having to explain what to him was obvious. "Jungle spirits." He peered at her. "You are aware of this?"

Leine straightened, her heart rate almost back to normal. "I know that some people believe everything has a spirit, and that these spirits sometimes help when there is a need. Is that what you're talking about?"

Although she'd been exposed to South American animism several years before in the form of a man who claimed he was a shaman, she didn't give it much credence. Her suspicion was vindicated after local authorities exposed him for conning tourists with false "healings." Belief in something she couldn't see or feel or touch that was believed to have the power to disrupt or help was anathema to Leine. She believed in herself.

Period. Anything other than that struck her as wishful thinking at best, self-delusion at worst.

Zolin studied her for a moment, then nodded. "You will see." With that, he turned and resumed his trajectory through the jungle.

Leine sighed and followed him. The shadows had lengthened to the point that it was difficult to navigate the rough terrain. "It's getting dark. Shouldn't we stop for the night?"

"My son needs me."

Leine stopped to pull her night vision goggles from her pack and slid them on. "I have an extra pair."

Zolin waved her comment away. "I have no need of them."

The two continued through the darkening jungle. Night sounds echoed through the still air, lending a mysterious soundtrack to their journey. Every so often, something deep in the bush would scream, sounding eerily human.

Zolin didn't slow his pace. Leine found it easier to track him through the NVGs, which allowed her to keep up.

"How long have you lived in the jungle?"

Without missing a step, Zolin replied, "Many years. Why?"

"Just curious. You've got amazing night vision. I wonder how long it would take to develop living in the wild."

"Not as long as you think. The human animal is an amazing organism. The ability to adapt far exceeds its limitations." He stopped and waited for her to catch up. He nodded at the NVGs she wore. "Technology inhibits adaptation."

Leine shrugged. "I don't expect to be here long enough to develop that part of my 'organism.' Beats hiking with a headlamp."

"I see." Zolin closed his eyes and took in a deep breath. He exhaled and added, "When you live in the wild, all of your senses are sharpened. You'd be amazed what your physical body knows."

"Understood. I'm sure it depends heavily on what kind of training you have."

"And the ability of the organism to let go of preconceived ideas."

Leine wasn't about to argue with a man who'd trained as a shaman. Her approach and his were polar opposites. But she'd always welcomed different points of view, gleaning insights from even the wildest beliefs. Zolin's beliefs wouldn't be any different.

Although, she'd been wrong before.

.

17

D ario ended the call and slid the sat phone into his pack. Herberto Rodriguez was a spineless *pendejo*, interested only in accumulating power in his tiny section of the Amazon. Iquitos was a shithole, a place people traveled through in order to access the bounty of the rainforest. Herberto was a big fish in an insignificant pond, but he defended his territory as though he was King of South America.

He was King of Shit, as far as Dario was concerned.

Dario had much grander ambitions. Ambitions that Herberto had unwittingly reignited with his last phone call. Dario had assumed kidnapping the woman was a one-off, a lucrative side job in addition to the drug trafficking empire he'd created. But Herberto had told him more by what he didn't say.

The so-called lost city of gold was a pipe dream, Herberto had insisted. Only a few artifacts, if any, were believed to be recoverable, and had value only to those who studied them. Herberto's boss had decided that if Martin was unable to locate the lost city, then they would return the woman, unharmed, and allow him to continue with his expedition.

Right.

Dario knew a lie when he heard one. Why go to the trouble of kidnapping the man's daughter if there wasn't something to the discovery? When Dario'd pressed Nancy to tell him what she thought they would find at the site of the lost city, she'd been vague—a sure sign she was hiding something.

Something valuable.

Obviously, Herberto was attempting to cut him out of the loop. Dario wouldn't allow that to happen.

Dario had worked hard all his life, from his years growing up in the slums of Lima, to the day he joined a gang at age fourteen. Like so many before him, Dario started out as the go-between for cocaine suppliers and buyers. The local crime boss recognized Dario's ambition, and he allowed the young recruit to catapult up the ladder of the organization. Within two years, Dario had his own crew and was known as a ruthless but fair leader.

But in the drug trafficking world, leaders become targets. Dario knew this and employed heavy security for both himself and his girlfriend, Liliana, who was expecting their first child. During a particularly hot summer day, Dario left his home to mediate a dustup between rival factions, leaving Liliana and his unborn child in the hands of trusted members of his crew.

When he returned later that day, he opened the door to horror—blood covered the walls, the floor, the shattered furniture. The six men tasked with protecting his family were all dead, tied up and shot twice through the back of the head, execution-style.

His heart heavy, he'd followed a trail of fresh blood into the master bedroom, where he found Liliana on the king-size bed, covered in gore, her belly split open. His unborn child had been ripped from her womb and hung over the side of the bed, its umbilical cord wrapped around its neck. Its tiny face had turned blue from lack of oxygen. Horrified, Dario fell to his knees in grief, vowing revenge.

Throughout the following weeks, he left a trail of bloody corpses in his wake before he disappeared into the jungle, never to return to civilization. From that point on, he never allowed himself to grow close to anyone or anything except money, and worked ceaselessly in his search for wealth.

Money insulated him against the world, against loneliness. Against memories of the past. When that didn't work, whiskey was a good runner-up.

The coca trade had been lucrative, to be sure. The route Dario had established through the jungle, along with the relationships he'd built with various tribes in the area, promised a steady income with little risk other than the normal dangers of the terrain. Creating the route had been relatively easy. The remote tribes he dealt with had already gotten word that more accessible communities had made lucrative deals with companies who supplied "authentic" Amazon experiences to eager tourists, and they wanted a share.

Enter Dario and his gang of armed traffickers. First at gunpoint, then at his insistence, communities would work the coca fields to the detriment of their traditional crops of manioc, corn, beans, and bananas. He would pay them from the proceeds of successful shipments north, which involved a chain of people from the coca fields and beyond. Fueled by the European and *Norte Americano's* addiction to cocaine, this supply chain held the participating tribes captive. The communities were no longer self-sufficient—they relied on cash from the coca shipments to purchase food and other necessities. It was a win-win.

For Dario, at least.

But the idea of a lost city of gold—the fabled *El Dorado*—fueled Dario's imagination. And gold lust. He'd been brought up on stories of Lake Guatavita in Colombia, where believers offered untold amounts of gold trinkets to the god of the lake. Stories of ancient tribes who sacrificed slaves and holy men and women to appease their gods, and of countless quantities of gold and precious stones scattered throughout Amazonia, just waiting to be discovered.

And now he had an opportunity to take control of what may be the fabled lost city. He'd be rich. He would take the treasure and move it out of Peru along his supply lines, find collectors for the rare pieces, and melt down the rest.

He could leave the rainforest and live in luxury for the rest of his days.

Something stung him and he slapped his neck. Damned mosquitos. He'd have to research where to go to avoid the malicious little beasts. Somewhere warm—an island, perhaps—where they didn't drive a man to drink.

Dario walked over to the raised platform where he kept the woman. She lay in a hammock, pretending to be asleep. He knew she pretended because she'd seen him coming and had only just put her book down.

"Kind of early for a nap, yes?" he asked. He kicked the hammock, making it swing.

Her eyes popped open. "What do you want?"

The barely concealed hostility brought a bubble of laughter to his lips. "Now, now. Is that any way to treat an *amigo*?" He took a step closer so he could read the title of the book. Something with a bare-chested man on the cover. His lip curled in a sneer. "I think it will be dark soon. You will need a light so that you can continue reading."

She narrowed her eyes. "Why are you being nice to me? I already told you I know nothing about your lost city."

Dario chuckled. "My mother told me that I would catch more flies with honey."

"You had a mother?"

He tensed. A surge of anger coiled in his belly, and his hand itched to slap her for such insubordination. *Easy, Dario. It is unwise to bite the hand that feeds you.*

Not that she was relevant to his ultimate end, but he'd have to play the part.

For now.

"I will have one of my men find a light for you." Dario left the woman in the hammock and descended the steps. The shadows grew long as the sun sank below the trees. His men should have checked in by now. He gave the two women one night in the jungle alone before they ran back to camp, tails between their legs. He didn't anticipate any problems with Mateo. Not when Hugo knew how to find his father. He expected at least Bobo to be back that evening. The other two would most likely be out for a couple of days as the three teams searched for the city.

Dario smiled to himself. Letting the expedition do the hard work of finding the lost city was a stroke of genius. He wished he'd have thought of it himself. Herberto's boss had demanded that Dario not interfere with anything Martin and his people did to find the city. According to Herberto, *El Jefe* was adamant Dario not obstruct their movement in any way. He'd also made it known in no uncertain terms Dario was not to surveil the group in any manner, which of course created the opposite effect. There was something big about this discovery.

And Dario was just the one to exploit it.

18

Zolin had finally relented and slowed his pace so Leine could keep up. She marveled at his ability to sidestep obstacles, to pick out animals, plants, and insects that Leine wouldn't have seen even if she'd known where to look.

"The ceiba tree stands at the center of the earth," he said at one point. They'd been having an intermittent discussion of the world's religions to pass the time. "Many spirits call the tree home."

"Your belief is similar to Norse mythology. They called their tree *Yggdrasil*, which encompasses nine worlds. A serpent lies at its base, nibbling away at its roots, while an eagle lives high in its branches."

Zolin nodded. "I have heard this before, from a friend of my son that he met at school." He grew silent, his thoughts taking precedence over his words.

"I'm sorry about your family." Leine recognized his sadness. Profound loss was quiet, powerful, a gut punch. When she'd lost Carlos, her first love, she'd been unable to function. She'd descended into a life of alcohol abuse and self-hatred, and neglected April, afraid to take her down with her. April had felt abandoned and left town as soon as she reached legal age, traveling Europe and avoiding all contact with Leine.

With help from Santa, Leine pulled herself from the abyss and found a new life and *raison d'etre* providing assistance to victims of human trafficking. Eventually, she and April managed to patch things up and were now on solid ground.

Zolin said over his shoulder, "You have lost someone close to you. A man."

Leine nodded. "I have."

He stopped and closed his eyes. His chest rose and fell with a steady breath. After a few moments, he opened them and stared directly at Leine. "The spirits have a message for you." With that, he resumed walking.

"What the—" Leine rolled her eyes and followed. When she caught up, she tapped him on the shoulder and said, "And?"

Zolin shook his head and kept walking. "Not now. First, we must find my son."

"How did you become a shaman? I assume you went through some kind of training."

"I learned from the Shipibo."

"I've heard of them. They're native to this area of the Amazon?"

Zolin nodded. "They are known as great healers."

"I'm not all that familiar with shamanism."

"That's understandable where you come from."

"How do you know where I come from? I haven't said."

"Your mannerisms and accent tell me you are a Westerner, most likely from the West Coast of the United States." He stopped and peered at her. "California?"

"Bingo."

He resumed their trek. "As I said before, living in the jungle hones your senses. Everything takes on a different cast. Where modern amenities like automobiles, televisions, and dish-washers are meant to make life easier, all they really accomplish is moving you farther and farther away from what it really means to be human."

"And what does it mean to be human?"

Zolin stopped and bent down to pick several leaves from a low-growing plant. "Have you ever watched an animal hunt?"

"I'm afraid I don't spend a lot of time outdoors with preda-tors." *Except for the human kind.*

He tucked the leaves in a leather pouch hanging from his waist before moving on. "You would learn from the process. Animals have an instinctual ability to notice slight disturbances in the earth's energy field."

"Ah. You mean like when a cat or a dog senses earthquakes. Or when birds migrate."

"Human beings used to have the same ability. But it's been bred from us. We no longer need to hunt to survive, and most of us don't spend significant time in nature. Instinct is like any other muscle. If you don't use it, it atrophies."

"You're saying you can tell when an energy field is disturbed?"

"And much more."

"Do you use drugs to achieve this state?"

"I have, yes. The plants help speed up the process. It will happen over time, though. Even if you don't partake in the ayahuasca ceremony."

Leine had heard of the ayahuasca vine and its psychotropic properties. The con artist shaman she'd known from years before had guaranteed a spiritual experience to anyone who would pay him to conduct the ceremony. Younger tourists flocked to him, believing he was the real deal. They definitely got an experience, and not always good.

The dream she'd had the night before came back to her, and she shook her head to clear it. She'd seen through the eyes of a predator stalking through the jungle. The imagery most likely stemmed from the close encounter she'd had with the jaguar.

Zolin took the lead again. Leine didn't recognize their surroundings and checked her compass to make sure they were still headed in the right direction.

"You haven't asked what happened to Mateo."

"He's been shot."

Leine stumbled over a root, but she caught herself. "I'm sorry?"

"The spirits sent a dream to tell me he'd been shot, here." He cupped his side indicating Mateo's wound. "I also dreamed you would take me to him, and that a young woman with long dark hair would be with him."

Leine's bullshit meter didn't know which way to swing. Zolin knew Mateo had a gunshot wound, which she hadn't mentioned. But she had told him April stayed behind to make sure he was safe.

"You don't believe in dreams?" Zolin asked.

"I believe dreams are your subconscious sorting through the information your brain has collected throughout the day."

"Interesting."

"Why is that? I suppose you're going to tell me that your definition of a dream is more accurate."

"Not at all. I just find it interesting."

"You know, you don't strike me as an ex-special forces kind of guy."

"Why? Because we just had a philosophical discussion? Would you prefer I grunt, scratch my ass, and throw a hand grenade?"

"That's not exactly what I meant, but point taken." Obviously she had some ingrained biases she needed to check at the door.

"So if you had a dream about Mateo, then you must know if he survives his wounds."

Zolin was quiet for a moment. "Some things are not meant to be seen."

Leine wasn't sure she liked the sound of that.

19

April's eyes snapped open. *What was that?*

Mateo hadn't stirred. She touched his face—he was burning up.

Infection had set in.

She grabbed her canteen and shook it. There wasn't much water left. She unscrewed the cap and poured some in her palm, then dripped it on his forehead and into his open mouth. He stirred, but didn't wake. They needed more water. Careful not to disturb him, she rose, picked up the assault rifle, and climbed down from their perch on the covered ledge. She skirted the cliff base and headed to the waterfall.

The moss-covered rocks near the small catch basin were slick and the handholds scarce. She picked her way forward to the waterfall where she held the open canteen underneath the cascade of cool water until it overflowed. She dropped in a water purification tablet and screwed the top back on. Then she turned and gingerly started back across the slippery rocks.

A troupe of howler monkeys filled the early morning calm with their demonic roars, and she froze. She'd heard them before on the hike into Martin's camp. They reacted when humans encroached on the simians' territory. But this time was different—she and Mateo had been sleeping under the overhang, so the monkeys weren't reacting to them. Hyperaware of being alone and the sole defender of an injured person deep in the Amazon, she knew the only thing standing between her and any number of predators was her rifle, ammunition, and her ability to use them.

Something moved in her periphery. A man in camouflage stood up from behind a clump of ferns, his rifle aimed at her chest. April's heart leapt and she instinctively went for her rifle. Seconds later, two more men appeared, one in front and one to her side, both of their weapons trained on her.

Restraining herself from glancing at Mateo, she faced the first gunman and raised her hands.

He barked an order at the other two and headed for the overhang. One of them took her rifle and patted her down, while the other covered her with his gun.

The first gunman headed straight to Mateo.

"He's wounded and sick," she yelled.

He ignored her. Mateo stirred and tried to lift his head.

April clenched her jaw, willing herself to remain outwardly calm, but inside she boiled with anger. These thugs were going to either kill them both or try to move them. Mateo was in no condition to travel. She turned to the gunman who had taken her weapon.

"He needs medicine. He won't survive."

He didn't respond—just stared. Frustrated, she called to the first gunman, "He can't be moved. He will never survive."

The first gunman grabbed Mateo under his arms and lifted him to a sitting position. Mateo groaned and opened his eyes. The gunman shouted at the second man to help him. The second gunman sprinted to the overhang and climbed up to help lift Mateo to his feet.

"You can't do that. He's going to die." April started for the overhang, but the gunman covering her shoved his rifle into her back as a warning. She closed her eyes and took a deep breath.

Getting herself killed wouldn't do Mateo any good. These men were obviously under orders to take them alive. She'd have to do what she could to make sure they both survived.

She raised her hands.

20

L eine checked her compass again. "We should be able to hear the water by now." She stopped and surveyed their surroundings. She'd found two of the markers she'd left behind as she hiked through the jungle, but hadn't found the third one signifying the last leg to the waterfall.

Zolin stopped and rummaged through a leather pouch that hung from his waist. He pulled out a small package made of leaves and opened it to reveal a brown powder. Leine watched as he tapped some onto the back of his hand and snorted it. He returned the small package to the pouch and sat on a nearby rock.

Maybe the guy needed a break. They'd been walking all night. The brown stuff was probably dried coca leaves, which would give him a boost. Leine had been fighting fatigue for the last couple of hours and hoped she hadn't steered them wrong. She made certain they'd kept moving east. Leine pulled out the topo map and traced their path from the last marker.

Zolin took a deep breath, closed his eyes, and in a low voice began to chant. The words were unintelligible. His voice pitched high, then swooped down to a baritone, then rose up the scale back to where he'd started. Fascinated, Leine wondered what he was doing. Some kind of ritual to assist a lost traveler? Or perhaps he was praying to the spirits to help his son.

Whatever it was, she hoped it worked.

Leine scanned the forest, looking for something familiar, but the terrain was similar to what they'd just come through. She checked the map one more time. There. Why didn't she see it before? The topography mirrored an area to their left.

Leine folded the map and waited for Zolin to finish. When he was through, he took a deep breath and sighed, then opened his eyes.

"Mateo is gone."

She gave him a sharp look. "Gone? You mean he's dead?"

Zolin shook his head. "He is gone."

"Mateo's in no shape to go anywhere. We need to get to the waterfall. I think I know where we are."

Twenty minutes later, the welcome sound of splashing water could be heard in the distance. Getting her second wind, Leine stepped up her pace and rounded a group of palms. There, across an expanse of ferns, was the waterfall. The overhang lay in shadow. She couldn't make out if April and Mateo were still there.

The two of them quickly covered the distance to the overhang.

They weren't there. Leine's heart dropped to her stomach. She climbed up to the ledge but found only the two ponchos. The packs were gone.

She turned to Zolin. "How did you know they wouldn't be here?"

"I called on the spirit of the waterfall."

"Where are they now?" The only explanation that made sense was that Dario's men had found them. She didn't think

April would have taken Mateo someplace on her own. He wouldn't have been able to go far.

"Give me something of Mateo's."

"There are only the two ponchos."

Zolin nodded. "That's fine."

"They have to be at Dario's camp." Leine handed him the taped-together ponchos. He draped them over his shoulders and grew quiet. She took out the map and compass and planned a route to Dario's camp based on Bobo's directions.

"There is death here." Zolin looked at Leine. "Their spirits cry."

He obviously meant the dead gunmen. "You were a soldier. If you were threatened, what would you have done?"

"I am no longer a soldier." He closed his eyes.

Leine put the map away and walked to the waterfall, where she refilled her canteen and splashed water on her face and neck. Time to rethink her strategy. Statistically speaking, operations rarely went according to plan, which was why she'd been trained to think on her feet and have a backup plan or five.

Dario was down three gunmen, as well as Hugo. How many more of his thugs had infiltrated Martin's camp? She glanced back at Zolin. According to Martin, he used to be Brazilian Special Forces. Could she count on him to use those skills to rescue his son?

His actions told her he'd left that life behind. Period.

Her main concern was to rescue her daughter. Next in line would be Nancy, then Mateo. Taking out Dario and his thugs would likely be necessary, but she didn't rule out exfiltration without exchanging gunfire.

First, she had to find Dario's camp. Bobo had given her a rough idea of where it was, but she couldn't be certain he'd been telling the truth. She took a deep breath and let it go. There was a hell of a lot of territory to cover between where she and Zolin were now and Dario's camp.

Leine screwed the cover back on her canteen and returned to where Zolin was folding up the ponchos.

"Anything?" she asked. She was willing to hear the shaman out—he'd known his son was no longer at the waterfall. He'd also known Mateo had been shot, and that there was a young woman with him.

Zolin handed her the ponchos, which she stuffed into her pack.

"Our children are still alive."

Relief swept through Leine, but she checked herself. His statement was not fact—it was akin to reading a horoscope in a magazine and believing the forecast had anything to do with anything.

For entertainment purposes only.

Still, his words ignited a small flame of hope that April was all right.

Jesus, Leine. Get a grip. Now you're going to take the assurances of a shaman that your daughter's alive? Time for a reality check.

She pushed the hope back into a corner of her mind and shouldered her pack.

"Let's hope you're right."

21

The first gunman took the lead, with April second in line. April glanced behind her to see how Mateo was doing. Blood soaked through his bandage, staining his shirt. Mercifully, he'd passed out from the pain. The other two gunmen dragged Mateo between them.

"You're going to kill him." Her outrage didn't move either gunman.

They walked for what seemed like hours. The humidity and soaring temperature added to the grueling death march. April made a point of stopping to drink from her canteen and insisted she be able to dribble water into Mateo's mouth. Surprisingly, the first gunman didn't object. That one allowance gave her hope that Dario wanted them both delivered alive.

A few hours later, when April thought she couldn't walk another step, the first gunman stopped and held up his fist. The two men holding Mateo stopped immediately. April scanned the area, wondering why they'd halted. She unscrewed the top of her canteen and was about to take a drink when she spotted white smoke curling through the air.

We must be at Dario's camp.

Gunman One cupped his hands around his mouth. The sound he made bore an uncanny resemblance to a toucan's call. A minute later the same call was returned, this time with a higher pitch. Gunman One's shoulders relaxed, and he gestured for the group to move forward.

The camp consisted of three raised huts, all with palm-thatched roofs and no walls, and various small outbuildings. A fire blazed at the center of the clearing, with what looked like a wild boar on a spit. Several armed gunmen were visible—two covered the perimeter, while the others—April counted six—lazed about on wooden benches and plastic chairs. She wondered if Dario was among them.

As they approached, a dark-haired man walked toward them, his expression unreadable.

"What have we here?" he asked Gunman One in Spanish.

"We found them several hours from here near a waterfall."

The man glanced at April and Mateo. "Where are Hugo and the others?" he asked the gunman.

Gunman One hesitated. "All dead, *jefe*."

Jefe's expression hardened. "Dead? How can that be?" He nodded at the two hostages. "One is near death himself, and the other is a woman. Don't tell me these two had something to do with such a massacre?"

"No, *jefe*. We believe they were waiting for help. One of the men saw the man they call Gunnar headed back to the other camp."

"I know this man. He is not a fighter." He narrowed his eyes at April. "What about her?"

April bristled. "What about me?"

The corner of *jefe's* mouth quirked up in a cruel grin. "I think you are a fighter."

"She had this." Gunman One slipped the AK-47 off his shoulder and handed it to him.

Jefe took the assault rifle and slung it over his shoulder. "I was right." He looked at Gunman One. "Where is the other woman?"

"Other woman?" Gunman One's face was a blank.

"There were two women sent to help Martin find his daughter."

April froze. *How did he know that?* Mateo had been MIA during part of their hike through the jungle, but he didn't appear to have any equipment that could have been used to contact Dario. Had he told the gunman he met in the jungle? Or had Hugo somehow alerted Dario? Maybe after Martin made the call to Lou for help.

"She was not there, *jefe*."

Jefe sighed. "Then she is a danger." He waved at the other men sitting around the camp. "Ready your weapons. Vigilance is paramount."

"What should we do with these two?" Gunman One nodded at April and Mateo.

"We will use them as bait. This one," he cupped April's chin with his hand, "is the other woman's partner. I do not think she will leave her to die."

April jerked her head away, her anger rising. "Don't touch me."

Jefe chuckled. "Like I said, a fighter."

"The other one is not doing well, *jefe*."

Jefe glanced at Mateo, who stood unsteadily between the other two gunmen. Sweat slicked his face, telling April his fever had gotten worse.

"He needs medical treatment," she said. "Antibiotics, fluids. I need to change his bandages."

Jefe considered them both for a moment. "We should keep this *cabrón* alive for a little while longer. Dead bait is not as effective." He turned and yelled, "Roberto, come here."

One of the gunmen who had been patrolling the perimeter peeled off from the group and jogged over to them.

"*Si, jefe?*"

"I need you to do what you can for this man."

Roberto glanced at Mateo. "*Que?*"

Jefe nodded at Mateo. "Keep him alive a while longer." Doubt filled Roberto's face. *Jefe* barked, "That is an order."

Roberto snapped to attention and slammed his heels together. "*Si, jefe!*" He jerked his head at the two gunmen holding Mateo. "*¡Vamanos!*"

Roberto led the way back to one of the platforms, gesturing for the other gunmen to drag Mateo up the stairs. April lost sight of him after that.

"What should I do with her?" Gunman One asked.

"Take her to the other platform and tie her up." *Jefe* moved his gaze slowly up her body, stopping at her eyes. "Be sure she can't escape. This one is like a snake."

"But *jefe,* that is where—"

"Yes, I know," he snapped. "We will move her."

With that, Gunman One grasped April by the arm and dragged her to the opposite platform. Someone was lying in one of two hammocks. April couldn't make out the person's face through the mosquito netting.

Gunman One shoved her toward a roof support. "Sit."

April slid down the support until she reached the floor. Her mind turned over possible escape routes, but each one ended with her dead. Besides, she didn't want to leave Mateo.

The gunman zip-tied her wrists together, then walked over to the hammock and lifted the netting.

"Get up. We're leaving."

The person sat up, giving her a clear view of their face. April's heart raced.

Nancy.

———

22

Leine and Zolin ducked behind the thick trunk of a tree. They'd been roughly following the topo map to where Bobo had indicated Dario kept his camp. The smell of smoke reached them first, telling Leine they'd found their target. Using the binoculars she peered at the camp through the leaves of an acai tree. Three gunmen were visible. One patrolled the perimeter while the other two each occupied a separate sector.

She scanned the two structures for April or Mateo. Both platforms were in shadow near the center, the darkness bleeding off at the edges. In the hut to her left, through the lengthening shadows of midafternoon, Leine could make out two empty hammocks strung between roof supports, with someone sitting on the floor, leaning against one of the supports. She couldn't be sure, but the figure appeared to be female.

Three hammocks hung in the structure to the right, one of them occupied.

She handed the binoculars to Zolin, who studied the scene before them.

"Three heavily armed gunmen." He gave her back the binoculars. "There are only two possible prisoners. Didn't you say you are searching for another kidnapping victim?"

Leine nodded. "The daughter of a friend." She held up the binoculars again. "I've got a bad feeling about this."

Zolin cocked his head. "A bad feeling? I thought you were only interested in facts."

Leine rolled her eyes. "I use a little bit of everything to assess risk. Some people call it intuition. I call it my gut. Whatever you call it, it's a combination of past experience, observation and training, and target knowledge."

Zolin shook his head. "You sound like my commanding officer."

"And that's bad?"

He shrugged. "Not when your life depends on it."

"So what does your training tell you?"

His expression grave, he said, "I've got a bad feeling about this."

"So we go in expecting a trap."

"These men look like drug runners. We'll need to watch for tripwires and viper pits."

"The same tactics the VC used against soldiers in Vietnam."

"Exactly. Jungle warfare works in any jungle. Punji stakes, spike balls, venomous snakes, you think of it, they'll know how to use it."

Leine and Zolin ducked back behind the tree trunk. Leine pulled out her knife.

"Never take a knife to a gunfight," Zolin chided.

Leine ignored the joke and brushed away a layer of leaves and other plant matter to bare ground. Then she used the tip of her knife to draw a rough map of the camp in the dirt.

"There are three guards visible, and two potential targets. If this is a trap, then the two people on the platforms could be armed decoys. But they could also be April and Mateo, or Nancy.

If that's the case, then there are probably gunmen concealed in the jungle. We have to be ready to defend ourselves from all quarters."

Zolin nodded, thinking. He pointed at three separate areas on her roughed-out map. "I'd booby trap here, here, and here."

"Duly noted."

"Too bad we don't have more firepower."

Leine smiled.

"What?" Zolin squinted at her.

She dug inside her pack, pulled out three frag grenades, and handed him two. Then she slipped the AK off her shoulder and handed it to him.

"What about you? A lone grenade won't be helpful at close range, unless you use it as a threat."

"Don't worry about me." She raised the hem of her shirt to show him the holstered 9mm.

"You're a woman of many surprises."

"I've found that having more weapons than you think you'll need is useful, no matter the circumstances."

"Exploding grenades may bring Dario and his men running."

"Who's to say they aren't here already? Create a diversion with one of the grenades. That'll be enough to bring out whoever's nearby," Leine said. "I'll take care of the three guards and anyone else who shows up, as well as identify who's in the huts. If we're overrun, use the second grenade."

"Let's hope we aren't."

"You still a good shot?"

Zolin gave her a baleful stare. "What do you think?"

"Just checking."

Zolin pocketed the two grenades and slipped from behind the tree, headed for the southwest end of camp. Leine waited to make sure he was in position before she headed northeast toward the farthest structure.

Using the abundant shrubbery and ferns as cover between herself and the three guards, she picked her way toward a clump of colorful heliconia located closer to camp, mindful of possible trip wires or other hidden dangers. Halfway there, she froze.

Something didn't look right.

She dropped to a crouch and studied a clump of ferns. Looking closer, she noticed fresh dirt. She picked up a nearby branch and used the end to gingerly lift a large section of moss. There was no resistance, telling her it had been disturbed recently.

There weren't any wires that she could see, so she lifted the section of earth higher, revealing a void. She turned the clump upside down and peered inside the deep hole. Several rows of barbed stakes pointed straight up.

Punji stakes.

Something moved inside the pit. Leine stepped back and pulled her pistol free.

Entwined around the sticks was a huge snake. Its triangular head and dark brown markings identified it as a bushmaster— one of the deadliest pit vipers in South America. It raised its head, its forked tongue testing the air. Someone had impaled the muscular tail to the earth with one of the stakes, imprisoning it in the pit. Leine backed away slowly, leaving the hole in the ground exposed.

Her heart rate had returned to normal by the time she reached her target location. She raised her hand, signaling to Zolin she was in position.

23

The explosion from the grenade shattered the air. Pandemonium erupted in the canopy, as birds and monkeys and every other kind of animal in the vicinity screamed, squawked, and howled in agitation. The three guards whirled toward the sound, guns raised.

Leine used the diversion to move in. She squeezed off rounds, hitting the closest guard in the back of the head. He dropped like a marionette with its strings cut. She slung his mini Uzi over her shoulder and moved to the next.

The second guard pivoted and aimed, but he was too late. Leine fired, hitting him in the throat. His rifle fell from his grasp and he hit the dirt. She picked up the AK and continued into the compound.

The third gunman had made it halfway to where Zolin had holed up in a stand of palms. Leine swept the compound with the AK, scanning for combatants.

The *rat-tat-tat-tat* of machinegun fire crackled through the air. She didn't know if it was Zolin or the third gunman. There was no gunfire from anywhere else, so she moved to the first hut and climbed the steps. A quick sweep of the platform revealed

April seated on the floor, her back to the roof support with her wrists tied together.

Leine moved to her and ripped off the tape covering her mouth.

"It's a trap," she gasped as Leine cut her free. "Dario's done something with Mateo—I don't know what. But I heard two of the guards laughing about it." She climbed to her feet, and Leine handed her the AK.

"Mateo's in the other hut." April touched Leine's arm. "I saw Nancy."

"Alive?"

"Alive. They took her somewhere. I'm not sure where."

"How many gunmen are there?"

"Several took off, but as far as I know, no more than half a dozen stayed behind."

More gunfire erupted on the other side of the camp. Leine and April descended the steps and made their way toward Zolin and the other hut.

Leine took the lead as they cleared the open space at the center of camp to reach the second hut. Leine gestured to April to check on Mateo, reminding her to be careful of traps. Then she circled behind the third gunman.

He had his back to her as she moved toward him, but she couldn't get a clear shot. Leine caught a glimpse of Zolin behind a stand of banana plants. He engaged the third gunman and fell back, keeping the other man's attention on him. Her finger on the trigger, Leine skirted the second hut, getting into position. There was movement in her periphery and she spun around.

A series of gunshots split the air above her. A fourth gunman, hiding behind a clump of ferns, grunted and dropped to the ground. Leine glanced up to see April swing her rifle toward the third gunman from her perch on the platform of the second hut.

She squeezed off another volley, and the third gunman fell.

Leine waited for more, but none came. She scanned above and behind but found no other threats. She waved at Zolin, who broke cover and started toward the platform.

She ran to the third gunman, but he was definitely dead. The round had penetrated the upper section of skull, exiting the forehead. She picked up his weapon and handed it to Zolin.

"Go and tend to your son. I'll check the other gunman. Watch for traps."

Zolin sprinted to the far platform.

The fourth gunman was still breathing and alert. Blood soaked his shoulder and stained the front of his clothes. The look on his face told her he was in horrible pain. She relieved him of his rifle and slung it over her shoulder. "What else you got?" she asked. Not expecting an answer, she covered him as she patted him down.

Other than a tactical knife, he didn't have any other weapons on him. She stepped back, aiming the barrel of the gun at his face. "Where did they take the woman?"

No answer. Again, she wasn't really expecting one. His insolent look told her he didn't understand what was coming. He'd break. They always did.

With a sigh, Leine went to work.

LEINE WAS RIGHT. THANKFULLY, IT DIDN'T TAKE LONG TO EXTRACT the information. The gunman died soon afterward. Dario had ordered Nancy moved to a second camp, not far from Martin's.

She climbed the steps to the platform two at a time and stopped abruptly. April and Zolin stood near Mateo, trying to get him to respond. He looked bad. His skin had a gray cast, and his shirt was saturated in blood.

Zolin lifted his son's chin, studying him with a practiced eye. "Do you know matico?" he asked Leine.

She nodded. "I believe so, yes." The plant was popular in the Amazon and had a chapter devoted to it in the book Leine had been reading on the boat.

"There is a large stand of them just outside of camp, near the banana plants. Gather several handfuls of the leaves and bring them to me."

Leine did as he asked, finding the leafy shrub easily. She stripped its leaves and hurried back.

"What does it do?" April asked, watching as he opened Mateo's shirt and removed the bloody bandage to reveal a wound filled with pus. The skin around it was an angry shade of red.

"It has antibacterial and antifungal properties," Zolin explained. He chanted as he crushed the leaves and applied the poultice to Mateo's wound. His movements were measured and deliberate, taking great care to cover the wound completely.

April leaned next to Leine and whispered, "What's he singing?"

"It's how he speaks to the spirits."

"Which spirits?"

Leine shrugged. "Plants?"

Zolin paused his chanting and said, "I need boiling water. And a bowl."

April sprang to her feet. "I know where they keep their drinking water." She hurried down the steps and disappeared.

Leine moved to the edge of the platform to scan the jungle for threats.

Continuing the eerie, unintelligible chant, Zolin rummaged inside the pouch hanging from his waist and pulled out a small bundle. He opened it and shook the contents onto the poultice.

A short time later, April reappeared with a steaming pot of

hot water and a bent metal cup. Still chanting, Zolin dropped several of the matico leaves into the hot water and swirled them around with his finger. April and Leine continued to watch the perimeter, both of them stealing glances at Mateo and his father.

After a few minutes, Zolin poured the liquid from the tea into the metal cup and held it to Mateo's lips, lifting him to a sitting position. He opened his eyes for a moment, but then closed them. Zolin murmured something in his ear, and Mateo took several sips of the brew.

Obviously exhausted, Mateo fell back in the hammock. Still chanting, Zolin set the cup down and again rummaged inside his pouch. He withdrew a bundle of dried herbs and lit them with a lighter from his pocket. He allowed the bundle to burn for a few seconds, then blew out the flame. The acrid smoke drifted toward Leine, reminding her of burned sage.

Zolin leaned toward Mateo and blew the smoke over his entire body, making sure to direct smoke toward the wounded area multiple times. When the bundle had burned to a nub, Zolin extinguished the embers and laid the remaining herbs next to the wound.

He stepped back from the hammock.

"What do you think?" Leine asked.

"I think he is very sick." Zolin rubbed his hands with the remaining leaves of the matico before discarding them. "His life is now in the hands of the spirits."

"May I ask what you were singing?" April asked.

"I was praying to the spirit of the matico to heal my son."

"That's amazing. Does every plant have a spirit?"

He nodded, a tired smile tugging at his lips. "That is my belief, yes. It's how we know which plants to use when we treat someone."

"They communicate with you?"

"Yes."

"Can only a shaman like you understand the plant spirits?" April asked.

Zolin studied her, his deep brown eyes searching hers. "I have seen it happen for others, so no, it is not only within the realm of the shaman."

"I would *love* to learn how to do that."

"It takes time and dedication." He glanced at Leine who gave him a slight shrug. "Of which we don't have."

"No, of course not now. Right now, we need to help Mateo recover."

Something caught Leine's eye, and she stepped closer to Mateo's hammock. A thin wire, barely visible, ran up the back side of the support post, high into the rafters above them.

"Uh-oh."

24

"What's wrong?" April stepped closer to Leine and followed her gaze.

"Take a look." Leine nodded at the post. She walked away from the hammock, eyes glued to the wire running across the ceiling. She followed it several feet and stopped. The line terminated at a series of detonators connected to several white blocks of what appeared to be C-4.

"Holy shit." April stared at the plastic explosives packed into the rafter. "Why didn't it go off when Zolin moved him to drink the tea?"

Leine walked back to the support to check the other end of the wire, which had been threaded through the hammock. She followed its length, testing it. "It's wired like a pressure plate."

"So if he gets out of the hammock, the bomb goes off?"

Leine nodded. She walked to the edge of the platform, climbed up, and stood on the railing. From there she hooked her arm around one of the rafters, swung her legs up and over, and moved across each one so she could use them as an improvised catwalk to make her way to the explosives.

She checked for a failsafe. Finding none, she followed the

wires to a small battery trigger hidden behind a rafter and disconnected them. Then she shunted the wires on the caps to prevent accidental detonation before removing each from the blocks of C-4. She double-checked to make sure there were no other backup explosives feeding into the hammock before she peeled the C-4 off the rafters and gave them to April.

No reason to leave it for the next guy.

Satisfied there would be no more surprises, Leine pocketed the detonators, before she backtracked through the rafters and slid down a roof support to the floor. "That explains why none of Dario's thugs came back here after the first grenade went off."

Zolin nodded in agreement. "So his men believe we are dead."

"That's enough C-4 to blow up a house, so yeah, I would say so."

"Then they probably won't be back, right?" April asked.

"Maybe, but I wouldn't count on it." Leine turned to Zolin. "How soon can Mateo be moved?"

He studied his son, who appeared to be sleeping peacefully. "I can't say. He needs to rest."

"I'm not comfortable staying here. We need to get him back to Martin's camp ASAP, as long as he can be moved without endangering his life."

"We could move him just far enough so that he can't be seen by anyone who might do him harm," April offered.

"That's a possibility. Zolin should make that call." She turned to the shaman. "Besides the explosives, I found a trap on my way into camp, and there may be more. The one I found had a bushmaster in a pit filled with punji stakes."

"Is the pit too deep for the snake to get out?"

"Someone drove a stake into its tail. It's stuck."

A look of alarm crossed Zolin's features. "Show me."

Leine and Zolin walked into the jungle, leaving April to watch over Mateo.

"Step where I step," Leine warned, "and we should be all right."

They continued to where Leine had seen the pit. She grabbed the branch she'd used to lift the covering off the hole and handed it to Zolin as he peered in at the hissing snake. An unmistakable rattling sound echoed from deep inside. He took a step back, muttering something unintelligible.

"What?" Leine asked, keeping her distance. There was no telling how far the coiled snake could strike. Bushmasters were known aggressors.

"The men who have committed this heinous act deserve to have the same done to them."

"I'd agree with you there."

Zolin removed his shirt and headband and approached the hole.

"What are you doing?"

Ignoring her question, he slowly sank to his knees and peered over the edge of the pit at the snake. The bushmaster hissed and rattled its alarm, but Zolin remained where he was, making no sudden moves. Soon, the snake calmed, and the hissing became intermittent.

"I may need your help."

"Okay." Against her better judgment, Leine joined him. "Just so we're on the same page, what's your idea here?"

"I'm going to free him."

"Yeah, uh-no. That is *not* a good idea, Zolin."

"You would leave him here to die?"

He had a point. "When you put it that way—"

Zolin tied his headband into a slip knot and, using the stick, carefully lowered it over the bushmaster's triangular head. With a quick movement, he raised the stick and cinched the noose tightly around the snake's neck. The snake writhed against the trap as Zolin pulled the snake's head up toward Leine.

"Wrap my shirt around his head so he can't bite."

Leine grabbed his shirt and dropped it over its head. She quickly pulled the material tight, wondering if the snake would suffocate.

"Tie it off and grab the stick. Be sure to keep the snake's head away from us both. I'm going to pull the stake out of its tail—be ready to fall back."

Shit. The man was serious. Once the snake was free, what would stop it from turning on either her or Zolin? Leine tied off the shirt, then grabbed the stick. The snake was strong—she could barely hold it steady.

Zolin reached into the pit, grasped the end of the stake embedded in the serpent's tail, and heaved. At the same time the tail came free, Zolin fell back. Leine released her hold on the stick and jumped clear. The snake immediately slithered out of the pit. Without a backward glance, it disappeared through the tall grass.

Heart pounding, Leine watched it go, leaving Zolin's headband and shirt in its wake. The shaman climbed to his feet and walked over to Leine. He offered a hand to help her up.

"Well, that was exciting." Leine stood and brushed off her cargo pants. "How did you know it wouldn't turn on us?"

Zolin shrugged. "I didn't."

LEINE AND ZOLIN FOUND SUITABLE TREES AND CUT THEM DOWN TO use for a travois frame, then brought them back to camp. April took down a hammock, which they lashed to the poles with some cord she found in a storage container underneath one of the platforms.

"Will he be all right?" April placed her hand on Mateo's forehead. "I think his fever broke."

Zolin nodded. "I believe so, yes."

Mateo's eyelids fluttered and then opened. His gaze flickered from April to his father, back to April.

April smiled. "Welcome back."

Mateo gave her a weak smile before returning his gaze to Zolin. "Thank you for coming."

"We were about to move you." Zolin slid his hand underneath his shoulders to help him sit up.

Mateo resisted. "Wait—the hammock is wired."

"Mom took care of that," April said. "You're safe."

He relaxed his shoulders and allowed his father to bring him the rest of the way up. April helped swing his legs over the edge of the hammock. "What happened to the other men?"

Leine wrapped his arm around her shoulder. Zolin took the opposite side to help him stand. "Your guards are dead. We're not sure about the others."

"They'll be back. They were expecting the explosives to go off when you came for me."

"Yeah, I wouldn't worry about that."

Mateo glanced at Leine with a puzzled expression.

"The grenade your father set off when we took the camp." She shrugged. "Sounds a lot like C-4."

"They still might come back—this camp is one of their main compounds. There have to be provisions."

"That's why we're moving you." Leine and Zolin walked him over to the steps.

"Nancy was here."

"We know."

"I think they took her to another camp."

Leine nodded. "Dario's main camp."

Mateo glanced at her. "How did you know that?"

"Don't ask."

Zolin remained quiet, his mood somber. Leine took note but didn't say anything. If he wanted to share his thoughts, he would.

They moved Mateo to the base of the steps and lowered him onto the travois. April and Leine secured him so he wouldn't fall off.

When she finished strapping him into the travois, April straightened and said, "I'm going to look for items we can use. I doubt they took everything, especially if they plan to come back. I think I saw something promising under the other platform."

Leine was about to do the same, when she noticed Zolin studying Mateo, his gaze sharp and penetrating.

Mateo must have noticed because he said, "What's wrong?"

Zolin made a sign in the air above him. "Your soul will not allow you to heal."

"My soul's fine."

The shaman shook his head, his expression grave. "You must unburden yourself."

Mateo rolled his eyes. "Why, do dark spirits hover near me?" He scoffed. "It's your imagination, old man."

"I know what I see. You carry a burden that is not truly yours."

Mateo's face flushed red. "And what would you know about burdens? When Mami and Celina died, you disappeared. I had no idea if you were alive or dead for *three years*." He narrowed his eyes. "How do you think that made me feel? Not only had I lost my mother and my sister, but in an instant I'd lost the only family I had left. You ran away from your responsibilities. *I* was your responsibility." The emotion in his voice said the wound was still fresh.

Zolin's voice softened. "I couldn't take living, Mateo. The pain of losing them was too great." He hesitated as though searching for the right words. "I found my salvation through healing others. This burden you carry will destroy you if you're not careful. Tell the truth. Allow your life to heal."

His face reddening, Mateo stared at the sky, his frustration at not being able to physically turn away from his father obvious.

"Mateo. Please."

April returned carrying a rucksack. She slowed as she approached, detecting the tension between the two men. "I found some tins of food."

Zolin held out his hand for the rucksack. "Give it to me."

April handed him the pack and raised her eyebrows at her mother. Leine gave her a look that said she'd fill her in later.

"Looks like we're ready to head out." Leine began to pick up the travois poles, but Zolin stopped her.

"He is my son."

"Then at least let me carry the rucksack."

Zolin nodded and handed her the bag containing the food. She shouldered her other pack and carried the Uzi in her free hand. April did the same with her pack and weapon, and they set out for Martin's camp.

25

Martin swatted at a mosquito and continued his inventory. Food was running low and so was the rum. The camp needed to replenish their batteries, along with gas for the generator.

Gunnar had returned late the night before, bringing with him news of Mateo's gunshot wound and the deaths of Hugo and the other gunmen. He relayed the information that Leine had gone in search of Mateo's father, Zolin, and that Gunnar had been tasked with bringing back what medical supplies he could to stabilize Mateo for travel back to camp. Unfortunately, most of the medical supplies had been in one of the cupboards in the mess area and had burned with the rest of the structure. All Martin had left was a portable first aid kit with some bandages and two ampules of antibiotics.

It would have to do. Gunnar had gone up to the sleeping platform to pack his gear, getting ready to go back.

Ignacio and Noah still hadn't returned with the supplies, which was odd. Normally a supply run took the two men between five and seven days, depending on weather and what was needed. It had been over ten since they'd left, and Martin was worried.

This was the jungle. Nothing ever ran smoothly—and so much could go wrong.

He'd decided to recount the remaining supplies to keep his mind off Nancy and where she might be. Dario's deadline was fast approaching. The others had to be back before then. Martin shuddered to think of what Dario would do when he didn't give him what he wanted. He could tell him about the fire and pretend the laptop and all his notes were destroyed, but Dario didn't strike him as a man who accepted excuses.

"What should I do with these?" Pablo pointed to two of the bins that had been partially melted in the fire.

"Are they empty?"

"Yes."

"Put them on the pile."

Pablo picked up both bins and headed for the pile of burned and melted equipment on the other side of the compound.

Thankfully, April had rescued the most important electronics, and anything else that had been consumed by the fire could be replaced, although not easily. Martin had taken care to only use the laptop when he was alone, so camp personnel wouldn't know he still had access to the information in case Dario and his men questioned them. Martin returned to filling out his makeshift spreadsheet by hand.

"What are you doing?"

Martin paused in his work at the sharpness in Pablo's tone. He put his pencil down and rose to see what was going on. Dario and two of his men appeared from behind the supply hut with Pablo between them. The man's face was white with fear. A third gunman materialized on the other side of camp, his automatic rifle aimed at Martin.

Martin's heart skipped a beat. Dario and his men were early.

The deadline was still a day away. His mind raced for an explanation. *Had Dario found out about Leine and the others?* Fear pooled behind his eyes and slid to his stomach. This was a scenario he hadn't considered.

Stupid, stupid, stupid. If the plan went the way it should have, everyone would be back by now. He hadn't considered Dario finding out about the ruse and then returning early.

Steeling his courage, Martin walked out to meet them.

"Where is the rest of your crew?" Dario scanned the camp. "There are very few people here, so I must assume you have sent them away from the danger, yes?"

Martin cleared his suddenly dry throat. "They are on their way back to Iquitos." He hoped Leine would be careful when they came back, and check to see if the coast was clear. If not, Dario would kill him and everyone else for the lie.

"Do you have the information?"

Martin shook his head. He had to convince Dario he was telling the truth. Even though he wasn't. "There was a fire. It destroyed my laptop, which contained the raw data needed to determine the city's location. I'm trying to recreate my notes, which were also destroyed in the fire." He watched Dario carefully to see whether the man had knowledge of the fire. His expression didn't change.

Dario smiled and shook his head. "Do you know what I think? I think that you sent them to find the treasure. I also think that you told them to take as much of the gold as they could so that there would be nothing left for me and my men when we got there."

"That's preposterous. The location is too remote—"

"So you do know where it is." Dario's expression hardened. "Give me the location. Now."

"I told you, everything was destroyed in the fire. Yes, I sent people out to search for it, but that's because you have my daughter. What else was I supposed to do?"

"I suggest you tell the truth."

"That is the truth."

Dario nodded at the two men holding Pablo. "Kill him."

One of the gunmen brandished a knife and held it to Pablo's neck. Pablo's eyes widened in fear. Beads of sweat appeared on his forehead.

"No—" Martin started toward him, but he was too late. With a flash, Dario's gunman slit Pablo's throat. Blood spurted from the wound, spilling down the front of his shirt as Pablo slumped to the ground.

"Pablo!" Renata screamed from across the compound, spearing Martin's heart. She raced to him and fell on his body, sobbing in anguish.

"Mi amore. No me abandones." My love—don't leave me.

Dario watched the sobbing woman with something akin to mild interest before turning his attention back to Martin. "As you were saying?"

Martin stared at Pablo and Renata in horror, his rage building at the killing of an innocent. "He didn't deserve to die," he said through gritted teeth.

Dario rolled his eyes and sighed. "Who among us does?" He gestured to his men. "Find the others."

The two gunmen nodded and ran off. The third gunman remained in an overwatch position.

Dario grabbed Renata by the hair, pulling her to her feet. "Stop your babbling, woman." Renata continued to cry, unable to hold her grief.

With a deep sigh, Dario pulled out his pistol and shot her point-blank through the head. Renata sagged to her knees, and Dario released his hold. Her body fell the rest of the way onto her husband.

"Oh my God—what are you doing?" Martin shouted, stunned. Would Dario kill everyone there? He purposely kept his attention from the sleeping platform, praying Gunnar was well hidden.

"When a great man is confronted with obstacles," Dario said, "he removes them. I am removing the obstacles." He shrugged.

"*Jefe,* look what I have found." One of Dario's men appeared, shoving Gunnar in front of him. Gunnar had his hands clasped behind his head. Martin sensed panic behind his stoic expression.

"Another member of your crew, eh, Martin?" Dario waved at his man. "Bring him to me."

The gunman prodded Gunnar to where Martin and Dario stood, keeping his weapon trained on him.

Dario pointed his gun at the prisoner's head. "You have seen what I am capable of. If you do not take me to the treasure I will do the same to this man and everyone else here. How many deaths do you want on your soul?"

Martin's shoulders sagged. He had no choice. Dario's men would tear apart the camp and kill anyone they encountered. The other camp members must have hidden as soon as they saw what was happening. What if Leine and the others determined Mateo was well enough to transport and returned early? He couldn't live with himself if he allowed Dario and his thugs to slaughter more innocents.

"Stop. I'll take you to the city."

"I thought you would see things my way." Dario lowered his gun.

The man covering Gunnar whistled. The other gunman reappeared and joined them.

Dario turned to him and said, "Burn the camp."

26

It was too quiet.

Leine walked ahead of the party to scope out Martin's camp. There was no obvious activity, and that had her worried.

The trip back to camp had taken longer than she would have liked, but at least they made it. Mateo did surprisingly well, dipping in and out of an exhausted sleep. His coloring looked better. Along the way, Zolin had attempted conversation with him but Mateo had resisted.

Leine quietly slipped into camp, gun drawn. The place was a shambles. Everything had been trashed, and whatever could be burned now smoldered. Contents from the supply shed had been scattered everywhere, the shed itself destroyed. The sleeping platform had been burned to the ground, its charred supports the only evidence of its existence. The generator still hulked in its spot. She checked, but there didn't appear to be any further damage to the equipment. With a deepening sense of dread, she continued through the camp.

It wasn't long before she found the bodies. They were hard to miss.

Pablo and Renata. The couple had been murdered on the same spot. Blood from the gash across Pablo's throat had dried, staining the front of his shirt a dark brown. Renata appeared to have been shot at close range.

Dario.

Leine walked to what remained of the sleeping platform. A piece of burned fabric from one of the hammocks poked through the ash. She lifted what was left.

A charred laptop stared back at her.

Leine opened the top and pressed the on button. Nothing happened.

She closed the lid and stood. Obviously, they wouldn't be able to access Martin's data.

Continuing her search, she walked the perimeter, checking for more bodies or, more hopefully, survivors. As she passed by a small stand of palms, the leaves rustled. She spun in place, her gun in her hand.

"Don't shoot." Renata's assistant, Esme, pushed through the bushes, her eyes wide with fear. Dried tears streaked her face.

Leine lowered her gun. "What happened? Are you all right?"

Her face white, Esme nodded. "Yes. But Pablo and Renata..." Her voice caught.

"I saw them. Was it Dario?"

The girl's expression turned dark. "That *pendejo* has no conscience. He killed them as though they were nothing."

"How were you able to survive?"

"I hid when they came. When I saw what they did to Pablo, I fled to the jungle." She glanced at the ground, her cheeks turning red. "I didn't have a weapon."

"You did the right thing. Trying to fight them would have gotten you killed. So it was Dario and how many other men?"

"Three."

"Where's Martin and the others?"

"Dario took Martin and Gunnar with him. I think Martin agreed to go to stop them from killing the rest of us. Everyone else has left. I think for good."

"Do you know where they're going?"

"I overheard Dario tell Martin to take him to the treasure."

If Dario only brought three gunmen with him to terrorize Martin, then the deaths of Hugo, Bobo, and the other two thugs sent to follow the search parties had made a dent in Dario's forces. April counted a half-dozen men at the main camp. Minus the two guards that died at the compound, that left four known gunmen. Dario would have to keep at least one, possibly two, to guard Nancy at the second camp.

But where had they gone? Had Martin really taken them to the lost city? Or was he leading them away from camp in a last-ditch effort to save the remaining crew when they came back? If that was the case, then both Martin and Gunnar were in grave danger.

"Wait here. It doesn't look like Dario left anyone behind. I need to tell the rest of the group what happened."

"Can I come with you?" There was palpable fear in Esme's eyes.

"Of course."

Esme nodded, relief obvious on her face. "Thank you."

The two women made their way back to April, Zolin, and Mateo.

"What happened?" April asked.

"Dario paid the camp a visit. He's gone now, though."

"Where's Martin?"

"They took him and Gunnar." She paused. There was no good way to break the news. "Dario killed Pablo and Renata."

Mateo closed his eyes, a pained expression on his face. "Anyone else?"

Esme shook her head. "Everyone else is gone. I ran into the jungle when I saw what they were doing."

"Where did the *cabrón* go?" Zolin asked.

"Esme overheard Dario demanding that Martin take them to find the city."

"But he doesn't know for sure that it's even there." April looked from Mateo to Leine to Esme.

"That doesn't matter," Leine said. "I think Martin was taking a gamble to get Dario and his men away from camp before we showed up."

"Or Ignacio and Noah."

"Yes."

Zolin picked up the travois poles. "We need to do something with the bodies."

They brought the travois into camp, and April and Zolin helped Mateo find a place to sit. Zolin then found a shovel, and proceeded to dig several shallow trenches to bury the bodies. Leine and April both offered to help, but Zolin shook his head.

"This is men's work."

Leine and April shared a look, but neither said anything as they joined Esme in clearing the camp.

Zolin prayed over the fresh graves, and April and Esme placed crosses at the head of each one. Leine was characteristically silent, preferring to pay her respects privately. From her early days as an assassin, death had become a constant companion. She no longer remembered her ideas about dying when she was younger, only that she was critically unfazed by the act now. Every living thing died. It was the way of the world, and she rarely questioned why.

It was easier that way.

"We need to go after Martin and Gunnar. Nancy will be all right as long as Dario thinks Martin will lead him to the lost city." Leine sighed. "Unfortunately, the laptop was destroyed in the fire."

Mateo gave Leine a sharp look. "I thought the laptop was destroyed before we left."

"During the chaos of the first fire, April hid it in my hammock. Apparently Martin decided her choice was effective." Leine nodded toward the smoldering remains of the sleeping platform. "I found it over there, in the ashes from the last fire."

Mateo looked stricken. "Then we are lost. I never saw the report."

"No, but Nancy did."

"But how will that help? Dario has her."

"April and I will find Nancy. Dario's camp isn't far. Zolin can stay here and take care of you."

"What about me?" Esme asked.

"Keep watch for Dario and his men." She slid her pistol free and handed it to Zolin, along with an extra magazine. "I know you prefer not to deal with guns, but I'd feel a whole lot better if you had this."

Zolin racked the slide to check for rounds, then slipped the 9mm into his waistband and stowed the extra ammunition in a side pocket. "I normally avoid the kind of situation where I need one. Since it appears to be unavoidable, I accept."

Leine pulled out the topo map and charted a course through the jungle to the area where Dario's gunman had indicated the second camp's location. She and April repacked their backpacks, adding dried fish and smoked capybara, and filled their canteens.

Zolin pulled a small bundle from the bag at his waist and handed it to Leine. "You look like you could use this."

Leine unfolded the packet to find several coca leaves inside. Zolin was right. She was running on fumes. Normally during an op, she resisted the urge to sleep until the critical phase was finished. A second wind usually kicked in about the thirty six-hour point. Even so, the coca leaves would be a welcome assist. She refolded the packet and slid it into her pocket.

She smiled. "Thanks. This will come in handy." She turned to April. "Ready?"

April nodded, her expression grim. "Let's go."

27

Martin stopped to take a sip of water from his canteen, but Dario's thug prodded him with his gun barrel to keep going. Dario and his men kept a grueling pace, obviously unaffected by the searing heat and relentless humidity.

Sweat rolled down Martin's face and forehead, and his clothes stuck to his body. Gunnar was in the same shape. They'd been hiking the better part of two days, being allowed to rest for only a few hours at a time. Martin was now closer than he'd ever been to where the LiDAR had depicted an anomaly in the forest. All around them was virgin jungle, jungle he was certain had never before been seen by foreigners.

Cascading waterfalls serenaded them at every turn. Wildly colorful birds streaked across the sky, squawking to each other and searching for their next meal. Orchids and ferns and unfamiliar flowers dotted the terrain, adding texture and color to an overwhelmingly green landscape.

This must have been how early explorers felt when they encountered the unmatched beauty of unspoiled forest.

Paradise.

Shaking himself from his reverie, Martin continued on. He hoped his gambit would succeed. Taking Dario to the second site he'd noticed on the LiDAR report would be a risky venture. Located midway up the cliff rather than at the top, the secondary site was most likely subordinate to the upper level. He could always profess ignorance if the area turned out to be nothing. Martin assumed the minor site was a feeder settlement, one that supplied slaves and other support to the larger settlement, higher up the cliff face. There was still the question of how the inhabitants climbed what appeared to be a sheer rock wall. Although still a climb, the secondary settlement should be easier to get to, which might go a long way toward convincing Dario of the futility of trying to find treasure.

But there was no telling how Dario would react. Which was the main reason Martin had led him away from the camp. Thankfully, Gunnar didn't know of the secondary site and hadn't seen the LiDAR report showing where the main site was located. Martin hoped the feeder site would satisfy Dario's appetite for treasure. If the area turned out to be a settlement, there would certainly be artifacts.

Either way, Dario would inevitably kill them all.

Martin untied his bandana and wiped his face. "I need to check the map again." He stopped and unfolded the topographic map to study the terrain. Dario had demanded to see the map but turned away in disgust when he saw only data points he couldn't interpret. Martin had at least done that right —only he knew where to look. Dario would have to keep him alive until they reached the site.

They were close. The base of the cliff was over a nearby ridge at the far end of the immense valley in which they now found themselves. He closed his eyes, envisioning the color-coded LiDAR report, and his heart quickened. If only Nancy was there, and this was a genuine search party—one that recorded the scientific facts and revered history.

Not a group of thugs who were only interested in enriching themselves.

How could he keep his promise to Taruca now? If Dario found nothing, he would accuse Martin of lying about the location and would most likely kill him. On the other hand, if they did find the lost city, Martin would be of no use to him and he'd certainly kill him. Even if there were no treasure Dario would try to profit by plundering and selling whatever artifacts he found.

Inevitably, word would leak of the discovery, and Martin would no longer be alive to stem the flow of interest in the region. Taruca's jungle would be overrun by tourists, and conglomerates eager for profit.

Profit. The quest for riches had moved many to subvert their better instincts. Governments were no different. A discovery of this magnitude would do one of two things: become a veritable bonanza in tourist dollars, or be swept under the rug to make way for oil and gas and timber concessions.

Martin glanced at the sky. How long before smoke from the fires to clear the jungle darkened the atmosphere? A handful of days during the previous week Martin had tasted the acrid poison sifting through the air.

It wouldn't be long.

Perhaps he was being foolish, trying to save this last, great place from the perverse greed of man. Martin closed his eyes, breathing in the damp earth, the green, growing things surrounding him. He felt old. Used up.

Ineffective.

With a sigh, Martin stowed the map and struck off toward the far end of the rugged valley. He remained alert for some way to take the kidnapper out, but Dario's insistence that Martin and

Gunnar not communicate with each other, coupled with three armed bodyguards, made that a risk that would end in certain death.

His. And Nancy's.

Several hours later, they reached the base of the cliff where the settlements were supposed to be located. Martin stood back and scanned the sheer rock wall, searching for a trail or some kind of clue as to how the original inhabitants had conquered the vertical cliff.

Halfway up he noticed a series of unusual depressions in the moss- and fern-covered rock face, and his heart raced. This was the closest he'd come to finding anything resembling a settlement. His previous sojourn elicited injuries and sickness, and he'd turned back, unwilling to put his crew in danger.

But now he was almost there. He could feel it—even taste it.

Dario followed his gaze. "What do you see?"

Martin pointed at the depression. "There. See the shadows that mark three equidistant depressions?"

Dario frowned and stepped back, craning his neck. "No." He paused. "Wait. Yes." He scanned the cliff face. "How do we get there?"

"I'm not sure." Martin moved away from the base and studied the rock, forgetting for a moment that he was in the company of criminals. The joy of discovery often made friends of enemies. "I suggest we look for evidence of a road or path. Some indication of how the inhabitants were able to climb this edifice."

Dario shouted at his men, ordering them to search for something resembling a road or path. Gunnar joined them.

How did the original inhabitants scale such a steep cliff? Martin searched the rock face, but the vegetation was too dense. The LiDAR had shown lines radiating outward from the larger site, like spokes on a wheel. Which could mean the inhabitants might have built raised roads similar to the Mayans.

But there should be evidence. Some kind of physical indication that a civilization had occupied the site.

Martin worked his way west, carefully scanning the rock face and surrounding plant life. Even though exhausted from the forced march through the jungle, the excitement of discovery spurred him on. Taruca's appeal to his better nature kept nattering away in the back of his head, but he studiously ignored it, willing it to go away.

He wasn't getting out of there alive. Dario had won, if only by superior firepower. Martin wasn't stupid. Four against two wasn't good. Unless something happened to even the odds, once Dario determined Martin or Gunnar were no longer of use, he'd kill them both.

Don't think like that. What will happen to Nancy? You must stay alive, and you must find a way to stop Dario and his men. Otherwise, his daughter would suffer a terrible fate.

His resolve returned, and he doubled his effort to find something, anything, that might pass for evidence of a pathway. He'd find a way to get rid of Dario.

He had to.

He'd overheard Dario talking with one of his gunmen about shipments needing to go out. Martin had a good idea what those shipments involved. What else, other than coca paste? The money was good and the work relatively simple: clear the jungle, plant the coca, tend the leaves. When it was time, harvest the leaves, turn them into paste, and transport them north to facilities that turned the paste into cocaine. Enough to fuel the addiction of the masses.

Martin pulled off his bandana to wipe his face again. The material was soaked in sweat and provided little relief. Hiking through the humid jungle was an exercise in endurance. To his left, a trickle of water coursed down the rock, pooling at the base. He walked over to it and dipped his scarf in the water, then squeezed it over his face and head, reveling in the short-lived relief. A flat, white rock poked out of some ferns next to the tiny waterfall. Weary, Martin sat down. He unscrewed the cap on his canteen and took a swig. Gunnar and Dario were farther east, assisting Dario's men as they wielded machetes to remove the dense undergrowth as they searched.

Martin leaned back and sighed. Under any other circumstance, this would be a phenomenal opportunity. Now that opportunity threatened his only daughter.

He screwed on the top of his canteen and set it to the side. Something caught his eye. He turned, wondering what he'd seen, and brushed away a thicket of ferns and moss.

Surprised, he got to his feet. He'd been sitting on a perfectly smooth stone. And there was another beside it.

Just like the stones he'd seen at Mayan sites in Central America.

Heart racing, he tore at the ferns, pulling them free, unearthing more stones. Could it be? Had he found a trail?

The more he uncovered, the more certain he became.

28

Thankfully the gunman Leine had interrogated had told the truth. Three hours later, Leine and April made their final approach to Dario's main camp.

The compound consisted of a number of wood structures covered in plastic tarps held together with bungee cords. One of the "buildings" had been erected on top of a platform approximately four feet above the jungle floor, ostensibly in case of heavy rain. Another structure had only a tarp roof and housed a row of tables covered in leaves.

People lined the tables, busily sorting what appeared to be dried coca leaves. To the left of them was a wide, plastic-lined pit filled with water. Beside that were several plastic fifty-five gallon drums. The smell of diesel permeated the air.

"Looks like Dario's involved in something other than kidnapping." Leine nodded toward the coca operation.

"Cocaine?"

"They're making paste for transport somewhere else. The next step is cocaine, but that's a more complicated procedure. A nearby airfield is a must-have. Since I haven't seen one, it's likely

Dario's using them as mules to carry the finished product across the border."

April waved her hand in front of her face. "Someone must have spilled a boatload of diesel."

"They use it to extract the cocaine."

"Really? And people snort that shit up their noses?"

"That isn't all." Leine gave her a wry smile. "Add ammonia and sulfuric acid into the mix, too."

"Gross. Remind me to never partake."

She certainly could understand her daughter's reaction. The coca leaves Zolin had given Leine had helped her remain alert and awake but were a far cry from the effects of processed cocaine. Coca leaves had gotten a bad rap in years past—indigenous cultures had chewed the leaves and made tea from the plant for hundreds of years. Once the leaves were processed into cocaine, the resulting drug became highly addictive. The leaves were much less so.

Leine scanned the rest of the camp, searching for Nancy. She spotted a gunman carrying a mini Uzi slowly walking the perimeter. She didn't see anyone else.

Yet.

One of the structures near the far end of the compound looked like it had potential.

"Let's recon the tarp-covered building on the far side." She checked the rounds on both Hugo's pistol and the Uzi, then replaced the Uzi's mag with a full one. The forty-five had two-thirds of its rounds, there was another full mag for the Uzi in her side pocket, and she still had a grenade. Satisfied, she returned the pistol to her waistband.

"We'll use the jungle for cover, head around back, and come up from behind."

April nodded. Leine led the way.

When they reached the far side of the camp, Leine held up

her fist, signaling April to stop. She scanned for other gunmen. This end of the camp was relatively quiet, with the activity concentrated in and around the processing tables. There were no other people that she could see.

April leaned in, keeping her voice low. "There aren't any guards."

Leine nodded. The absence of Dario's gunmen could mean a number of things: either Nancy was being held somewhere else, or she was inside and Dario had her restrained in some way so she couldn't escape.

Or she was already dead.

April must have come to the same conclusion. "Do you think she's even here?"

Leine shrugged. "We won't know unless we check. Cover me. If you see someone headed this way, toss something on the roof. The tarps look brittle from the sun. It'll be loud."

April set up her rifle on the fallen limb of a tree and hunkered down to take the overwatch position.

Leine crept to the rear of the raised structure and listened for movement. Three sides of the tented building had walls made of weather-beaten silver and blue tarps, held in place with thread-bare bungee cords. She rounded the corner to the front. The wall facing the camp was partially open to the outside. Several stacked barrels blocked the view into the processing tent, allowing her to remain hidden from the workers.

Coming in low, she moved to the steps. Quietly she mounted them, pivoting as she climbed to scan the terrain.

She reached the top of the steps and swept the darkened interior. Plastic tubs stacked four and five high stood to her left, with rusted metal shelving filled with gallon jugs and tinned food to her right. At the far back of the space stood a cot surrounded by mosquito netting. A book by a popular romance author lay on the mattress. Next to the cot was a milk crate sporting a cracked ceramic cup and a battery operated lamp.

Leine continued her recon, giving the shelves a cursory glance, but there was nothing of value. She walked back and descended the steps, moving around to the side facing the jungle, where April could see her. With a series of gestures she indicated that she was continuing into camp.

As Leine turned to resume her search, something moved in her periphery. She slipped behind one of the platform supports and waited.

There was a rustle of leaves as someone broke through the jungle and walked toward the platform.

Nancy.

Leine waited until she reached the steps before she eased in behind her. She slipped her hand over the woman's mouth and at the same time wrapped an arm around her torso. Nancy went rigid.

"It's Leine," she whispered. "Your father sent me."

29

Nancy relaxed and Leine slowly released her. She turned around, her eyes wide. She looked surprisingly good for being held prisoner by a drug trafficker. Her clothes were relatively clean and she seemed healthy. Score one for Dario, Leine thought. At least he had the decency to keep the hostage in good shape.

"How did you know—?" Nancy started to say.

"Shh." Leine took her by the arm. "Come with me." Making sure there were no guards in the vicinity, she led Nancy behind the platform, back into the jungle.

April rose to greet them as they approached. Nancy balked at the AK-47 in April's hands and looked a question at Leine.

"She's well trained," Leine said, by way of explanation.

"Oh, my God." Nancy's knees gave out, and she grabbed Leine for support. Leine eased her onto the fallen tree limb.

"Are you all right?"

Nancy nodded. "Yes. I'm fine. I'm just overwhelmed that you're here." She glanced at Leine. "Back at the other camp. There was an explosion—"

"I'll tell you about it later. Right now we have to leave." The rescue operation had gone well. Too well. Leine didn't want to tempt fate.

April offered Nancy a drink of water from her canteen.

"Thank you." Nancy took a sip and handed it back.

"Well, *that* was anticlimactic," April said, attaching the canteen to her belt with a carabiner. "I thought we'd have to shoot somebody to get you out of here."

"Be glad." Leine picked her canteen up off the ground. "I'm surprised Dario didn't have a guard on you."

Nancy shrugged. "Where am I going to go? I don't have any idea where I am, or where our camp is. They blindfolded me when they brought me here."

Leine helped Nancy to her feet. "We'd better head for camp. I'd like to be back before dark."

"Is it far?" Nancy asked.

"About three hours."

"What time is it?" Nancy's gaze darted back to the platform.

Leine glanced at her watch. "Twelve thirty. Why?"

Nancy's eyes widened. "This is when they bring my meal."

"Shit. Come on. Let's move."

Behind them, someone shouted in Spanish.

April grabbed Nancy by the arm and pulled her deeper into the jungle as Leine pivoted toward the man's voice.

One of the coca sorters stood near Nancy's tent, holding a plate of food. Eyes riveted on Leine's Uzi, he dropped the plate and raised his hands.

The guard Leine saw earlier sprinted toward them from the other direction. The man with the tray didn't appear to have a weapon. Leine adjusted her aim to take out the guard.

Leine tracked him and fired as the gunman dove for cover behind a fifty five gallon barrel.

The barrel erupted in a spray of clear liquid, soaking the

gunman. With a scream, he rocketed out from behind it, ripping his clothes from his body as he ran.

Sulfuric acid? Leine pivoted and aimed at the unarmed worker. He shook his head and closed his eyes, muttering what sounded like a prayer. Leine lowered her weapon, then raced after April and Nancy. She caught up with them several minutes later and took the lead. Neither woman asked what happened. Leine didn't go into detail.

About one hundred meters from camp, Leine veered north onto what looked like a well-used trail. Sensing something wasn't right, she stopped abruptly and raised her fist. Nancy almost walked into her but stopped in time.

"What is it, Mom?" April asked.

"Someone's been here." She nodded at a patch of ground that appeared to have been disturbed. Leine squatted and peered in front of her. A thin wire, barely visible, stretched across the trail.

"Tripwire." She lowered herself onto her belly to see where it led. The wire ran from the nearby clump of ferns, across the path, and terminated at a sapling, twisted around the trunk.

Leine climbed to her feet and carefully stepped over the wire, indicating the other two do the same.

"Keep an eye out," she said.

"Aren't you going to cut it or something?" Nancy asked.

"Disabling the wire might trigger another mechanism, and we don't have time to figure it out."

Once Leine was certain they weren't being followed, she stopped so Nancy could rest. She doubted the professor was used to hiking through the jungle in the sweltering heat and humidity. Nancy gratefully accepted April's offer of her canteen once more, then handed it back.

"How's my father?"

Leine and April exchanged looks.

"What is it?" Alarm swept across Nancy's features. "Is he all right?"

"We don't know. Dario raided the camp, killing Pablo and Renata. Your father wasn't there."

Tears filled Nancy's eyes. "No."

"We think Dario is forcing him to lead him to the lost city," April added.

"Has he found it?"

"We don't know," Leine answered. "A fire destroyed Martin's notes, as well as the laptop. Once we bring you back to camp, we'll head out after him." She paused. "That's if you can remember enough of the report to chart a path to the area."

"I—I can try." Nancy squeezed her eyes closed, her face a mask of misery. "What about Hugo? And the others?"

"Hugo's dead. Dario took Gunnar with them. Mateo was wounded, but he seems to be doing better." Leine held out her hand. "Look, we really need to go. Now."

The tears in Nancy's eyes spilled over onto her cheeks. "I can't—I can't take it all in."

"You'll be able to mourn when we get back to camp." Leine checked her compass.

"How did Mateo get shot? And Hugo? How did he die?"

"Hugo was working for Dario," Leine answered.

"How do you know that?"

"He tried to kill April and me, and he shot Mateo."

"So you—killed him?"

Leine held her gaze. "I did."

Nancy shuddered. "My God. Does my father know?"

"He does now, yes."

"He was so sure that everyone who worked for him was loyal.

And honest." Nancy stared into space. "You just can't believe anyone anymore."

Leine wasn't about to argue. She'd learned long ago that even friends couldn't be trusted. Fallout from her days as an assassin, certainly, but also the byproduct of a violent and ruthless world.

In a way, trusting no one made life easy. But also much, much harder. Case in point: Santiago Jensen.

Don't think about that now.

Leine shouldered her weapon. "It's getting late." The shadows had begun to lengthen, signaling the early onset of dusk.

Nancy nodded. "How much farther?"

Leine checked the topo map. "A couple of hours."

"My God, it's hot." Nancy slapped her neck and checked her hand. "Damned mosquitos. You'd think someone would come up with a bug spray that actually worked on the little terrorists."

April reached into her bag and pulled out a wad of netting, which she handed to Nancy. "Drape this over your hat and tuck it into your collar."

Nancy did as instructed. "Thank you. I spent as much time in bed at Dario's camp as I could stand."

"That was pretty civilized of them to give you netting," Leine said. "Drug traffickers generally aren't quite so solicitous."

Nancy shrugged. "He probably got sick of me complaining."

Leine studied her for a moment. "Probably."

They continued on to Martin's camp without incident, reaching the perimeter as night descended. Nancy and April stayed behind as Leine reconned the area.

Zolin came out to meet her before she managed to get very far. "We've got company."

30

Two torches had been lit, illuminating a large portion of camp. A couple of electric lanterns glowed next to a man in a buzz cut sitting on a makeshift bench. Leine set her pack down and walked over to him. He stood at her approach.

He sported the alert, relaxed expression and stance of a seasoned operative. An MP5 submachine gun and standard issue, military-style backpack lay on the ground beside him. He didn't appear to be a gym rat—he was more wiry than bulked up. The patch on the shoulder of his jungle fatigues depicted crossed arrows and the silhouette of a sniper rifle on a background of green. Underneath were the words *Base One*.

She held out her hand. "Leine Basso. Lou sent you?"

They shook. "Dave Cooper."

"Where's the rest of your team?" She distinctly remembered Lou saying he'd hired more than one person to help them.

"I'm it. Our unit began taking fire right after we landed. The helo took off, and *bam!* A group of guerrilla fighters pinned us down. I'm damn lucky to be alive."

"How many casualties?"

"Seven." Dave flexed his jaw. "It's like the bastards knew we were coming."

"I'm so sorry." Leine paused. "Where are you from?"

"Montana, why?"

"Have you ever seen the geysers erupt?"

"You mean the ones in Yellowstone?"

"I thought they were in Yosemite."

Dave shook his head. "Yellowstone. My brother and I went camping there with my dad every summer."

Leine nodded.

Nancy frowned and cocked her head. "What does that have to do with anything?"

"Just making sure he is who he says he is," Leine replied. Dave got the exchange right, using Montana and the geysers as verification, but she still wasn't comfortable. "What about coms? Were you able to contact anyone?"

Dave reached in his pocket and took out a sat phone. He turned it toward her. A bullet hole had cracked the screen. "Not much good now."

"Is that the only phone your team had?" Lou had mentioned that Austen Newell was footing the bill for everything on the rescue operation. She doubted the billionaire would skimp on equipment.

He shook his head. "The team captain and second in command both had sat phones. This is the captain's. I couldn't find the other one."

"What about the enemy?" April asked. "Surely they used something."

"And you are—?"

"April."

He leveled his gaze at her. "Well, April, I didn't have a lot of time to check. I didn't know if they called in reinforcements.

Figured the best bet was to get out, fast, find you, and let you know what happened."

Leine nodded. "What about support? Someone must have called in the attack."

"Nada. Nobody came. It was a fucking disaster." He rubbed his eyes, then shook off the memory. "Somebody needs to go in and recover the bodies."

"I'm sorry. It's never easy to lose your team." Leine paused a moment before changing the subject. "Did you neutralize the guerrilla fighters, or are they still at large?"

"All but one. He managed to escape."

"Pretty doubtful a lone survivor is going to come after you." She motioned to the rest of the small group. "You've met April. That's Nancy," she said. "I assume you've met the others. Nancy is Martin's daughter."

Obviously surprised, Dave asked, "The woman we're supposed to rescue?"

Leine nodded. "The objective has changed. Dario, the man responsible for kidnapping Nancy, has taken Martin. We think he's forcing him to locate a so-called lost city."

"Do we know where?"

She glanced at Nancy. "We might."

"I'll do my best," Nancy replied. April pulled out the topo maps and handed her a china marker. Nancy selected one of the maps and went to work.

"What exactly are we up against?" Dave asked. "At our last briefing we were told that rescuing the daughter was objective one."

"Let's just say events are fluid at the moment. We need to find Martin, and at the same time keep Nancy safe." She turned to Esme. "Why don't you get Dave something to eat? I'll bet he's hungry."

"Of course."

Dave picked up his pack and followed Esme across the compound to the makeshift mess area consisting of a couple of semi-melted chairs. The camp's food had been stored in a container high in a tree out of reach of wildlife. Dario and his men must have missed it.

Zolin watched them leave. "What do you think?"

"He had the right code, but it worries me that he's the sole survivor."

"We'll keep an eye on him, then."

"I need to send a message to Lou to tell him about the massacre. I'll ask him if he has any insight into our guest."

Zolin nodded. "Good idea."

Leine glanced at the topo map. "Is it coming back to you?" she asked Nancy.

"The primary and secondary sites are on a cliff somewhere in this area." Nancy pointed at the map, indicating an expanse of dense jungle several kilometers east of them. "But I can't visualize exactly where." She sat back in defeat. "That ridge is long. As my dad would say, it's a needle in a haystack scenario."

"What about the elder tribesman Martin mentioned? Do you have any idea where he is?"

"You mean Taruca?" Nancy shook her head. "If he knew, Dad kept it a secret. He told me a number of times he was afraid someone would inadvertently leak his location to the world." She closed her eyes for a moment, then sighed. "He meant me. That I would tell my colleagues."

"So we search the area," Leine said, "and take our chances. It's not ideal, obviously, but we don't have much choice."

"What about Mateo?" April asked. "It's not safe to leave him. We don't know when or if Dario's coming back."

Nancy asked, "Has anyone heard from Noah and Ignacio?"

"Not yet." Leine thought through various scenarios, discarding all but one. "Mateo needs time to heal. He shouldn't be moved. It isn't ideal, but if we rig a shelter, Esme can stay here to feed him and dress his wounds."

"But what if Dario or his thugs come back? Are you willing to risk their lives?" April crossed her arms and gave her mother a familiar look.

She'd made up her mind.

"We'll leave one of the guns with Mateo," Leine said, "along with plenty of ammo."

"I'm staying."

The determination on April's face brought Leine back to when she was twelve—no, make that three—years old. Stubborn wouldn't begin to describe her daughter growing up. There was no use trying to change her mind.

With a sigh, Leine nodded. "All right. Keep the AK." She reached in her pack and pulled out one of the two remaining grenades. "Take this, too. Just in case." She turned to Nancy. "If we're going to get within a football field of this place, you'll need to come with us."

"I intend to. This is as much my discovery as my father's."

Leine glanced at April to see if she'd noticed Nancy's apparent lack of concern for her father's well-being. April raised an eyebrow, signaling she had.

"That's it then." Leine shouldered her pack. "April, you'll stay with Mateo and Esme and keep them both safe. That way you'll be here in case Noah and Ignacio show up. Dave, Zolin, Nancy, and I will search for Martin. Anything else?"

Zolin cleared his throat. Leine looked at him expectantly.

He waited a beat, as though weighing whether he should say something. Then, "I know where to find Taruca."

31

Martin wiped the perspiration off his forehead with his sleeve—sticky, itchy sweat that never dried and failed to cool. The afternoon sun blazed across the sky, the humidity brutal in its intensity. He searched out pockets of shade created by the rocks but soon moved on, driven by the brutish behavior of his captors. They were almost to the secondary site. The climb had been slow going as Dario's men hacked at the dense vegetation to clear the way up the increasingly steep route.

The cleared path and his burning quadriceps reminded Martin of his trip to Machu Picchu the previous year when he climbed the "Stairs of Death"—a steep set of steps leading to the top of Huayna Picchu, a peak near the famous Inca site. In ancient times, the high priest was said to have ascended the stairs each morning before sunrise to greet the dawn. The man must have been in amazing condition to make that precarious climb every day.

Martin's months of living in the Amazon hadn't done him any favors. Actually the opposite. Typically he'd be in great physical shape from hiking and hacking his way through the terrain. However, since he'd started using the drone to map the jungle, he'd put on weight and lost muscle tone.

He surveyed the forest below him. It was amazing to think that five hundred years before, people used these steps. And here he was, one of the first people in centuries to do so again. His heart raced, and not just from the steep climb.

"Keep moving," Dario yelled from above. He was climbing behind two of his men, who had the unenviable job of clearing the overgrown vines. The third gunman brought up the rear, most likely to ensure that Gunnar and Martin didn't try to make a run for it. All six were roped together for safety. Although if one fell, he could drag the others down with him.

The second gunman used his machete to clear whatever the first gunman missed. Gunnar was directly behind Martin. If they could take out the third gunman and cut him loose, that would even the odds. Gunnar and Martin against the remaining three —except Dario and the other two gunmen had automatic weapons.

There had to be a way to disarm them.

He caught Gunnar's gaze. Gunnar gave a slight shake of his head, as though he knew what Martin was thinking. Throughout the forced march, Martin had been looking for a private moment that he and Gunnar could use to devise a plan of attack, but Dario had proven to be an astute kidnapper and didn't allow them to be alone for any length of time.

Martin sighed and resumed his climb. What would Dario do if there were no artifacts at the secondary site? Would he decide Martin and Gunnar were no longer needed and kill them both?

He had to come up with a reason to keep himself and Gunnar alive—something other than his knowledge of the location of the main settlement at the top of the cliff. To protect Taruca's people, Martin couldn't let on about the larger site above them. If Dario found out he'd been trying to keep him from the main site, the man would surely kill him.

He'd most likely keep Gunnar alive to help him decipher any symbols or carvings they found. As an ethnobotanist, Martin was expendable.

They continued their slow ascent. Martin pushed through the pain of searing lungs and burning thighs, keeping his mind focused on the possibility of discovering a new site. Sadness surged through him as he thought of his daughter. Nancy should be here, with him, as should everyone at the camp who had worked so hard for this day.

The gunman at the front of the line shouted. Dario had caught up to his two men.

Gunnar joined Martin. "They found something." The men were excitedly cutting away the last of a curtain of vines covering the cliff.

"We need to get up there before he and his thugs destroy any artifacts."

"No talking," the gunman behind them growled. Gunnar and Martin exchanged a glance before both men resumed the laborious climb.

By the time they reached Dario and the other men, most of the vegetation had been cleared away, revealing a dark tunnel of stone.

Martin's heart raced with excitement. Carvings covered in moss depicted stylized versions of local animals and insects, with the jaguar in pride of place above the entrance. Its jaws open in a snarl, the carved jaguar's teeth were clearly outlined, as were its long claws.

Dario flicked on his flashlight and directed the beam into the darkness, strafing the stone with light. The tunnel, or cave, stretched far back into the cliff, the light falling off in the darkness. Dozens more carvings dotted the walls, some with versions of the animals seen on the outer stones, some with symbols Martin had never seen before. Strikingly, the red, blue, and yellow paint the ancients had used to decorate the figures was still vibrant.

Dario grinned and turned to Martin. "We have found the lost city." He glanced behind Martin to Gunnar. "You." He beckoned him forward.

Gunnar looked surprised. "Me?"

"Yes. You."

"Martin should go in first—"

"You're not in a position to argue." Dario raised his rifle to emphasize his point.

The last gunman untied the rope at Gunnar's waist. With a muttered apology Gunnar slipped by Martin and stepped into the tunnel.

"May I see your torch?" he asked Dario.

"Give him yours," Dario commanded the first gunman, who did as he instructed.

Walking slowly, Gunnar swept the walls with the flashlight, illuminating the carvings. No longer tethered to each other, Dario, Martin, and Dario's men followed close behind. Dripping water echoed in the narrow space, giving Martin the disorienting sensation of being deep underground.

Several yards in, Gunnar stopped and trained the light on a particular stone. "Martin. Come here."

Martin looked a question at Dario, who nodded, giving him the go-ahead.

"What is it?" Martin asked, squinting at the stone. Water trickled down the face of the rock, pooling at the base. The brilliant paint of the carving stood out against the gray, lichen-covered stone.

"What is that?" Gunnar asked.

Martin leaned in closer to get a better look. Next to a stylized version of a jaguar and one of an anaconda was a carving of a tiny blue and yellow amphibian. "Looks like the sinchi poison dart frog."

"I figured it was a dart frog. I've never seen one with those particular colors before."

"That's because it's rare. It's found in one specific area of the Amazon, about ten kilometers west of here."

"Where they're burning?"

Martin shook his head. "This section is farther west and was burned over two years ago. According to Herberto, the government awarded the concession there to one of their favorite gas companies. They've been drilling for some time now."

"If the frogs' habitat is so narrow, they must be considered endangered, right?"

"They are, but were conveniently categorized as a common amphibian by Peru's Department of Agriculture, which of course allowed the drilling to move forward. Since then, the sinchi frog has been MIA." Martin sighed. "Pit a tiny population of frogs against big money, and money wins every time."

"What have you found?" Dario came up behind them and squinted at the stone carving. "A fucking frog? What do I care about a frog?" He shook his head. "Keep going. We need to find someplace to make camp."

"We're staying here?" Martin asked, eyeing the narrow space. Good thing he wasn't claustrophobic.

"You want to climb back down the cliff in the dark?" Dario asked. "Be my guest." When Martin didn't respond, Dario snorted. "I didn't think so. Keep moving."

Gunnar continued down the dark corridor, with Martin close behind.

"This site is all he can know about," Martin whispered.

Gunnar glanced at him sideways. "What do you mean? This *is* the only site, right?"

Martin shook his head. "There may be a larger site above this one."

"Stop talking," Dario barked from behind.

Gunnar nodded at Martin and continued on.

They'd just rounded a corner when Gunnar stopped abruptly and drew in a sharp breath. Martin eased past him, his gaze following the flashlight beam.

"Holy shit."

32

L eine, Dave, Zolin, and Nancy set out from camp early the next morning. Leine left the sat phone with April, in case she ran into complications with Mateo. Unfortunately, Lou hadn't yet replied to her earlier message informing him of Dave's survival and asking about his background.

She'd just have to play it by ear.

Half an hour into their trek, Zolin stopped abruptly and held up his fist, signaling everyone to halt. Leine walked forward to see what had made the shaman pause. She followed his gaze and froze.

Two naked men had been staked to a tree, their corpses bloated and covered in blood. Each man had a gaping hole cut into his chest, as though someone had removed their hearts. Bits of white rib poked through the wounds.

Nancy gasped. "Oh, my God." Retching, she turned and vomited into a bush.

"Gruesome," Dave said. "Native handiwork?"

Zolin shook his head. "Not in this part of the Amazon."

Leine, Zolin, and Dave made their way to the dead men. Nancy opted to hang back.

"They've been dead for some time." The shaman studied the bodies. "The organ removal is crudely done." He motioned to the jagged cuts and broken ribs. "The tribes in this area do not participate in human sacrifice. They also generally keep their weapons razor sharp. This cut was made with a dull edge."

Leine added, "The man on the left has a modern haircut. The other one is hard to tell. Any idea who they are?"

Zolin shook his head. "No."

"Any idea who these guys might be?" Dave called over his shoulder, directing his question to Nancy.

Nancy edged closer to the bodies. As she got closer, the blood drained from her face. "No."

Alarmed, Leine asked, "What is it?"

"It can't be." Her knees buckled and she stumbled. Tears welled in her eyes as a sob escaped her.

Leine sprinted to her. The others did the same. She took Nancy's hand. "Don't look."

Nancy shook her head, misery obvious in her eyes. "Noah and Ignacio..."

Leine glanced sharply at Zolin. "The men Martin sent on the supply run?"

Nancy nodded, tears coursing down her cheeks. "No one was supposed to die." Great, wracking sobs spilled from her as she hung her head.

Leine studied the woman. Was she referring to the danger of the expedition?

Or did she mean something else?

LEINE, DAVE, AND ZOLIN CUT THE TWO MEN DOWN AND DUG shallow graves for each. Out of respect for her grief, they left Nancy alone with her thoughts for a few moments. When she was finished, they resumed their trek through the jungle to find Martin and Gunnar.

Zolin led them along a narrow tributary enclosed on both sides by towering ceiba and palm trees. There'd been no rain the past few days and the normally robust river was running low, allowing them to hike along the rock- and mud-covered shore-line with relative ease.

By Leine's calculations, they'd traveled several kilometers. Without notice, Zolin veered off into the jungle on a path she would have missed even if she'd been looking for it. Eventually they came to a clearing that had a number of raised, palm-roofed structures. Scruffy chickens scuttled about the area, pecking at the ground, while a group of young children ran after them, giggling with delight. They skidded to a stop at the sight of the small party. The oldest one shouted something in his native language.

An ancient woman with multiple tattoos appeared at the door of the larger structure to see what the commotion was about. When she saw Zolin, she grinned, revealing a missing tooth, and beckoned him forward. She shouted to whoever was inside the hut. A moment later, an even older man with long gray hair, and his neck draped with strands of beads, followed her down the steps to greet them. A younger couple dressed in T-shirts and shorts followed him.

"The kids' parents?" Dave asked out of the corner of his mouth.

"Maybe," Leine answered.

The older man's clothing had been dyed to match the bril-liant birds they'd seen on the way there. Bright feathers and bleached bones hung from a thong at his waist, with more feathers cascading from a headband reminiscent of Zolin's. The woman was dressed similarly, although with less plumage.

The two men embraced and began conversing in a language

Leine had never heard before. She looked at Nancy and Dave and asked, "Either of you understand them?"

Dave shook his head.

Nancy shrugged. "I don't understand what they're saying, although I've heard a form of it spoken before. Its language family is referred to as Tucanoan, and there are two dozen variations. Many of these tribes live in isolation and have cultivated their own language. Although these days most are multilingual —either Spanish or Portuguese—allowing them to trade with each other."

"I take it he's the man we're looking for?"

"I assume that's Taruca," Nancy said. "By the way he's dressed, he would be the tribal elder."

The older woman said something to Taruca and disappeared inside the hut.

Zolin gestured to the rest of the party to join them. "Taruca and his wife have invited us to share their meal."

Leine glanced at the sky. "We don't have a lot of daylight left."

Zolin said something to their host, who nodded and laughed.

"He says we're not going anywhere tonight. Rain is coming." Zolin turned and followed Taruca inside.

Leine and Dave exchanged glances.

"We should make it quick," Dave said, eyeing the white, puffy clouds above them. "We could cover a lot of ground between now and sunset."

"You want to argue with a tribal elder?" Leine asked. "It's generally a good idea to listen to the locals. They know a lot more about their home than we visitors do."

"I agree with Leine," Nancy added. "He's lived here all his life. He knows the jungle."

The frustration on Dave's face would have been comical,

except Leine understood. Any delay in finding the city meant more danger for both Martin and Gunnar. But trying to make camp in a storm in an unfamiliar area had its share of danger too.

"Look," Leine said. "We'll wait out the storm, have a good meal and a few hours' rest, and get as much information from Taruca as we can. That way, we'll be fresh. The topo shows pretty rugged terrain. I don't know about you, but being well-rested and well-fed sounds like a sensible plan. Besides, we really don't have a choice." She glanced at the doorway where Zolin had disappeared. "Neither of them will likely give us directions before we finish the meal."

"Yeah, you're right. I just hate sitting on my ass when there's something that needs to be done."

"Believe me, I know what you mean." Although, if she were being honest, this time she welcomed the slight delay. Leine had run out of the coca leaves she'd gotten from Zolin, and the lack of sleep was catching up with her. She couldn't remember the last time she'd slept more than an hour. Add intense heat and humidity and you had a recipe for making mistakes.

Mistakes that could be costly.

If nothing else, the evening would be interesting, and she looked forward to experiencing another culture. She wished April could be there, though. She hadn't wanted to leave her guarding Mateo, but her daughter insisted. Through the years, Leine had learned to pick her battles, even though technically Leine was April's superior. Damn Lou and his decision to send the two of them into the Amazon on her daughter's first major operation. Yes, she'd done a few smaller ops, but she'd had a lot of help and support along the way.

She was so vulnerable in the jungle.

Leine stopped herself. *Your daughter is well trained. She's about as vulnerable as the AK and the grenade you left with her.*

Feeling slightly better about leaving April in such a precarious position, she followed Zolin inside the darkened hut to meet Taruca and the rest of the family.

33

"Holy shit," Martin said again.

The tunnel opened onto a large cave, its walls lined with stone carvings. The beam from Gunnar's flashlight landed on a life-size statue of a jaguar, poised to spring from the center of the room. Its sharp fangs and claws gleamed in the artificial light. The black stone eyes glowered at them, giving the carving a jolt of realism. Martin and Gunnar stared slack-jawed at their discovery.

"What? What did you find?" The excitement in Dario's voice preceded him. He pushed past the two men into the room. "A statue of a jaguar," he said, his voice flat. He glared at Gunnar and Martin. "I thought you found gold."

"I told you not to expect too much." Martin wasn't about to tell him the statue alone would be worth a fortune to a museum or a collector of Amazonian artifacts. The less he thought the carvings were worth, the better.

Dario grabbed the flashlight from Gunnar and proceeded to walk the perimeter, pausing at intervals to peer into corners and crevices. At one point, he stopped to study something. Below, a stone bench jutted out from the wall.

"You." He gestured to Gunnar. "You know ancient languages and symbols. Tell me what this says."

Gunnar walked over to him and glanced at the carving. "Bring the light up so I can read it."

Dario raised the flashlight.

Curious, Martin started toward them. In unison, Dario's gunmen raised their rifles, barring the way.

"What is it, Gunnar?" he called, his frustration getting the better of him.

"It looks like a map of some kind."

Don't tell him anything else, Martin thought. That map could show the existence of the primary site, which, judging by the lack of treasure in the room they now occupied, could conceivably contain what Dario craved.

"To what?" Dario asked.

Gunnar studied the carving for a moment, then said, "If I'm reading this right, there's another, larger site above this one."

Martin clenched his jaw. It was as if someone had kicked him in the stomach. *What was he doing?* Gunnar was screwing everything up.

"Another site—" Dario stepped back and looked at Martin. "Did you know of this?"

Martin shook his head. "No, I—"

Gunnar gave the flashlight back to Dario. "He did. In fact, he told me not to tell you if we found anything."

"That's not true." Despite the cool interior of the room, sweat flowed down the sides of Martin's face. What was Gunnar's end game? Was he playing the odds, hoping Dario wouldn't kill him if he cooperated? Martin had to act fast. He couldn't let Dario think he was trying to keep something from him.

Dario shined his flashlight in Martin's face. Martin held up his hand, shielding his eyes from the direct beam.

"You lied to me." Dario's words fell like lead between them, sending a chill down Martin's spine.

He was going to kill him.

"Gunnar is lying, Dario. Not me. I had no idea about another site."

"I'm not lying," Gunnar insisted. "Think about it. This site isn't at the top of the cliff we just climbed. The details from the LiDAR report were taken from the sky, not shooting straight on to the face of the cliff."

"I see." Dario lowered the light. "So there's no reason to keep the good doctor around."

Dario's gunmen closed in, blocking Martin's path. The glint of a knife flashed in one of the men's hands.

"Wait." Martin's mind scrambled for something, anything, that he could say to make Dario and his men back off. Dario held up his hand, signaling his men to wait.

"Well?"

Martin swallowed, his dry throat making it difficult to speak. "I—I'm the only person who knows the true worth of the site."

Dario scoffed. "And why would I believe you?"

"Because I'm the only one who spoke with Taruca. He told me the secret." Martin sucked in a deep breath. He would only tell these thugs part of what the elder tribesman confided to him during their talk. Martin would be skating close to the truth, but if he held back just enough, perhaps Dario would be satisfied once they reached the main site.

If there was treasure buried deep inside the larger site as Dario believed, then Martin would have to watch as Dario and his men plundered rare artifacts, destroying everything. Martin would cease to be of value, and would most likely be killed.

He had to do something. If he was killed, then Nancy would also cease to be of value. He was prepared to risk everything, even his life, for his daughter.

"Fully one half of the Peruvian rainforest is leased under oil and gas and timber concessions," Zolin said. "People don't understand what is at stake." He looked at Leine. "Their ignorance will be the end of humanity."

"Can't argue with you there, Zolin."

They had finished dinner and the four of them were sitting in a circle, talking quietly, listening to the storm that Taruca had predicted. The rain fell in thick sheets outside the hut. Deep, rumbling thunder, punctuated by occasional bright flashes of lightning, added to the remoteness of the village. Taruca and his wife had retired after dinner and were in the back of the hut, fast asleep in their hammocks.

Dave shook his head. "It's all bullshit."

Zolin brought out a pipe and bundle and proceeded to fill the bowl with what Leine assumed were either herbs or tobacco. "Why do you say that?" he asked.

"Because, even if the changing climate *is* manmade, we're fucked. Since when did the human race ever come together to fix something that didn't have a payoff?"

"My daughter would argue that there's a huge payoff." Leine accepted the pipe from Zolin but refrained from smoking and passed it to Dave. The scent reminded her of burning sweetgrass.

While Leine did what she could to lessen her impact on the environment, she tended to take a more observational stance than one of direct activism, believing that this was one fight that needed buy-in from governments across the planet. Of course, April rode the other end of the spectrum. She believed with the fervor of someone who hadn't been jaded by life that healing the planet and helping curb global warming were still viable outcomes. She also believed that shining a light on problems would be enough to dispel the darkness.

Leine hoped so. For everyone's sake. But she didn't have much hope for humanity, even when factoring in an existential threat like climate change. People had surprised her before, though.

Just not usually in a good way.

"I'm talking a monetary payoff, not existential." Dave took a deep hit off the pipe and passed it on to Nancy, who declined and gave it back to Zolin. "Think about it this way. Even if we could make a difference, it would require the mobilization of multiple countries on a scale that hasn't been seen since the Second World War. Tell me you see *that* happening."

"Not if China, the United States, and the other developed countries don't take the lead." Nancy shook her head. "And that's a long shot, anymore."

"Not if the military takes control." Dave took a drink from his canteen.

Leine narrowed her eyes. "Are you suggesting a military coup? In the United States?" His statement advocated a different worldview than she'd assumed he held. She wished Lou had answered her text about the guy, but it was too late now.

"Nah. Just puttin' it out there as another option. People go where you tell them to go."

"Until mankind learns to respect the earth, they will continue to experience a disconnection from nature. This disconnection brings them farther away from their true selves." Zolin took another hit off his pipe and nodded at Nancy. "Taruca asked me to relay something."

"Yes?"

"A member of his tribe confessed to setting fire to your camp."

"I'm sorry?" Nancy appeared confused. She glanced at Leine for clarification.

Surprised that it hadn't been one of Dario's men she'd seen running away the night of the fire, Leine asked, "Did he give a reason?"

Zolin nodded. "He was trying to stop the expedition from finding the lost city. He thought destroying Martin's research would accomplish that."

"He came close."

"Yes, well, Taruca would like to offer Martin and Nancy his sincerest apologies. He's offered to send a team to the camp to rebuild. I asked him to wait until we find Martin and Gunnar. He agreed." He tapped the ashes into his hand and put the pipe away. "It's getting late. I will see you all in the morning." He rose from the floor and disappeared into the back of the hut.

"Sounds like a good idea to me." Nancy got up and stretched. "We've got a long, hot day tomorrow."

"Goodnight." Leine smiled as Martin's daughter followed Zolin.

"So, Leine." Dave scooted closer to where she was sitting. "What's your story?"

His hooded eyes and partial smile told Leine he was looking for something other than a conversation.

She locked in on his gaze and said, "My story isn't relevant. Yours might be."

He leaned back with a frown. "What? Because of my comment about the military?"

"Where are you from? I assume it isn't Montana, since that was the code phrase."

"Oklahoma, born and bred."

"Go Sooners, right?"

A brief look of confusion lit his eyes before he recovered. He smiled and said, "Yeah. Go team."

The Sooners were the men's basketball team from the University of Oklahoma, and it was clear he hadn't known that.

"I think those two had the right idea." Leine stood. "See you in the morning."

"Sure."

By the tone of his voice he wasn't a happy camper. She was pretty sure it wasn't because she didn't want to play with him.

Leine moved to the back of the hut and spread the mosquito netting hanging over one of the empty hammocks Taruca's son had prepared for them. Having second thoughts, she quietly crossed the floor to a section of the hut that acted as a window. From there, she had a good view of the center of the village and the steps leading to their platform.

A few minutes later, her instincts were rewarded. A shadow moved down the steps and underneath the hut. The rain was still coming down in sheets, so she could barely see who it was, although the man's height gave him away.

Dave.

Why would he lie about where he was from? What was he hiding?

She watched through the veil of rain for a moment, surprised to see an orange glow illuminate his face. Holding something with both hands, he looked down at the bright screen in the familiar stance of texters everywhere.

He had a sat phone. The phone he'd shown them had a round that pierced its screen, rendering it unusable. Apparently he had a second one, or the damaged one still worked. Another lie.

She'd have to watch him. Closely.

34

"You will tell me what you know." Dario's hot breath skated across Martin's cheek. He pressed his knife to Martin's throat. "Or I will personally torture your daughter. Then I'll have my men kill every surviving member of your camp."

Martin swallowed carefully. "Why would I trust you? You already killed Renata and Pablo. What's to stop you from killing me and Gunnar and everyone else if we find the other site?"

Dario smiled. "Nothing. You will have to trust me." He stepped back. "I am a man of my word." With a sweep of his hand, he gave him a short, mocking bow.

One of the gunmen chuckled. Dario's eyes gleamed in the dim light as he ripped his gun from its holster.

"Do you think I am funny?" he asked, aiming at the man.

The gunman stiffened. "No, *jefe*. Of course not."

The stress radiating from Dario's guy was palpable. *Maybe I can play them against each other,* Martin thought. He would have to be careful—going too far would likely end in death.

His.

"Are you going to allow a bodyguard to disrespect you? I pegged you as a strong leader."

"You think he is my bodyguard?" Dario aimed his gun at Martin. His lip curled in a sneer. "As you can see, I don't need a bodyguard."

Martin put up his hand. "My mistake." *Strike that idea.*

Dario lowered his pistol. "You should watch your mistakes." He glared at the gunman who had chuckled. "As should you."

"*Si, jefe.*" Nodding, the gunman lowered his gaze in deference.

"Now. Where were we?"

Gunnar piped up. "The primary site."

Martin gave him a warning look, but Gunnar ignored him.

Dario nodded. "Yes. The primary site. We will make camp here tonight. Early tomorrow morning, we will head back to the steps and clear a way to the top." He motioned to the first gunman. "Tie them together."

"I'm not going to try to escape," Gunnar protested. "I'm as intrigued as you are about the other site."

Dario shrugged. "You will act as anchor for the good doctor."

The two gunmen seized Martin and Gunnar and proceeded to tie them back to back.

It was going to be a long, cold, uncomfortable night.

"Wake up."

The solid kick landed on the side of Martin's leg, punctuating the gunman's command. Martin grunted and raised his head, his eyes still blurry from a fitful night's rest. Weak light from an electric lantern cast the cave-like room in deep shadow. Dario and the second gunman were nowhere to be seen.

"Can you untie us?" Martin asked. "I can't feel my hands." *Or my legs,* he thought.

The gunman bent down and cut through the rope with a knife. Either they had more rope than they needed, or Dario didn't anticipate having to tie them up again.

Which didn't bode well for Martin. Maybe even Gunnar.

Martin rubbed his arms, trying to restore his circulation as he and Gunnar followed Dario's thug through the tunnel, past the carvings and into the warmth and light of the new day. Being a pragmatic optimist, Martin normally loved mornings—the dawn smacked of fresh starts and new endeavors.

The AK-47s hanging from the gunmen's shoulders did not.

During the night, Martin had made peace with the idea of not surviving to see his daughter again. He just hoped he could do something to keep her safe. What that would be, he had no idea, but he knew at its core it meant killing Dario. He'd have to stay alert to anything that might help him do that. He would willingly sacrifice his life for hers.

Any remaining optimism he felt came from being able to see, at last, what he'd come to the jungle for—an as-yet unknown ancient settlement, its existence recorded in the conquistador's own hand, detailing a miraculous cure. If his attempts to kill Dario ended in his own death, Martin wouldn't be able to report back to Austen. But he sure as hell would keep his promise to Taruca. Whatever happened, Martin was going to neutralize Dario.

Do that one thing, and all would be well. His daughter would be safe, the site would be protected, and Taruca's request would be honored. If he survived, then his commitment to Austen Newell would also be completed.

The only other question was what to do about Gunnar. Martin didn't think he would alert the government of Peru, facilitating the destruction of what could turn out to be the key to ancient Peruvian heritage. The man was a scholar, not a criminal.

At least, he hoped that was the case. Once Martin got rid of Dario, Gunnar would be free to go back to his handlers in the government and tell them the site's location. Hopefully, Austen Newell would figure out a way to get what he wanted before that happened.

Dario and the two gunmen had already begun to hack away at the vegetation above the steps they climbed the day before. More steps leading up the cliff face had emerged, though these were cut at a steeper angle.

Martin's heart rate ratcheted up with excitement. The possibility of discovering a new site was still top of his list, despite Dario and his thugs. What would they find? Like many before him, the elder tribesman, Taruca, had warned of evil spirits protecting the site. But in all his travels, Martin had yet to see one of those "warnings" play out. Often, indigenous tribes would default to dire warnings in order to keep interlopers and adventurists from desecrating their sacred sites.

He didn't blame them. Most of the so-called treasure hunters weren't interested in preserving artifacts, only selling them. It was rare for such groups to partner with the host country's government, unless it was mandatory. Even then, many South American governments accepted cash payouts to look the other way.

Working for Austen Newell had been a boon for Martin and his group. The Peruvian government saw the same thing, assuming the billionaire's immense wealth would be a boost to their economy, incorrectly thinking that Newell would invest heavily in infrastructure, bringing tourism to whatever site they found.

Austen Newell was only interested in one thing: a cure. But that made him a threat to the site, nonetheless. Martin doubted he'd care what the government did with the site once he had what he wanted.

A pang of guilt flickered through him as he thought about all the money Austen had poured into the expedition. If they found evidence of the cure at the site and Martin didn't survive the day, Austen would be left in the cold, still searching.

Would there be treasure waiting for them? From what Taruca had said in their private conversation, it appeared that there might be something to celebrate.

He just wasn't sure what it was. The elder had been vague in his answer when Martin asked him what to expect if they found the site. He'd only said that it was guarded by evil spirits and that anyone who breached the entrance would die an excruciating death.

A standard warning, to be sure.

The third gunman removed the ropes tying Gunnar and him together and pointed to a mound of freshly cut vegetation. "You're on cleanup."

"Both of us?" Gunnar asked.

"What do you think?"

Martin and Gunnar started work, throwing aside the clumps of plants, while the gunman stood behind them, rifle at the ready. Martin kept a watchful eye on a break in the man's concentration, hoping for a window of time to speak to Gunnar, but that didn't happen.

Dario and the other two gunmen continued their progress. Martin and Gunnar had to dodge the shower of plants and dirt as they worked. The higher the other men climbed, the more debris ended up caught in the steps.

"You," the third gunman said to Gunnar. "Climb up there and clear the piles. Your friend will stay here."

Gunnar gave a nod and climbed the steep rock stairs. He paused when he came to a pile of plants and shoved them out of the way. Under the watchful gaze of Dario's thug, Martin continued to clear the narrow path that led to the secondary site.

Martin stopped to take a sip of water from his canteen. He shaded his eyes so he could see where the others were—they were close to the top. He had to figure out a reason to join them, or he'd never get rid of Dario. Leine's advice about acting like the soldier he once was came back with a force that nearly blindsided him.

She was right.

"Look," he said to the third gunman. "I'm not a young man. I'll wear out fast if I keep this up for much longer." He nodded toward the top of the cliff. "It looks to me like your boss and compadres are almost to their objective. How about you and I climb up there and join them?"

"I don't think that is a good idea."

"You can bring up the rear, keep me in your sights." Martin screwed the cap back on his canteen. "C'mon. Aren't you curious to see what's up there?" He shrugged. "I know I am."

The gunman appeared to consider the suggestion. "Don't try anything."

"What am I going to do?" Martin eyed the assault rifle in his hands. "You've got the firepower. I'd be an idiot to try anything."

"No, you would be dead."

"Good point." Martin squinted against the bright sunlight streaming through a break in the enormous trees surrounding the valley. "Do we have a deal?"

The gunman gave him a short nod. Martin turned back toward the cliff and hoisted himself up the first step before grabbing the next. He'd climbed several steps before the gunman mounted the first set of stairs to follow. Apparently, what he'd said about wanting to see the other site had rung true for him, as well.

Curiosity killed the cat. At least, Martin hoped so.

35

Leine and the rest of the group set out from Taruca's camp at dawn the next morning, navigating through the mud created by the storm the night before. Leine asked Dave to bring up the rear so she could speak with Zolin privately. The commando's questionable behavior had her worried, and she wanted to make sure Zolin knew about him.

Leine waited until she and the shaman were several yards ahead of the other two before she broached the subject. "We need to watch Dave," she said in a low voice. "I've caught him in a few lies."

Zolin nodded. "What do you propose?"

"Nothing yet. He's on Lou's list of operators, so I'm trying to give him the benefit of the doubt, but he used a sat phone to send someone a message last night."

"I thought his phone had been destroyed."

"He lied. The question is why?"

"That may be. But he's a soldier. He was most likely checking in with his superiors."

"But with whom? If he was sending a message to Lou, why

wouldn't he tell me?" Leine couldn't justify his actions. "He's reporting to someone—just not who he should be."

"What about the man who is funding the expedition?"

"Austen?" Leine thought about it for a moment before responding. "Possible. Although I'm not aware of him sending someone specific along on the operation. Lou would most likely have told me if that was the case." It was good protocol to know people's loyalties.

Still, it was a possibility. Even so, the question remained the same: why didn't he tell Leine?

Several hours later, Zolin called a halt to their hike. Leine spread out the topo map to check their course.

"We're close. Judging by our progress, I'd say we're approximately two hours from the base of this cliff." He pointed to a spot on the map showing several lines running close together, indicating a steep incline.

Leine took note of the sun's position. "That should put us there a little after dusk. Which means if we do find a way up we're going to either have to wait until morning, or we climb in the dark."

"Which do you prefer?" Zolin asked.

Dave glanced at the map. "I'm game for a night ascent."

"You know that if there are steps, they'll be extremely steep, right?" Nancy asked. "Like scary steep?"

Dave scoffed. "How steep can they be? Seriously. I've climbed steep." He nodded at the map. "Frankly, this looks like a cakewalk. Besides, we can rope up."

His bravado rankled Leine. "I think it's best if we approach with caution. Yes, we have climbing gear, but only enough for three. Steep climbs may be easy for you, but may not be for others. We still need to be vigilant. We won't know exactly what we're up against until we get there. It might be a cakewalk, it might not. Especially in the dark."

"Yeah, but there's a full moon tonight, so we'll have plenty of ambient light."

"Depending on what time we decide to go." The full moon was both a plus and a minus. The ambient light would help them on the climb, but would also help if Dario's men were keeping watch. Leine continued. "Moonrise is at eleven o'clock, so we'll need to time our ascent accordingly."

"Can I be one of the three that rope up?" Nancy asked. "I'm afraid I'll be the weak link here. I've climbed a lot of ancient sites in my time, but always in full daylight."

Zolin put a hand on her shoulder. "You will be fine."

Nancy nodded, but it was obvious his assurances didn't dispel her fears.

HIGH UP THE CLIFF FACE, MARTIN LEANED BACK AS FAR AS HE dared, trying to catch a glimpse of where Dario and the other gunmen were. The steps had grown steeper. On more than one occasion Martin stopped himself from losing his footing and plummeting to his death.

The other men's jungle fatigues made it a challenge to find them among the vegetation, but a slight movement caught his eye. Martin focused on Dario and the other gunman near the top of the cliff, hacking away at what appeared to be the last of the steps.

"Looks like they made it." Martin said it loud enough for the gunman behind him to hear. Gunnar was too far ahead of them to catch anything he said.

The sound of the gunman's labored breathing grew closer. Martin waited. During the climb, he'd found out the man's name was Guillermo and that he wasn't married. Martin played up the possibility of finding treasure, and the gunman had responded like most people—growing more and more excited with the chance of discovery.

Martin was counting on it.

"Have they found the entrance?" Guillermo asked as he reached the step behind Martin, straining to see where the other men were. The friendly banter had lowered his guard.

Martin shook his head and turned as though he wanted to say something, then shoved Guillermo with as much force as he could muster. The gunman's eyes saucered and he windmilled his arms, attempting to regain his balance.

He didn't.

He plummeted dozens of steps to the first site, his body and rifle bouncing off the rocks. Guillermo landed where they'd started that morning, his leg bent at an unnatural angle. Martin waited to see if he moved. When he saw no signs of life, he yelled.

Higher up the cliff, Gunnar turned to see what happened. Martin didn't have to pretend to be horrified.

He'd just killed a man.

Obviously distressed, Dario gestured angrily at Martin and the body below. He said something to the nearest gunman, who nodded and started down the steps.

Martin was struck with the possibility of getting rid of the second gunman but quickly discarded the idea. Dario would be suspicious of one gunman's death. Two would be much more difficult to explain.

Martin glanced at Dario and their eyes met. Martin looked as surprised as he could, trying to communicate his horror at the man's death. Dario stared at him for what seemed like an eternity. Eventually, he turned his focus on Gunnar.

"You," he shouted. "Come here."

Gunnar nodded and scrambled toward him, stopping to

allow the second gunman to maneuver around him and continue down the steps.

Once the other gunman had made it past him, Martin resumed his climb.

One down, three to go.

36

B y the time Martin reached the top of the steps, Dario, Gunnar, and the other gunman had cleared a huge pile of vines and other vegetation. Their efforts had revealed what Martin both hoped for and dreaded: an entrance, rectangular in shape and rimmed in stone carved with sculptures of jaguars, pumas, snakes, odd human figures, and celestial bodies. Tree roots hugged the opening, giving the site a primeval look.

Gunnar tossed the last of the vines onto the pile then flicked on his flashlight, directing the beam into the interior. The light dropped off, illuminating only a few yards.

"Looks like we found it," Gunnar said. "Shall we?"

Dario strode forward and turned on his own flashlight. He studied the carvings and what he could see of the interior. "Not yet."

Martin and Gunnar both looked at him.

"Why are we waiting?" Gunnar asked, voicing Martin's thoughts.

Ignoring his question, Dario walked back to the stone steps and yelled down to the other gunman. "Julio—come."

Dario returned to where Martin and Gunnar waited. "Only a fool would go into a confined space with two enemies and only one guard."

"But you have weapons," Gunnar protested. "We don't."

"And you would do well to remember this."

Julio reappeared, his face red from the exertion of climbing the steep steps. Dario waved him to the entrance.

Julio's eyes widened, and he gave Dario a skeptical look. "We are going in there?"

"Yes, idiot." Dario scoffed. "This is what we came for."

Julio visibly swallowed. "*Si, jefe.*"

The other gunman guffawed. Dario gave him a withering glance, and he clapped his mouth shut.

Gunnar stepped forward. Dario stopped him.

"I think the good doctor should lead."

His disappointment obvious, Gunnar nodded, allowing Martin to go first.

Dario gave Martin a menacing look. "Don't try anything foolish." He tapped his rifle for emphasis.

Heart in his throat, Martin took Gunnar's flashlight and stepped through the opening. He'd heard stories of booby traps, a form of ancient security to keep enemies from breaching valuable sites. His hands became slick with sweat as he hugged the wall, searching for anything that might serve as a trigger.

Dario's choice of having Martin go first took care of two problems. If there were traps, the person at the head of the line would be on the receiving end of whatever the former inhabitants dreamed up to stop their enemies, saving Dario, his gunmen, and Gunnar from injury or death. It would also save Dario from wasting a bullet.

Martin continued along the dark corridor, his senses heightened by both fear and the excitement of discovery. As long as he avoided triggering any mechanisms planted along the way to stop unwanted visitors, he'd be the first to set eyes on whatever treasure might be waiting for them. Again, he thought of his daughter, wishing she was there instead of Dario.

This was what they'd both been working toward. If he didn't find some way to thwart the kidnappers, then Dario would most likely have both Martin and Nancy killed to be rid of loose ends.

He couldn't let that happen. But what could he do?

Martin walked carefully, visions filling his mind of hand-dug holes too deep to escape, lined with sharpened bamboo, which would either kill or maim an unwary victim. Either way, escaping from a pit was often impossible, and if the fall didn't kill the victim, then starvation would. Martin shook his head, trying to push the frightening images from his mind. Worrying didn't do any good.

The corridor jogged left, then continued on. The others kept their distance behind him. Dario had pushed Julio to second position in front of Gunnar, with the remaining gunman fourth in line. The damp air had grown close and thick, giving the impression they were heading underground. Water trickled down the sides of the tunnel, its eerie echoes accompanying the sound of their progress. Martin wiped the sweat from his eyes and kept going.

The ceiling lowered, forcing the men to duck as they walked. The odd angle made it difficult to see ahead. Something pierced Martin's shoulder, tearing his shirtsleeve, and he drew in a sharp breath at the sudden pain. He aimed the flashlight so he could see what had caused the cut. Some kind of root had forced its way through the rock and stuck out into the corridor.

"Two o'clock," he called over his shoulder, before stopping himself. *Don't warn them, idiot. Let them find out for themselves.* Gingerly, he touched his shoulder. His fingers came away wet with blood.

Better than a puncture. At least the blood would flush bacteria from the wound. He aimed the flashlight in front of him to see what lay ahead. There was another turn, this time to the right.

At that moment, a faint thud sounded. Martin froze, straining to hear. A barely audible clatter followed. A moment later, the ground beneath Martin's feet started to shake.

Something was headed their way.

Without thinking, he dropped flat and covered his head. A split-second later, something whooshed over him, leaving a breeze in its wake.

Julio's screams were cut short. A heavy weight brushed Martin's calves and settled, partially pinning him to the floor. He raised himself to his elbows and field-crawled out from under the crushing mass, leaving one of his boots behind. Martin scrambled to his feet and directed the beam of his flashlight behind him.

A rough clay ball the size of a boulder, embedded with sharp spikes, blocked the corridor. Blood dripped from the bottom. The lower half of Julio's body was wedged between the ball and the floor, keeping the ancient booby trap from swinging back the way it had come.

"What the hell happened?" Dario's anger reverberated through the small space.

Martin took a step back. Dario, Gunnar, and the remaining gunman were on the other side. If he continued on without them, what would he find?

More importantly, would he be able to escape at the other end?

He couldn't leave Gunnar.

A shuffling sound echoed through the tunnel.

"Grab him, here—"

Martin redirected the beam of light toward the ball and studied the spikes. A dark stain covered several of the tips, and it didn't look like blood.

"Wait."

The shuffling stopped. "What?" Dario's tone told him the kidnapper's patience had grown thin.

Part of Martin didn't want to say anything, allowing Dario and his thug to make a grave mistake, but the other part had to warn Gunnar, even though he'd betrayed their mission. "Be careful of the spikes. I think they've been dipped in something."

"Shit." Gunnar's hushed expletive sounded loud in the dark space.

"Just grab his fucking arm," Dario said. "We have to move him to get past this thing."

Martin directed his flashlight above him. A channel ran along the stones that made up the ceiling, allowing the spiked ball to swing freely along the corridor. The rope holding the ball was several centimeters thick. It would take a sharp knife to sever.

"If you free the ball it may swing back, but it could also still block the tunnel."

"What do you propose?" Gunnar asked.

"I'll go on ahead. If it looks worthwhile, I'll come back and we'll figure out some way to move the ball."

Dario answered, "I have a much better idea."

Flashes from Dario's rifle strobed the tunnel as a barrage of rounds splintered the ball. Gunnar yelled at him to stop, but he kept firing. Spent brass pinged against the rock walls and the thick pottery, as the rounds chipped away at the ancient booby trap.

A sharp pain pierced Martin's calf as he jog-limped to the end of the tunnel and threw himself around the corner.

He sat up and checked his body for additional damage. Using his flashlight, he directed the beam at his calf.

A dark stain saturated his pant leg. Gingerly, he rolled up the cuff. Blood ran down his lower leg from what appeared to be a deep cut. He felt the skin around it, and his fingertips brushed something sharp. He grasped the object and pulled, wincing from the pain.

He held it up to the light. A small piece of bamboo had embedded itself in his leg.

Shit. He checked to see if it was one of the tips with a poisoned end, but the piece was covered in blood, making it difficult to determine. He let the bamboo fall to the ground.

There wasn't much he could do if it was, other than hope the blood cleared the poison from the wound before it entered his bloodstream. He dug inside his pocket for his bandana to clean up, but it wasn't there. He tried ripping his shirtsleeve, but the material was too sturdy. He'd just have to bleed.

Using the rock wall for support, he climbed to his feet and tested the weight on his leg. It hurt like a mother, but he'd manage.

The automatic gunfire had become sporadic. Dario must have been clearing out smaller sections of the "death ball." Martin turned back, intending to continue.

And gasped.

Huge, open jaws with rows of teeth and pointed fangs both top and bottom reared out of the darkness like a monstrous predator. Heart hammering in his chest, Martin swept his flashlight toward the ceiling. Two stone-cold eyes gleamed back at him.

My God. It looks like the open jaws of a jaguar.

Stunned, Martin studied the enormous sculpture. The teeth had been carved from white stone, giving them a realistic appearance in the dim light.

The same type of carving had been discovered on the Mayan Peninsula at a site called *Ek Ba'lam*, but the sculptures, though spectacular, weren't nearly as large as what stood before him now.

The gunfire ended, leaving an eerie silence in its wake. Martin stared in disbelief at the masterful carving. He was about to step through the jaws when Gunnar rounded the corner and stopped. He crossed himself and muttered something in Spanish.

The beam from Dario's flashlight announced his arrival. He trained the beam on the impressive sight and said, "Now we're getting somewhere."

37

"Have you ever seen anything like this?" Gunnar asked.

"There is a Mayan site northeast of *Chichen Itza* called *Ek' Balam* that has a similar entrance, but nothing this large."

"*Ek' Balam,*" Gunnar repeated. "Black jaguar."

Martin nodded. "You know your Mayan."

Dario motioned with the barrel of his rifle toward the entrance. "Keep moving."

Martin raised his flashlight, and the men stepped through the jaws.

Gunnar glanced at Martin. "You're limping. Are you all right?"

"Just a cut. I'll be fine."

They proceeded through a tunnel lined with hieroglyphs painted in deep blue and red. A faint light could be seen at the end of the corridor.

Gunnar stopped to decipher a section of glyphs, but Dario prodded him in the back with his rifle. "Keep going."

The tunnel ended abruptly, opening onto a cavernous room. The remnants of a block ceiling littered the floor, the space now covered in massive tree roots, weaving their way into and out of the walls and meeting overhead. Weak, late afternoon sunlight filtered through dense vines, painting the space with a gentle glow. At the far end of the room stood another doorway, this one not nearly as large or as ornate as the jaguar's jaws. A rectangular stone slab, about the size of a minivan, stood in the center of the space. A series of carved monoliths surrounded the slab, which was covered in decaying plant matter. What appeared to be bones poked through the detritus.

"Inca?" Martin wondered aloud. The ancient tribe's propensity for sacrifice might explain the bones.

"Possible," Gunnar said. "The stones remind you of anything?"

Martin nodded. Although much smaller, their placement resembled the prehistoric site of Stonehenge in England. His excitement building, he started for the monoliths.

Dario kept his distance as did the other gunman, who covered them with his rifle.

"Where is the gold?" Dario asked.

Martin made his way to the stones. Each had hieroglyphics carved into its face. He didn't recognize them and motioned for Gunnar to join him. "Can you make out what these say?"

Gunnar stepped closer to get a better look. "It appears to be of Jivaroan and Inca origin."

"But the Jivaroans repelled the Incas." Fierce warriors and known headhunters, the Jivaroan tribe had lived in the Amazon for millennia. The Inca failed to conquer them. To Martin's knowledge, the warring parties had never joined forces.

Gunnar nodded. "True, but that doesn't mean they didn't communicate with each other." He pointed to one of the glyphs in a line of hieroglyphics. "There's your frog again."

Martin leaned in closer. The carving was indeed a pictorial

representation of the sinchi dart frog, similar to the one they'd seen at the secondary site below them.

"Look. A jaguar and an anaconda."

"Can you make sense of what it says?" Martin moved closer so he could whisper to Gunnar without Dario being able to hear. He had to trust him. "There's two of us and only two of them."

"Step back," Dario warned, aiming his rifle at Martin. Martin did as he was told.

"It appears that this place was used for religious purposes." Gunnar paused for a moment. He hadn't acknowledged what Martin said. "Many of the ceremonies were performed to heal large groups." He pointed to another glyph. "This represents a well-respected shaman-priest rumored to cure terrible diseases. According to this, he was in high demand."

Martin's heart skipped a beat. Could it be? Had they found the conquistador's city? He took a slow, deep breath to calm himself. Gunnar didn't know Austen Newell had tasked Martin with finding the cure mentioned in the conquistador's manuscript, only that they were looking for a lost city.

As an ethnobotanist, Martin had been prepared to discover a combination of herbs and other plants shamans used to heal the conquistador. But there weren't any references to plants other than the psychotropic ayahuasca vine so prevalent throughout the Amazon basin. These stones depicted only animals.

Could Austen's cure be of animal origin?

"The Inca used gold in their ceremonies." Dario spread his hands. "Where is this gold?"

"Perhaps the site has already been looted," Gunnar suggested. "It happens more often than not."

Martin turned his attention to the skeleton lying on the stone slab. The brownish skull was elongated, similar to remains discovered in the Paracas region of Peru. Egyptian mummies had also been known to have longer skulls than normal. Members of fringe societies believed the unusual shape of the skulls signified alien ancestry. The scientific community, however, believed that wherever these elongated skulls were found, the inhabitants prized skeletal modification, either for religious or ceremonial reasons. Parents would bind their babies' heads, sometimes using boards to facilitate the variation. As their children grew, their skulls would display the preferred elongation. The ritual struck Martin as similar to the Chinese practice of binding women's feet.

Fascinating, but also disturbing.

Careful to preserve the skeleton's placement, he removed the plant matter to get a better look at what may have caused the person's death. A large hole marred the skull. Blunt force trauma appeared likely. Martin searched the area for an object that might have created post mortem damage to the skull, but there wasn't anything nearby.

Hairline cracks crisscrossed the femur and tibia. The leg bones were thin and light, and the interior had an odd, honeycomb appearance, giving the impression of severe osteoporosis. The rest of the skeleton appeared normal. Doctors had treated Austen Newell for osteoporosis and osteoarthritis in his legs, but the treatments did little to arrest his decline.

Martin was certain he'd found a clue to Austen's condition, but he needed Gunnar to read the rest of the carvings.

A twinge in his shoulder reminded him of the cut he received going through the tunnel. The bleeding had stopped, but the area around the injury was warm and had turned red. He needed to clean and bandage the wound, but Dario had the first aid kit. The pain in his leg ebbed and flowed, whether he put weight on it or not.

"I need to clean the cut on my shoulder. Infection is setting in," Martin said to Dario. "You have a first aid kit, right?"

Dario shook his head. "Not until we find the gold. It's getting late and we're running out of daylight. I want to see the rest of this place now, while we still can." He nodded at his gunman. "Take a position at the entrance. I don't want any surprises."

"*Si, jefe.*" The gunman nodded and disappeared through the main entrance.

With Gunnar in the lead, Dario brought up the rear as the three men headed for the doorway at the far end of the room.

38

The arduous trek brought Leine, Zolin, Nancy, and Dave to their destination just before sunset.

Zolin pointed to the steep cliff at the end of the valley. "That's it."

Leine scanned the base of the cliff through binoculars, looking for signs of activity. She almost missed it, had to backtrack and zero in on a specific spot near a small waterfall. Clumps of vegetation had been scattered at the base. She scanned what appeared to be a series of stone steps leading to a ledge halfway up the face of the cliff. More steps and another ledge were visible near the top. There were no signs of life. She handed Zolin the binoculars.

"Halfway in, near a small waterfall, then straight up."

He studied the area. "I see it." He lowered the binoculars. "We should be able to achieve the base of the cliff in less than an hour." He glanced at the sky. "I suggest we wait until dark. Dario may have posted a lookout."

"Agreed." She turned to Nancy and Dave. "You guys good with that?"

Dave nodded. "Roger that."

"I'm just following you guys," Nancy said.

Leine set her pack on the ground and opened the top. "We only have enough climbing equipment for three. Since Nancy has the least experience, she gets one set." She gave Dave a look. "What about you?"

"I'm going to free climb."

"Okay. That leaves Zolin and me. Dave, you take the lead."

"Roger Wilco."

Leine still wasn't sure about Dave, and preferred to be behind him so she could keep track of his whereabouts. She figured he wouldn't want to be tied to two other climbers. This way, if Nancy stumbled, Leine and Zolin would be able to arrest her fall.

"I'll take the first aid kit and the pistol. You take the Uzi," she said to Zolin. "All set, Dave?"

Grinning, Dave patted his MP5.

As soon as darkness fell, they headed for the cliff. Zolin's uncanny ability to navigate through the dark jungle along game paths helped them move quickly by avoiding the necessity of hacking through the thick vegetation. Leine had loaned Nancy the second pair of NVGs since Dave had his own, allowing them to navigate almost as well as Zolin.

The full moon hadn't yet risen, giving them cover from anyone standing guard above or below. Zolin slowed his pace as they closed in on the section of the cliff where the stairs began.

Once they reached the cliff base, Leine, Zolin, and Nancy donned their climbing gear and waited until Dave began his ascent. Once he'd climbed several feet, the other three began. Zolin took the lead with Nancy in middle position. Leine brought up the rear.

At first, the steep stairs took some getting used to, but after a while, even Nancy kept pace.

Halfway up the first section, Nancy lost her footing. Zolin and Leine acted quickly, arresting her fall.

"Are you all right?" Leine asked.

"I'm fine. Thanks," Nancy muttered. She took a deep breath before grabbing the next step with shaking hands.

"You're doing great," Leine assured her.

Dave reached the landing area and turned to give Zolin a hand up. In turn, the shaman helped Nancy onto the narrow pathway. Leine came last. Nancy removed her climbing harness and handed it to Leine, who stuffed it into her pack.

"I'd like to stay here," she said, her voice shaky. "I'll just slow you guys down."

"Dario may have left a guard," Leine warned. "Wait until we clear the interior."

"All right."

Leine asked Zolin, "Would you mind staying with Nancy?"

"Of course."

Dave headed toward the entrance. Leine slid her gun free and joined him, glad for the NVGs. "Watch your step. The tribes in this area are known for creating traps."

Several yards in, Dave stopped abruptly. "Looks like the first casualty."

"Who is it?" Leine asked, steeling herself for bad news.

"Some guy in jungle fatigues."

She moved past Dave and glanced at the dead gunman. One of Dario's men. Relieved, Leine let out a breath. He'd been propped against the side of the tunnel. One of his legs stuck out at an odd angle. "There's no evidence of a gunshot wound." She checked his skull. The section near the occipital ridge had a mat of dried blood and hair. "Blunt force trauma."

"Maybe he fell."

"From the looks of his leg, that's a good possibility." Leine searched the man for weapons and found a pistol strapped to his ankle. She checked the magazine and the chamber for rounds before she slid it into her waistband.

They continued through the long corridor and around the corner.

Dave pulled up short. "Damn. That's realistic."

Leine studied the life-size jungle cat sculpture. "Menacing. It's obviously meant to scare off unwanted visitors."

"Which would be us."

"I'm going to light up the place." They slid their goggles off, and she swept the flashlight's beam around the dark interior. The center of the room was largely empty. "Looks like a place for a ceremony of some sort."

Dave continued to the back of the cave, aiming his flashlight along the wall, illuminating a series of carved stones.

Leine continued into the space, searching for an exit or indication of another room or passageway, but found nothing but carved stone. She walked in the opposite direction, searching the perimeter, when her foot landed on something soft. She aimed her light at the material and bent down to retrieve it.

"Whatcha got there?" Dave asked.

"Bandana." She shoved it in her pocket and scanned the floor. Several footprints marred the ground. "Looks like they were here."

"Maybe they spent the night." Dave went back to the carving.

The absence of blood was good. She'd expected signs of struggle. She continued her circuit of the cave until she met up with Dave.

"Find something?"

Dave lowered his light and smiled. "Just some interesting carvings. Should we go back out and let Nancy and Zolin know it's clear?"

"It may be clear, but I figure Dario and his boys will be back to fetch the dead gunman."

"Not if we get to them first."

He had a point. They retraced their steps back outside where Zolin and Nancy waited. The moon peeked above the surrounding trees.

"Well? Can I go inside?"

"It's empty," Leine said.

"Let's just say there isn't anybody alive in there," Dave added.

Nancy gasped. "Is it—?"

"We ran across one of Dario's thugs." Leine gave Dave a look. He shrugged.

"Oh. Thank God." Nancy blew out a breath. "Wait. Does that mean Dario might be dead, too?"

"Not necessarily," Leine replied. "There was only one body, and it looks like he died from a fall."

Nancy shivered. "That could have been me."

Leine added, "According to Esme, Dario had three gunmen with him. Better odds for Gunnar and Martin, but remember Dario and his thugs have weapons."

"You're right. I—I'm just so worried."

Leine squeezed Nancy's shoulder. "We'll find him."

Nancy touched Leine's hand and nodded. "I know you will. Thank you." She looked at Zolin and Dave. "Thank you all for your help. I don't know what I'd do." Her voice cracked, and she cleared her throat. "What does it look like inside?"

"Nothing earth shattering," Dave answered. "It's a big cave with a life-size jaguar and some carvings on the walls. That's about it."

"Is it all right if I take a look?"

"If you do, stay alert, in case one of Dario's men shows up. We need to establish some kind of signal to let you know it's us when we come back."

"How about the phrase King Tut?" Dave suggested.

"That works." Leine eyed the steps leading up the cliff.

"We've got the element of surprise. We should be able to make short work of the bad guys as long as they're still above."

"Just don't shoot my dad. He'll be the one *not* wearing camo."

"Don't worry."

Nancy looked back at the entrance to the tunnel. "I have to go inside. I promise I won't stay long." When she saw Leine's look, she added, "I've been searching for this site for months." She nodded at the stairs. "And I may not ever make it up there. Surely you can see that?"

"Take this." Leine handed her the dead gunman's sidearm. "There are six bullets left in the magazine and one in the chamber. You know how to use it?"

Nancy took the gun from her and nodded. "I do. Is there a safety?"

Leine demonstrated how to use the pistol, then turned to the other two. "Ready?"

Both men nodded. "Ready."

39

"What the hell is this?" Dario stared into the smaller room, his flashlight strafing the walls.

Dozens of purple crystals winked back at them. During daylight hours, their placement would have bathed the room in a serene, violet light. Gunnar scraped away some moss covering the floor, revealing opaque black stone, similar to obsidian. What they could see of the ceiling boasted stones of forest green shot through with black. Four benches had been erected along the walls, with plaques depicting jaguar, anaconda, the poison dart frog, and human figures. The center of the room was open.

Gunnar studied the carvings. "Look at this."

Martin joined him to see what he was talking about. His neck and shoulders wrapped in what could only be described as a huge snake, a man dressed as a priest held a stylized frog over a person lying on the bench.

Gunnar nodded at Martin. "Your frog again."

"More frogs," Dario scoffed. "Where is the treasure?"

"There may be more to see here. I doubt these two rooms are

all there is." Martin's instincts were kicking in, telling him to keep Dario's interest piqued, or he and Gunnar would be dead. "If this was a major religious site, which it may well be, then there will undoubtedly be gold somewhere nearby. Indigenous tribes used gold extensively, especially in their ceremonies."

A spark of interest lit Dario's eyes. "We'll see." He turned to Gunnar. "Come with me."

Gunnar hesitated. "I'm going to need Martin's expertise if we find anything of value."

Martin's spirits rose. Maybe Gunnar was on his side, after all.

"He will only slow us down."

"How about I bandage his wounds?" Gunnar gestured toward Martin. "You heard him. The cut on his shoulder is infected. I won't be able to consult with him if he's dead."

Dario's sharp gaze took in Martin's appearance. After a moment, he grunted and removed his pack. He rummaged inside and tossed the first aid kit to Gunnar. "Don't waste too much time on him, *comprende*? Just enough to keep him alive. For now."

"Sure." Gunnar opened the kit.

Martin removed his shirt and set it aside. Gunnar handed him some antibiotics, then tore the top off a packet of ointment and spread it on his shoulder.

"It doesn't look good, brother," he said in a low voice.

"I'm more worried about my leg, to be honest."

"No talking," Dario barked.

Gunnar bandaged the cut. Whispering, he said, "Pull up your pant leg so I can see the wound."

Martin gingerly raised his pant leg, wincing from the pain. Gunnar peered at his calf with his flashlight.

"Holy Jesus."

"That bad, huh?" Martin said drily.

Gunnar brought his gaze to Martin's. "What caused this?"

"A piece of shrapnel from the spike ball."

Gunnar blanched. "But you said the tips had been—"

"I did. By the look on your face, they were."

"How long?"

Martin shook his head. "I don't know. That poison is likely over five hundred years old. I have no idea how toxic it is, or what kind of bacteria might have been growing on the spikes."

Gunnar redirected his focus to cleaning and bandaging the wound. "Well, this should help."

When he finished, Martin lowered his pant leg. "Thanks."

Gunnar returned the first aid supplies to the kit. "I gotta ask..." he glanced at Dario, whose attention seemed to be elsewhere. "Did you push that guy?"

Martin studied him, searching for a sign that he was genuinely curious and not trying to find out intel for Dario. Something told him to stay quiet about what he'd done.

He shook his head.

Gunnar seemed to accept his answer and nodded. "I didn't think so." He finished packing the kit and stood. He and Dario exchanged a glance too quick for Martin to decipher.

"Don't try to leave, Doctor. Remember who has the gun, yes?" Dario patted his rifle. He followed Gunnar out.

Martin climbed onto one of the stone benches and gently massaged his calf. The skin and muscles were numb, dashing his hope that the neurotoxin had lost its potency. Zoological studies had shown that toxin from the golden dart frog could last up to a year. Five hundred years seemed a stretch, but few had studied the sinchi frog due to its rarity. Could its poison be even more toxic than that of the golden frog? That was assuming the venom used would have been from the frog in the carvings.

He stretched out on his back and stared into the darkness. Falling asleep would be difficult. If the neurotoxin continued to spread through his body, more lethal symptoms would develop. He'd read stories about people experiencing hallucinations and seizures. If the sinchi frog was anything like its golden cousin, eventually its poison would overwhelm his respiratory system. What if he woke up and couldn't move? Couldn't breathe?

How much longer did he have?

40

Leine made it to the top of the cliff first, followed by Dave, then Zolin. The full moon had crested, blanketing everything in a blue-white glow. Leine slid on her NVGs and scanned the terrain.

They were alone.

"Looks like an entrance," she said in a low voice. "Let's go."

"I'm going in first," Zolin said. "I have experience with ancient sites. I know what to watch for."

They gathered at the opening and entered the corridor— Zolin in the lead, with Dave and Leine in second and third position.

The night vision goggles painted everything an eerie green. To Leine's relief, the small group was quick, silent, and moved as one unit, as though they'd been on dozens of operations together. The stark difference between trained operators and amateurs like Nancy or Mateo couldn't be overstated. To be fair, Martin's daughter had never been anything other than an academic, yet she'd conducted herself admirably.

But neutralizing the enemy was dangerous and required professionals. She was glad to see that Dave was a real pro.

The corridor zigged and zagged, eventually leading to a stretch scattered with debris. A second dead gunman dressed in fatigues like the man they'd discovered below had been shoved against the wall. Dried blood dotted the body, and pieces of bamboo were embedded in his skin.

Careful of the barbs, Dave checked the corpse for weapons but found none, so they continued on. Leine glanced at the items on the floor as they passed—dozens of sherds of pottery and splinters of bamboo mixed with spent brass from an automatic rifle. Zolin pointed out a length of shredded rope hanging from a deep channel in the ceiling.

Talk about a gruesome death, Leine thought.

As they approached the next turn, Zolin slowed his pace. He eased around the corner, and Dave followed suit. Leine waited a beat before she did the same.

A pair of gaping jaws loomed at her and she caught her breath. The impressive carving of the large cat's fangs would have certainly done what the ancient inhabitants wanted—terrify intruders.

A glow emanated from beyond the jaws. Both Zolin and Dave had disappeared. Leine eased up to the entrance and peered into the dimly lit room.

A torch burned at one end, its flames flickering eerily against the walls. Dave covered one half of the perimeter, while Zolin did the other. In the center, several monoliths surrounded a slab of rock. Trees had taken root throughout the space—nature reclaiming its ownership—transforming the ruins of the building into a natural setting.

A body lay off to the side near the rock slab. It wasn't obvious if the person was dead or sleeping. Leine scanned the rest of the space, searching for others, but didn't see anyone else. She moved toward the body, expecting them to be dead. Zolin acknowledged her and continued his recon.

She knelt down to shake the person's shoulder when a voice behind her stopped her cold.

"Drop your weapons."

The order was in Spanish. Leine eased her hand back and slowly stood. The body on the floor sat up. It was Gunnar.

Eyes wide, Gunnar scrambled to his feet. He was about to say something, but before he could the man behind Leine barked an order.

"I said drop your weapons. Now."

She placed her pistol on the ground, raised her hands, and backed away, then turned to see who'd spoken.

A wiry, dark-haired man in jungle fatigues stood at one end of the room, his AK-47 aimed her direction. *Dario.* Another gunman in similar dress had his rifle trained on Dave and Zolin. She scanned for more gunmen but didn't see any. Depending on Gunnar's allegiances, it could be three against three, or four against two.

Good odds, either way.

"Search them. And bring the goggles to me."

She gave Zolin and Dave a look. Gunnar stepped forward with an apologetic expression and proceeded to pat her down. His hand brushed the combat knife in the sheath next to her ankle. He raised her pant leg and slid it free. When he straightened, she snatched the knife and twisted his arm behind him. Holding the blade to his throat, she dragged him behind a monolith.

Dario fired, the rounds pinging off the stone. With Dario's attention diverted, Dave bum-rushed the other gunman, knocking him off his feet. Dario pivoted and fired again, this time near Dave and the gunman. The rounds kicked up dirt where the two men wrestled, but it did no good—they continued to struggle.

"Don't fucking move," Dario shouted, his head on a swivel. "*Or everybody dies.*"

Zolin raised his hands. His voice calm, he said, "I know where to find the treasure."

Dario scowled at him and waved his pistol between the shaman and the monolith where Leine had dragged Gunnar. At the same time he kept his rifle trained on Dave and the other gunman. Dave appeared to be winning. "What the fuck did you say, *pendejo*?"

"The treasure you seek. I know where to find it."

Gunnar struggled, but Leine pressed the knife into his flesh. "Don't even try it."

"I'm on your side," he said in a raspy whisper.

Leine tightened her hold. "Is that why you took my knife?"

"Please. You must believe me."

Ignoring him, she turned her attention to the drama unfolding between the other men.

Dario frowned at Zolin before shifting his focus to the two men fighting. Dave had the other gunman in a full nelson but kept the man's body between himself and Dario, frustrating a clean shot.

"I will *kill you both*," Dario bellowed. The words echoed in the large space.

Straining against Dave's hold, the gunman struggled to catch Dario's eye. "No, *jefe*. Please. I beg you—"

Dario fired at the ground between the man's feet. The round ricocheted, pinging the wall nearby. With a yelp, the gunman scrambled to move his legs out of the way, but Dave wrenched his arms back and pushed down harder on his neck, shifting him so that Dario couldn't target Dave's own head or torso. Dario narrowed his eyes, his finger curled around the trigger of the AK.

Shit. He was going to do it.

"Let him go, Dave," Leine called. "He'll kill you both." She shoved Gunnar out from behind the stone before she followed. She let the knife fall to the floor. Gunnar stooped to pick it up.

There'd be another chance.

There had to be.

41

D ave glared at Leine as he released the gunman and shoved him away, clearly pissed off that she'd given up when he'd had the upper hand. Dario tossed the AK to his man, who immediately turned the weapon on Dave.

He'll thank me later, Leine thought. A round from an assault rifle that close could have easily pierced the gunman's body and entered his, in turn killing, or at least seriously wounding, both men. Leine assessed risk and reward in absolute terms—if an action would result in unacceptable loss, then it was time to abort and find another way. Assuming he was on their side, the possibility of Dave being killed was an unacceptable risk. They needed Dave alive, or the odds of overpowering the two diminished considerably.

If Dario killed Dave, there would also be one less person to help get Martin and Nancy to safety. Better to allow Dario to believe he had the upper hand.

Zolin cleared his throat.

Dario's gaze cut to him. "Well? Where is this treasure?"

"Not far. I will take you there."

He narrowed his eyes. "Why should I believe you?"

Zolin nodded. "Your suspicion is understandable. I have lived among many of the tribes in the Basin."

"And I employ several. What has that got to do with anything? No one has ever spoken of treasure with such surety."

"You are an outsider. I travel between worlds and have seen that which you seek."

"Ah." A spark of understanding lit Dario's eyes. "A shaman, then." He scoffed. "You sell your questionable magic to heal people. If you fail," he shrugged, "you blame evil spirits. If you are successful, then of course it's all your doing."

Zolin shook his head. "My services are free."

"Sure they are." Dario lifted his chin. "Fine. Show me where to find this treasure. But only you." He gestured to his gunman. "Put them with the doctor."

Was Martin still alive? Or was that Dario-speak for "kill everyone?" Leine didn't think Dario would have them all taken out. If Zolin led him to a cache of gold, he'd need help removing the treasure.

Dario wouldn't have them killed.

Yet.

The gunman took their NVGs and herded Gunnar, Leine, and Dave toward a doorway at the far end of the cave.

"Give me the goggles," Dario ordered. The gunman handed him a pair, and he slid them on. Then he followed Zolin out through the immense jaws, back into the dark tunnel.

Gunnar stepped through the doorway first, followed by Leine and Dave. The gunman strafed the room with his flashlight, illuminating purple crystals and stone benches. A man lay on a bench to their left.

Martin.

"Sit," the gunman said, his tone gruff.

Leine and Dave exchanged looks. She gave him a slight nod.

She stumbled, focusing the gunman's attention on her for a split second.

Dave lunged for the gunman, twisting the weapon from his grasp. At the same time, Leine pivoted and jabbed him in the throat, then slammed her foot into the side of his knee. There was a sickening *crack* and the gunman went down. Eyes wide, he doubled over and wheezed as he tried to suck in a breath, and at the same time grasped his leg.

Gunnar ran toward him. "I've got him."

"Not so fast, Gunnar." Leine barred his way forward. "Back away. Now."

Gunnar stopped. "I told you, I'm on your side."

"Sure you are." Leine moved toward the gunman. "Dave, if he moves, shoot him."

"Will do."

Leine searched the gunman for weapons, taking his pistol, an extra magazine, his flashlight, and a handful of flex cuffs. She wrenched his arms behind his back and wrapped one of the cuffs tightly around his wrists.

"Watch them both," she said to Dave. Leine crossed the floor to the stone bench to check on Martin. His skin had a gray cast, even in the artificial beam of the flashlight. Martin stirred and opened his eyes to slits. The motion appeared to take too much effort. With a groan, he closed them.

She checked Martin's vitals. Rapid pulse, flushed and sweating. Skin hot to the touch.

"He's burning up." She raised his pant leg and pulled a corner of the bandage free. Pus oozed from the ugly wound. The skin around it appeared to be necrotic. "Martin." She patted his cheeks, attempting to revive him. "What happened?"

Martin shook his head, his eyes still closed. Sweat soaked his clothing. "Jaguars...snakes..." he moaned.

"A piece of bamboo from the trap got lodged in his leg,"

Gunnar said. "We think the tips were covered with a compound from a poison dart frog."

"But that would have been hundreds of years ago. The toxins would be neutralized by now."

Gunnar crossed his arms and nodded. "That's what we both thought. It's possible descendants of the tribe that built this site reapply the poison." He shrugged. "No one knows for certain. The tribes are notoriously closed mouth about sacred sites and rituals."

"Can you blame them?" Leine said, turning back to Martin.

Martin thrashed and rolled his head from side to side. "Must tell...Nancy..."

"Nancy is close by, Martin," Leine said, keeping her voice low. "She's down at the lower site. What do you want to tell her?"

He stopped moving and opened his eyes to slits, then closed them again. "Not plants..."

Leine looked at Gunnar. "Do you understand what he's saying?"

Gunnar shook his head. "Unless he's talking about the carvings we found."

"You mean those?" She nodded at the stone plaques above them.

"And the ones at the lower site."

"Is there some sort of significance?"

"Only in what's missing."

Leine glanced at the plaques above them. "No plants are represented. That's unusual, isn't it?"

Gunnar nodded. "It is, especially for a culture that relies so heavily on the natural world for medicine. Martin thought that was a clue to something. What, I don't know."

"Maybe this was where they sacrificed animals," Dave suggested. "Didn't the Incas do that a lot?"

"They did. But there are small animals represented here too, like frogs and insects. Normally larger species were sacrificed."

"More bang for the buck?" Dave snorted. "Yeah, I can see that."

Leine lifted Martin's eyelids and shined the light at his pupils, checking for dilation. "I'm not sure that a large dose of antibiotics could even stop the infection, but we have to try. He needs intravenous delivery." She turned to Gunnar. "Is there a first aid kit somewhere close by?"

"Dario has one, but it's in his pack. He took it with him when he and the shaman left. I gave him some antibiotics, but I'm not sure how old they were. Dario did allow me to bandage his leg and shoulder."

"So he obviously wants to keep Martin alive, at least until he finds what he's looking for." Leine pulled Martin's shirtsleeve away from his shoulder and peeked under the bandage. The wound didn't look nearly as bad as the one on his leg, although the skin was red and hot to the touch.

"Nancy—" Martin thrashed on the stone bench.

Leine looked at Dave. "Think we can trust him?" she asked, referring to Gunnar.

Dave shrugged. "He did try to help Martin."

"Believe me when I tell you—I am on your side," Gunnar said. "I've been working with Martin for months. Why would I do anything to hurt him?"

Leine studied him. She was going after Zolin and Dario, and needed Dave to stay and keep watch over the gunman, as well as be ready to fight in case Dario slipped by her and returned. But Nancy needed to see her father, now.

"Nancy's at the lower site. Tell her she needs to get up here, now. We left the climbing ropes down below. I don't know how long he has."

"On it." Obviously relieved, Gunnar stood and sprinted from the room.

Leine turned her attention back to Martin. Unless they did something, fast, Nancy's father was going to die.

42

Dario kept his rifle trained on the shaman's back as they walked along the tunnel leading outside. He was wary, but the other man didn't appear to be much of a threat. Shamans rarely threatened anyone physically. No, these witch doctors used their so-called magic to thwart their enemies.

Dario didn't believe in magic. He believed in work, and violence.

The two men reached the end of the tunnel and emerged into the stillness of early morning. The monkeys and parrots were calm, with only the occasional screech or squawk punctuating the silence. It wasn't yet dawn, and the jungle wore darkness like a veil.

"Where are you taking me?" Dario asked.

The shaman glanced skyward and said, "To the treasure." He turned to look at Dario, his gaze penetrating. "That is what you want, isn't it?"

Uncomfortable under the man's scrutiny, Dario didn't meet his eyes. "Of course. What do you think?"

The other man considered him for a moment. He didn't

appear afraid. *Stupid pendejo,* Dario thought. *He doesn't realize he'll be dead before the sun rises.*

The shaman nodded. "Follow me. It's not far."

"Good. I don't have time to fuck around."

The two men walked back to the stone steps, but instead of descending, the shaman turned left and disappeared into a vine-covered thicket.

Hurrying so that he wouldn't lose him, Dario ripped apart the vines and stepped through.

A faint path was the only route visible through the heavy vegetation. Cursing the shaman and his own stupidity, he followed the trail, angrily pushing past the vines and other plants in his way.

After several yards, Dario stopped to catch his breath. The shaman was nowhere in sight. Furious at being deceived, he turned back. A second later, the other man appeared. Relieved, but still fighting his anger, Dario waved the barrel of his rifle at him.

"Stay where I can see you."

The shaman's expression betrayed no emotion other than idle curiosity, giving Dario the impression that death was not a threat to the man. He'd have to figure out a threat that *would* mean something.

"This way," the man said, and walked away.

Cursing under his breath, Dario followed him.

A short while later, the vines thinned, revealing a small clearing surrounded by stone. Dario scanned the perimeter and noticed a shadow between two boulders near the far end. He nodded at it and asked, "Is that it?"

The shaman nodded. "It is the entrance to a cave. The treasure you seek is within."

Dario studied him for a moment. "Lead the way." He wasn't

about to go in first. Not when he had no idea what lay beyond the opening.

The shaman nodded and struck out across the clearing with Dario in his wake.

Surrounded on three sides by immense stones, the clearing formed a kind of bowl, insulating the place from all sound other than the two men's footsteps.

The silence was unsettling.

A moment later, an owl hooted. Owls were rare in the Amazon. Spooked, Dario looked over his shoulder, expecting to find the ghost of an ancient tribesman. The stories from his childhood came flooding back—tales of gruesome deaths and curses to all who sought Inca gold. A shiver ran up his spine. He shook it off.

Stop being superstitious. The shaman's presence had obviously instilled a measure of fear in him, what with his disappearing and reappearing, and leading him to this odd place.

"There had better be treasure, old man," Dario warned. Calling him an old man brought back a semblance of confidence, even though the man looked like he was in better shape than Dario.

But Dario had a gun.

Recovered from his momentary bout with fear, Dario followed the shaman into the cave. The NVGs lent a greenish hue to the rock walls and ground, but the farther they walked, the more the ambient light diminished. Dario turned on the NVGs' infrared capability, giving him a better view of the terrain.

How the hell did the shaman navigate the cave without night vision? He didn't use a flashlight but avoided obstacles like he could see in the dark.

Dario cleared his throat, the sound echoing in the closed space. "How is it that you can walk in the dark?"

"I've been living in the jungle for a long time. The longer I do, the better my night vision has become."

At that moment, a fluttering sound came at them from behind. The shaman immediately flattened himself against the rock wall and slid to a crouch. The noise grew louder, and Dario turned to see what it was. To his horror, a raucous, writhing cloud of bats appeared, headed straight for him.

He screamed and covered his face with his arms as the bats flew past, heading deeper into the cave. Dozens hit him, and he batted them out of the air. Many dropped to the ground, dead. Some recovered and flew off. Dario fell to his knees, but he was too late. More bats came, relentlessly filling the air with high-pitched squeaks and flapping, leathery wings. Dario crouched, shielding his face and head, and waited them out.

They had to stop sometime, didn't they?

After several minutes, the last of them flew past. Not convinced they were finished, Dario remained on the ground. The shaman tapped him on the shoulder.

"You can get up now."

Dario climbed to his feet, but when he tried to look through his goggles, he couldn't see a thing. He took them off and slapped the sides, then checked the battery, hoping they'd start working again. Nothing helped. The bats had ruined them.

"Fuck." Dario threw the goggles to the ground, disgusted with their failure. He'd thought they were military grade.

Obviously not.

His anger boiled into rage, and he kicked furiously at the pile of dead bats on the ground.

"Fucking flying rodents." Dario retrieved his flashlight and turned it on. A weak beam illuminated the shaman. Of course. The batteries were running low. He turned it off. He'd need it for the way back. The shaman would no longer be with him. Not after they found the gold.

"Here." The shaman handed him the end of a rope. "Hold on to this."

Dario gripped the lifeline. The rope became taut in his hand, but he balked.

"How much farther?" Disoriented, Dario couldn't even see his hand in front of his eyes. Had the man lured him into the cave in order to leave him there? Dario's chest tightened at the thought of dying alone in the dark. He'd kill the shaman before that happened.

"We're almost there."

"I don't believe you." Dario let go of the rope. He raised his rifle and aimed it where he thought the other man stood. "Either you take me to the treasure, or we go back. Now."

"If you wish to go back, then we will go back."

Despite the cave's chill, sweat broke out on Dario's upper lip. He wiped it away. What if he really was taking him to a treasure? They'd already come this far. A little farther wouldn't hurt anything. They'd only changed direction twice during the entire trek through the cave, and Dario had counted his footsteps between each turn, so he felt fairly confident that he'd be able to find his way back with or without the shaman.

"No. If we're close, we will keep going."

"Whatever you wish."

The shaman handed him the end of the rope once more, and they proceeded.

A few minutes later, the shaman stepped up his pace and they rounded a corner.

"Wait here." The shaman handed Dario the rest of the rope and walked away.

"Wait—"

The flare of a lighter illuminated the darkness. A moment later, that flame turned into a larger one when the shaman lit a torch.

"Follow me."

Relieved he didn't have to rely on the shaman's rope anymore, Dario did as instructed. They walked along a narrow corridor, which opened onto a much larger space.

Dario's breath caught as he stared before him. The shaman strode to the center of the large cave and stopped. The light from the torch illuminated mountains of gold: jewelry, masks, figurines, cups, plates, headdresses. The shaman stood next to a solid gold jaguar.

"Is this what you seek?" the shaman asked.

"Oh my God, yes." Dario crossed himself as he staggered to a pile of shimmering gold cups. Stunned by the wealth that surrounded him, he handled every item he could reach, marveling at his good fortune. No one would be able to touch him. He was now one of the richest men on the planet. A deep reservoir of relief bubbled up inside of him, and he started to laugh.

All of the stories he'd heard growing up were true. He removed his pack and set it on the floor. He'd jettison anything he didn't need and fill it with gold.

Unable to stop himself, he raced from one pile of treasure to another, handling each piece as though it would break, his imagination running wild at the price he'd be able to command on the black market.

Sobering, he remembered he wasn't alone. He placed his finger on the rifle's trigger and turned.

The shaman had disappeared.

His guide had stuck the torch inside a tall urn but was nowhere in sight.

Dario searched the room, but the man had disappeared without a trace. Was he lying in wait for him, or had he left, assuming Dario couldn't make it out of the cave? Alert for movement, he made his way to a nearby pile of treasure and filled his pockets. When he had more than he could carry, he went for the torch, intending to use it as long as he could before it burned out. Then, he'd turn on the flashlight to make it to the cave entrance before the batteries died.

He doesn't think I'll be able to find my way back. Won't he be surprised when I find the bastard and kill him?

Better get moving. He didn't want the shaman to get too far or to warn the others.

The gold he'd already picked up would be treasure enough to pay for someone to help move it.

Maybe it would be better to do this himself. That way, no one would know the location, and he could keep the rest of the treasure there, accessing it when he needed the money. Like a bank.

Dario grinned.

Perfect.

He grabbed the torch and lifted. The handle was stuck. Dario moved the wood base back and forth, trying to dislodge it, and finally pulled it free. The urn fell apart, the pottery disintegrating at his feet. Something sharp jabbed him in the thigh.

"Aughhh." Dario looked down. A gold shaft about the size of a pub dart stuck out at a right angle. Blood welled around the insertion point. He grasped the end and tried to pull it free, but searing pain radiated down his leg and he stopped.

"Fuck." He tried to shake off the pain. Luckily, he'd brought a first aid kit. He limped over to where he'd left his pack, but it was no longer there. Dario spun in place, searching for his bag. The bastard had taken that, too.

He'd just have to make his way back to the primary site and get help there.

Dario limped to the other end of the room, intending to leave the way they'd come. As he approached the entrance to the tunnel, there was a far-off clicking sound. Puzzled, he strained to listen, trying to source where it was coming from. Maybe the shaman was still there.

The noise grew louder, surrounding him.

Dario scanned the cave. Movement caught his eye, and he spun in place. In the low light of the torch, the ground between the piles of treasure appeared to churn. He blinked, hard, in an attempt to clear his vision, but it didn't help. The clicking grew louder as the dark mass flowed toward him across the ground.

Dario waved the torch so he could see. Light splayed over thousands of gigantic centipedes undulating toward him.

He whirled around and race-limped toward the tunnel over the insects, their bodies crunching underfoot as he hurled pieces of gold at them, hoping to delay their roiling advance.

They kept coming.

He didn't watch where he was going and tripped over a pile of dead bats, landing face first. He scrambled to his hands and knees, but he was too late.

The first wave of centipedes found him.

43

Thankfully, Martin had quieted somewhat, giving Leine the impression that the hallucinations had stopped for the time being. She checked his wound again.

It looked worse.

"I'm going after Dario and Zolin," she said to Dave. "Martin needs that first aid kit." She stood and grabbed her canteen, preparing to leave. Dario's gunman had left both her canteen and Dave's with them. There was enough left in Dave's for the two men, although Martin hadn't been able to keep much liquid down. "Unless Dario took them both, there's still a pair of NVGs out in the main room somewhere. I'll use the flashlight to find them, and then bring it back." She fastened her canteen to her belt.

"Roger that." Dave gave her a mock salute.

Leine found the night vision goggles on the floor outside the room, returned the flashlight to Dave, and followed the passageway outside. Dawn had broken. The surrounding jungle glowed with a gentle morning light. The birds and monkeys were just beginning to awaken, their calls filling the calm morning air. Leine ignored the heat and unrelenting humidity—

by now she'd gotten used to it. Thankfully, most of the biting insects left her alone. Either that was because she'd doused herself with enough DEET that the chemical had become a permanent component in her bloodstream, or the nasty little buggers were no longer attracted to her body heat.

She reached the steps to the lower site and hesitated. She had no idea where Zolin took Dario. She scanned the area. Some broken vines to her left caught her attention. Curious, she walked over to inspect them and discovered a faint trail. Two pairs of footprints could be seen in the dirt.

Leine followed the prints as far as she could through the heavy vegetation and eventually came to a clearing surrounded by boulders. Movement at the far end caught her eye.

Zolin. She looked, but there was no sign of Dario. Wary, she moved closer to see what he was doing. He swept a path through the dirt with a palm frond, backing up as he did so. He paused in his work and looked up. Their eyes met.

Zolin straightened and tossed the frond away, then headed toward her.

"Where's Dario?" she asked.

"He found what he was looking for."

Leine studied the shaman for a moment. "So should I take that to mean we don't need to worry about him anymore? Or do I need to find him?"

Zolin gave her an enigmatic smile. "We should go back."

Leine nodded at the backpack he wore. "Is that Dario's?"

"Yes."

"Good. Gunnar said there's a first aid kit inside." Remembering the grenade, she slid it from her pocket and held it up. "Can you use this?"

Zolin contemplated the explosive, but shook his head. "That won't be necessary." He looked behind him and added, "The spirits have their way of taking care of things."

Leine followed his gaze. Several vines covered what appeared to be an opening between the base of two boulders. To her, it looked like an entrance to a cave.

She didn't want to know.

"We need to get back." She headed toward the trail. "Martin's not doing very well."

They returned to the crystal room to check on Martin.

Dave took Leine aside. "Where's Dario?"

"He won't be a problem."

Dave nodded, his expression implacable. "Gunnar and Nancy haven't come back yet. I think I should go down there and see what's going on."

"Go. We'll take care of Martin," Leine said. It was obvious by his pallor that his condition had deteriorated. "Be sure to tell her to hurry."

Dave left. Leine found a syringe and a vial of antibiotics in Dario's pack, which she administered to Martin. Without a word, Zolin left the room, returning a short time later with a handful of leaves, which he crushed into a paste and spread on Martin's festering wound. Then he began to chant in an other-worldly voice, burning herbs as he did so.

The doctor's breathing had become more labored, and he moved in and out of consciousness. By the sound of his intermittent rants, the hallucinations had returned. It took both Leine and Zolin to keep him still.

He grew quiet for a time, and they took a break.

"Think he'll make it?" Leine asked, keeping her voice low so that Martin wouldn't hear her.

"It's up to the spirits."

"What were the leaves that you gave him?"

"An antitoxin."

"How effective is it?"

"It's hard to say. If given within six hours of ingesting the poison, survival rates can be upwards of fifty-fifty. But I don't know how long Martin has had the compound in his system."

Martin started to thrash again. "Nancy..." he moaned.

Leine wiped the perspiration from his forehead as Zolin tried to keep him still. "She'll be here soon, Martin. Hold on."

Zolin leaned down to listen to Martin's chest. He straightened, a grave expression on his face. In a low voice he said, "He does not have long." He began to sing a different chant, one that sent chills down her spine.

C'mon, Nancy. She had to get there before her father died. Leine wasn't with her dad when he was killed in action. The pain of not being able to say goodbye never left. Nancy shouldn't have to go through that.

Footsteps sounded in the outer room. Nancy appeared in the doorway, looking the worse for wear. Aside from her sweaty, beet-red face, her clothes were ripped and dirty. When she saw Martin, she rushed to his side.

"Daddy—" She clasped his hand in hers as tears welled in her eyes. "Daddy—I'm here."

Martin stirred. His eyes opened for a brief moment, then closed again. He tried to speak, but could only produce a dry, smacking sound.

"Here," Leine said, handing her a canteen.

Nancy tipped it to his mouth, and he managed to swallow a few drops. She handed it back to Leine. "What happened to him?"

Leine recounted what Gunnar had told her about the poison-tipped bamboo.

She turned back to her father. "Daddy, please don't die." Tears fell freely down her cheeks. "I didn't mean for anyone to get hurt." A deep sob escaped her and she bowed her head.

"It's not your fault." Leine squeezed her shoulder. "You couldn't have known Dario was going to kidnap you."

Nancy raised her head. Misery painted her face. "You don't understand. I—we set up the kidnapping." Sobbing, she wiped her eyes.

"You what?" Leine froze.

"When Dad refused to give me the coordinates to the city, I —I called Austen. We both decided that I should fake my abduction to put pressure on him."

"Austen's involved?"

Nancy nodded. "He hired Herberto to stage the kidnapping. When Dario and his men showed up, I almost didn't go through with it. But the plan had already been set in motion. Too many were involved. I couldn't back out."

Her anger growing, Leine took a deep breath and let it go. Getting mad at Nancy wouldn't help anything. But so many people had lost their lives.

For what?

Nancy turned back to her father. "Daddy, can you ever forgive me?" Choking out a sob, she laid her head on his chest.

Martin opened his eyes. He ran his hand gently through her hair. "Don't worry, Love-bug," he whispered.

"I love you, Daddy. I didn't...I didn't mean for this to happen."

Martin closed his eyes and nodded. "I know." He groaned, wincing from some inner pain. "Tell Austen...it's the frog. The sinchi..."

Nancy frowned. "The blue and yellow one?"

He nodded as he struggled to take a breath. "Taruca told me. The frog is the key..."

Zolin glanced at Leine. "The frog he speaks of no longer exists."

"Are you sure?"

He nodded. "I used to see them occasionally when I traveled through a particular part of the forest west of here. The poison they produce is revered amongst shamans. Taruca taught me how to harvest the special compounds, but warned me to use it sparingly and only in the direst of circumstances, as that particular species was known to be quite rare. But I haven't seen the creature in years. Certainly not since the government allowed drilling in the area."

"Did you hear that, Daddy?" Nancy said. "He says there aren't any more frogs..."

Martin groaned and started to thrash. Zolin held him down to keep him from falling off the bench.

Alarmed, Nancy stared at her father. "What should I do?"

Leine took her arm and gently led her away. "I'm afraid he doesn't have long."

Nancy widened her eyes. "No." She raised her hand to her mouth. "That can't be." A fresh round of tears came. "What have I done?"

With a deep sigh, Leine pulled her in and wrapped her in a hug. Nancy sobbed her grief into Leine's shoulder.

Comfort would be hard to find in the nights to come. Guilt from her part in her father's death and the deaths of the others would eat at her until she either succumbed or found help. Leine had experience with the corrosive power of guilt.

Too much experience.

She held her until Nancy's sobs slowed to occasional tears. At the moment, Martin was resting quietly, but his breath came in short, irregular gasps. The neurotoxin had reached his lungs. It wouldn't be long. Zolin continued to chant in a quiet voice.

Compartmentalizing her own grief at failing to rescue Lou's brother, Leine's mind turned to the matter of moving Martin's body. But Dave hadn't returned yet. They'd need him to help get the body down the cliff.

"Where's Dave?" she asked Nancy. "I assume he came with you."

Nancy pulled away and shook her head. "He stayed below. He said he'd be right up, but wanted to check something."

"Did you talk to Gunnar?"

"No. I didn't see him."

"He left to get you before Dave did." So she'd been wrong about Gunnar. She shouldered the rifle they'd taken from Dario's gunman. "Can you handle things?" she asked Zolin.

Zolin nodded.

"I'm going to find Dave, see if he saw Gunnar."

Something told her he hadn't.

44

"What did you find?" Gripping the sat phone, Herberto paced the marble floors of his home, his excitement building.

"You'll want to utilize whatever contacts you have in pharma," Dave said. "According to Gunnar, they found evidence of the cure."

"And why are you telling me?" Herberto asked, even though he already knew the answer. Although Dave was Austen's man on the ground, he'd gotten wind of a lucrative payday and didn't have a problem going behind his employer's back to make his own deal.

"I think that's fairly obvious," Dave drawled. "You do right by me, and I'll do the same for you."

Herberto stopped pacing. If they'd found a potential cure for Austen's paralysis, the pharmaceutical industry would pay handsomely for the information. The cure for one kind of medical condition could conceivably be used to cure others. He envisioned an auction scenario where the bids grew exponentially.

"How about a five percent finder's fee?"

"I think you need to go a tad higher there, Herbie. Look, I'm taking the bigger risk, by far."

Herberto's hackles rose at the man's familiarity. *Relax. If this pans out, the payday is going to be phenomenal.* "All right, all right. How about we raise it to seven?"

There was a long pause. Herberto wasn't sure if it was because of the delayed response of a satellite call, or because Dave had hung up.

"Are you still there?" he asked, wiping the sweat from his forehead. He had to secure this deal before Dave sold the information to Austen.

"I think thirty sounds about right."

Shocked, Herberto blurted, "Thirty percent? Are you fucking crazy?"

"Aw, jeez, Herbie. I think the satellite's moving out of range. I didn't hear your last transmission."

With a deep sigh, Herberto replied, "Thirty. Yes."

"Great. I'll keep you in the loop, buddy."

"What do you mean? I can't take this to my people if you don't give me the information."

"Well, I would, but I still need to see what Austen comes up with."

Enraged, Herberto stopped himself from slamming the expensive satellite phone on the tile floor and shattering it into a million tiny pieces. *Calm down.* He could always ensure Dave had an accident.

"Fine. Keep me posted. Make certain you remove any loose ends before you leave."

It appeared that Martin was on his way out. The two women Lou Stokes sent were baggage he didn't need. Hugo and the other deaths had been unfortunate, but the price of business. Hired thugs were a dime a dozen. Nancy would be a simple fix.

She could either continue with the ruse and become a celebrated professor at her university, or die.

"That would be an affirmative, Herbie. Don't you worry your pretty little head."

Dave ended the call. Herberto set the phone down on his desk. A fiery anger simmered just below the surface. Dave's demands were pure extortion.

He needed to be taken care of, now.

Herberto drummed his fingers on the mahogany desktop, furiously working through how to stem this despicable betrayal. There was only one thing left to do.

He picked up his other mobile and dialed *El Jefe*.

"What?" demanded the voice on the other end.

"You should know that Dave is going to call you shortly with a business proposition."

"And?"

"He says he has information on the cure."

"Really?" Austen Newell's tone told Herberto he was interested but had decided to play it cool.

"He offered it to me first—for a fee."

"Did he give any indication what this cure might be?"

"Not one word."

"How much did he ask?"

"An exorbitant fee."

Austen chuckled. "He knows I can double anything you agree to."

"But you won't."

"Oh? And why is that?"

Herberto smiled to himself at the ice in the man's tone. He was getting to the billionaire. Perhaps he would be able to wrest fortune from the jaws of defeat.

Time to deliver the *coup d'état*.

"Because I have recorded every conversation with you, Mr.

Newell. Not only that, but I hired a digital forensics investigator to comb through your business dealings. I'm sure the United States government would be quite interested in your Chinese contacts. I doubt you've revealed the full extent of your dealings with the Communist regime."

"Be careful, Herberto." The billionaire's icy tone had turned positively glacial. "I have evidence of your connection to Dario and his drug smuggling enterprise, as well as your failed attempt to kill two United States citizens. Women, no less. I think the State Department would be very interested in my information."

"Is that a threat, Mr. Newell?"

But Austen Newell had hung up.

45

L eine found no sign of Dave or Gunnar outside the tunnel on the lower level. She scanned the jungle below, but didn't see anything. She doubted they'd be inside the site. There wasn't anything there. Had they both left? That didn't seem plausible unless...

She searched her memory for any indication that the two men somehow knew each other. They didn't act as though they'd met before, but that didn't mean anything. Were they working together? If so, who did they work for?

Her earlier suspicions about Dave came flooding back. Lou hadn't replied to her message requesting information on the members of the team he sent to help them, so she didn't have much to go on. And what about Gunnar? Martin seemed to trust him, as did Nancy. But they'd also trusted Hugo, and he'd been working for Dario.

Leine slid on the NVGs and entered the tunnel, walking past the dead gunman they'd first encountered. She continued along the corridor until she came to where it opened up into the larger space. Hesitating, she paused and listened. Her senses heightened, she raised the rifle and eased around the corner.

The space appeared empty. Skirting the jaguar statue, she swept the area, but didn't find anything. She turned back toward the tunnel. Something moved in her periphery. She raised her rifle and aimed. Dave's large frame filled the entrance.

"I've been looking for you," she said, lowering her gun.

"And I've been waiting for you." He casually checked the tunnel behind him. His body language told her he was anything but relaxed. "Where's Zolin?"

Instantly alert, Leine edged toward the jaguar statue. "On his way," she lied. "Martin's not doing well. We're going to need help moving him."

Dave checked the tunnel behind him once more. When he turned back, his hand moved, and something sharp struck her torso.

"What the—?" A sharpened piece of bamboo had embedded itself in her chest.

Shit.

She ripped it free and dove behind the jaguar as the first barrage of rounds from the MP5 ricocheted off the rock floor, barely missing her. A steady stream of bullets pinged off the stone jaguar as Leine sprawled on her belly and returned fire. Dave took cover behind the entrance. He popped out and fired, peppering the base of the sculpture with bullets.

One of them found her. Leine bit back a scream as the searing shock of hot metal dug into her flesh.

Dammit.

Adrenaline-fueled anger and shock muted the pain. The green glow of Dave's face appeared around the corner, and she emptied the Uzi in a volley of gunfire. He dropped back. She low-crawled to the stone bench near the wall, ejected the spent mag, and reloaded.

Silence.

She waited, working to slow her breath.

He didn't come at her again.

Had she hit him?

Grimacing from the pain, Leine pushed herself up off the floor and onto the bench. Alert for movement, she kept one hand on the gun while she explored the wound with the other.

Blood soaked her thigh, but she didn't feel the bullet. She untied the bandana around her neck and cinched it tight above the wound, stanching the flow as best as she could.

She pulled her shirt up to see the puncture wound. How long before the neurotoxin paralyzed her respiratory system?

Dave still hadn't shown himself.

Who was he working for? Obviously not Lou.

Austen? Herberto?

Too many questions. She had to get back to Zolin. He'd mentioned that the first few hours were critical for the antitoxin to work. She pushed herself to stand. Pain radiated through her leg, stealing her breath.

Had Dave left her there to die, intending to kill the others?

She took a step and her leg buckled. Blindly, she reached for the bench, averting her fall. Standing the rifle on its barrel as a makeshift cane, she tried again.

This time she was able to hobble a short distance before she had to stop and regroup. Her range of vision tunneled, then widened, then tunneled again.

She was losing consciousness. Either she'd lost more blood than she thought, or the poison was already taking effect.

Exhausted from the effort, she stared at the entrance, willing herself to keep going.

"You can do it, Leine," she told herself. "Just get to the tunnel."

She made it a few more steps before she had to stop. Black spots appeared before her eyes. Struggling to remain upright, she took another step.

The floor rose to meet her as everything turned black.

LEINE STRUGGLED TO THE SURFACE, THEN DROPPED BACK INTO THE deep. She was swimming in a sea of viscous liquid.

No. That wasn't right.

She was flying through the air.

Where was she? She floated above her body, looking down. Oddly, there was no pain.

Hadn't she been shot? She should feel something.

Shouldn't she?

Had the neurotoxin already spread? Is that why she couldn't feel her legs?

The cave shifted and morphed into Santa's living room. But she wasn't there—she was in South America.

Right?

Zolin appeared before her and offered her a drink. Although she didn't understand what he said, his muted voice held a reassuring tone, so she took a sip before dropping back down into the void.

Like falling down a rabbit hole.

Suddenly, she was surrounded by dozens of rabbits. Dozens turned into hundreds, then thousands. Like computer generated replications. All of them with round, pink eyes.

Echoes of laughter filled her mind, and it took some time to realize it was her laughing. Which made her laugh even harder. Vibrant color filled her vision, and the rabbits disappeared. Swirls of fire engine red, royal blue, sunflower yellow, and dark, forest green cascaded before her. The colors were sound.

She was *seeing* sound.

She raised her hand to her face, marveling at the intricacy of her veins. Her fingernails began to stretch and grow, then became the roots of a giant ceiba tree.

She *was* the tree. The energy within the trunk astounded her. As strong as a hydroelectric dam, she rode the wave to the sky.

A low, menacing growl broke the vision and she plummeted to earth. She turned to meet the piercing yellow eyes of a jaguar staring her down, its tail swishing erratically behind it, the body poised to spring. It opened its mouth and said something she couldn't understand.

It disappeared.

She found herself in a long hallway filled with dozens of mirrors. Something moved and she spun in place, trying to catch sight of what had captured her attention, but the mirrors only reflected her face. She reached for her pistol but came up empty. She tried to touch the glass, but the mirror melted, turned into water, and gushed to the floor.

Leine looked up and came face-to-face with an old enemy— the Frenchman. A gaping black hole filled his eye socket. Orange smoke drifted lazily upward, dispersing in a gentle breeze. The Frenchman disappeared, and another man she'd killed years before took his place. His neck boasted a bloody red gash where she'd slit his throat. He opened his mouth as if to speak, but someone else shoved him out of the way.

Soon, dozens of kills from Leine's early life as an assassin appeared, leering at her with rage and bloodlust in their eyes. Leine blinked to clear the vision, but still they came, surrounding her, closing in.

"Leine," someone said.

She whirled to look behind her, her heart leaping at the familiar voice. Warmth radiated through her body.

"Carlos. Is it really you?" Her voice echoed in the empty chamber, sounding strange to her ears. She reached for him, but he dissolved. Her heart thudded in her chest and she glanced down. She could see her heart through her shirt, pumping as it should, and marveled that it could still be in one piece.

Santa appeared and she smiled. He pointed to her beating heart.

"See?" he said, returning her smile. "It works, just like I told you."

She was about to answer him, but a searing pain rocketed up her thigh and she gasped. She looked down to see vines wrapping themselves around her leg, then climbing upward, covering every inch of her body. She tried to move her arm, but it wouldn't budge.

"What the hell?"

An indigenous woman with flowing black hair and dressed in shades of green and brown materialized before her. Another wave of warmth flooded Leine.

"I'm dying, aren't I?" she asked. Not answering, the other woman touched her finger to her own lips before she shimmered and disappeared.

In her place, Martin appeared. Sadness etched his face.

"Martin. You're still alive." She tried to touch him, but he shook his head.

"I had to save Nancy," he said. Sadness radiated from him in waves, hitting her full force. Behind Martin, Austen grinned and nodded. "He'd do anything for her."

There was something about the billionaire that didn't seem right. His eyes were too far apart. Or maybe it was his clothes. They didn't fit. He shimmered and disappeared, leaving nothing but wisps of smoke.

Overcome by exhaustion, Leine closed her eyes and slept.

46

April returned from her circuit around the camp's perimeter to check on Mateo. Esme sat on a partially melted plastic chair next to his hammock, darning clothes. She'd been a big help to April, scavenging items from the camp rubble and making sure April drank enough water and ate something.

"Go ahead and take a break, Esme," April suggested. "I've got this."

Esme nodded and stood. "We're running low on water. I'll fill up the jugs and bring them back here."

April leaned her rifle against the upright. "Be careful." She checked her watch. Her mother and the rest of the rescue party had been gone a long time. Too long. She itched to go after them.

She glanced at Mateo. Although his coloring had improved and he seemed to be on the mend, she didn't feel comfortable leaving Esme in charge. She was a lovely woman but didn't know how to fire a gun with any accuracy.

She sighed. She'd have to wait a while longer.

"What are you thinking about?" Mateo asked.

Startled, April smiled. "I didn't know you were awake."

"Well?"

"Well what? I wasn't thinking anything in particular."

"Right." He rolled his eyes. "You want to go after them, don't you?"

April shrugged, nodded. "They should have at least sent word by now." She stared into the jungle. "I've got a bad feeling."

"Didn't you tell me your mother was—what did you call her —a badass?"

April allowed herself a tiny smile. "I did."

"Then she will take care of herself. I *know* my father can." He reached for her hand. She put hers in his and grinned.

"All right, Mr. Sunshine. I'll believe you. This time."

Their gazes locked. April resisted the urge to kiss him. She could lose herself in his eyes.

"Would you—" Mateo began. He looked uncomfortable.

Concerned, April stepped forward. "Are you in pain? Can I do something?" She started to change the position of his pillow, but he waved her away.

"No. I'm fine. I was going to say...would you ever consider staying?"

"You mean here? In the Amazon?"

Mateo looked down. "I know, I know. It's not Los Angeles. Let's forget I even asked."

"Hold on. What would I do? I'm not going to play house, if that's what you're getting at." What was he proposing? Her mother's warning about South American machismo came back with a vengeance. She had zero desire to become some man's appendage.

Ever.

His cheeks flushed red. "No, of course not. When my father returns, I—I'm going to ask him to train me in the ways of the forest. You said you were interested. If you like, I will ask him to consider training you, also."

"Oh." She didn't know what to say. She'd watched Zolin with fascination as he performed ceremonies and healings, and remarked several times that she'd like to learn. But what Mateo was suggesting would mean not only that she remain in South America, but she'd specifically live in the jungle. She'd be giving up a comfortable life and a lucrative career as an instructor at the SHEN academy. Not to mention she wouldn't see her mother very often.

Still, it was an intriguing idea.

Mateo's smile vanished and he turned his head. "Did you hear that?"

Instantly alert, April scanned the surroundings. "No, what?" It was too early for Esme to have made it back from the river.

"Shh." He put his finger to his lips. They both strained to hear.

Someone was coming.

April picked up her rifle and moved quietly toward the source of the sound, hoping to see her mother. A figure broke through the palms surrounding the camp.

"Gunnar." Swallowing her disappointment, April lowered her rifle.

He strode to her and stopped. "Martin's been hurt. I came back to get the first aid kit."

"Where's my mother? Is Dario still alive?"

"Your mother's fine." He started to walk back to the camp. "Martin's been poisoned."

"What about Dave and Nancy?" she asked, noting that he didn't answer her question about Dario.

"They're both fine."

April stopped. Her mother's knife was tucked in his waistband. Leine would never willingly give up her knife.

Gunnar turned to see why she hadn't followed.

She aimed her rifle at his chest. "Why are you alone? What happened to the others?"

Gunnar put up his hands. "Wait a minute. We're on the same side, remember?"

April narrowed her eyes. "Are we? Why do you have my mother's knife?"

He lowered his arms. "Look, I don't know why you're being paranoid, but I need the first aid kit, now."

"You didn't answer my question. Where's Dario?"

"Your mother went to search for him. She hadn't come back by the time I left."

"What about Nancy? And Martin?"

Something shifted behind his eyes. *He knows something.*

"Why do you have my mother's knife?"

Gunnar sighed. With a shrug, he said, "She let me take it in case I ran into Dario's men."

"Bullshit."

"Give me the gun, April." He took a step toward her.

Her finger firmly on the trigger, April stood her ground. "Don't come any closer. I *will* shoot you."

Gunnar scoffed. "No you won't." His eyes snapped with anger and he moved in. April sidestepped his advance and spun as he reached behind him for the knife.

April fired.

The report echoed through the jungle. A flock of parrots launched in unison from a nearby tree.

Gripping his chest, Gunnar staggered toward her before he dropped to his knees. A red stain blossomed on his shirt. His face ashen, he stared at April. "Why did you do that?"

April nodded at the knife in his hand. "Because you lied."

A moment later, Gunnar was dead.

47

The dull, throbbing ache woke her.

Leine forced her eyes open and looked around. She was lying on the stone bench next to the wall in the cave on the lower level. Nancy sat nearby, a flaming torch flickering beside her.

Leine raised her head, and the room spun. She took a deep breath, trying to right her world. Her temples pounded as though she'd been trampled by a herd of buffalo.

The dull ache came from her chest.

"Nancy." The word stuck in her desiccated vocal cords, coming out in a croak.

Nancy immediately came to her side. "You're back. Oh, Leine." She called out, "Zolin—she's awake."

A few moments later, Zolin appeared. He shined a flashlight in her eyes, checking her pupils. "How do you feel?"

Leine attempted to get up. Zolin and Nancy helped her to a sitting position.

She waited for the room to stop spinning before she replied. "All right, I think."

Zolin offered her his canteen, and she took several sips.

When she finished, she wiped her mouth and locked eyes with him. "What the *hell* did you give me?"

Zolin raised his eyebrows at the intensity of her tone. "Ayahuasca."

"That explains the visions." Her anger spiked. Where did he get off giving her a psychotropic drug without her consent? "Why on earth did you give me ayahuasca?" *Calm down, Leine. He did it to help you.* She really hated not being in control. Giving her a drug that induced hallucinations was the epitome of losing control.

Zolin gave her a serious look and took her hand. "When the antitoxin didn't have any effect, I realized something very serious was obstructing your healing."

"And?" What the hell was he talking about?

Nancy took up the narrative. "You should have seen him, Leine. He went into a trance and spoke to the jungle spirits. I've never experienced anything like it. It sent chills down my spine, it was fascinating. I just wish—I wish Dad could have been here."

Forgetting Zolin for the moment, Leine turned her attention to Nancy. "I'm so sorry, Nancy. Is he—?"

Tears welled in her eyes as she nodded. "He is." She took a ragged breath. "He died doing what he loved. I'm just so sorry..." A sob escaped her, and she buried her head in her hands.

Zolin continued. "When you didn't return, I came to find you. You were on the ground at the entrance to the tunnel. You'd lost some blood, but that wouldn't have explained your other symptoms."

Memories of shooting at Dave flooded back. "Dave tried to kill me."

He nodded. "He's dead. He'd been shot multiple times."

"So I did hit him." She closed her eyes and took a deep breath, then let it go. "So how did you know I'd been poisoned?"

"You were displaying many of Martin's symptoms. I found the barbed bamboo with blood on the tip and assumed that's what had happened."

"I think I got shot, too, but I couldn't find the round."

"I checked the wound in your thigh. There was nothing but torn flesh."

"A ricochet, then." The old saying *dodged a bullet* flickered through her mind.

Well, sort of.

Zolin closed his eyes and spread his hands, holding them over the crown of her head. After a few minutes, he dropped his arms to his sides and looked at her intently.

"How do you feel?"

"I'm good." She did feel pretty decent for having been poisoned and shot at. She raised her shirt to get a look at the puncture wound. A sticky paste covered the bamboo dart's entry site.

There was still a high probability of infection.

"So what was this serious thing you said was affecting me?"

Zolin leaned closer. His gaze bored into hers. "I sensed a shadow on your soul. The ayahuasca called on your spirit animal to consume it for you."

"My spirit animal?" *Okay, this is getting weird.*

Zolin nodded.

The solemnity with which he said the words told Leine he was dead serious. In deference to his beliefs, she tamped down the sarcastic remark that sprang to her lips. But then the memory of what she saw during her hallucination came back with a vengeance.

Carlos. Santa. A jaguar. Rabbits.

Rabbits?

She struggled to her feet. Zolin wrapped his arm around her

shoulders to help her stand. She put weight on the affected leg, but her knee buckled.

Zolin eased her back onto the bench. "Your body is weak from the poison."

Shit. Climbing down the cliff was going to be a tough proposition. If only there was another way.

"Did Dave still have the sat phone on him?" she asked the shaman.

He nodded.

"I sent a message to Lou," Nancy added, "but we haven't heard back yet."

"When's the last time you checked?"

"About an hour ago."

"Check again." Being stuck in the Amazon with an open wound or two was a recipe for disaster. Not discounting Zolin's healing ability—he had brought her through the worst, and for that she was grateful—Leine leaned heavily toward modern medicine when it came to serious issues. "And, if you could, try contacting April to tell her we're all right." She recited the number. Nancy repeated it back before she retrieved the phone from Dario's pack and disappeared down the tunnel.

Mild curiosity pushed her to ask the shaman, "What's this 'shadow' on my soul that you alluded to?"

The flickering light created by the torch intensified Zolin's already penetrating gaze.

"I've only seen it once before," he said. "In a man I treated many years ago. The 'shadow of a thousand deaths,' he called it. An appropriate name."

Leine searched his eyes. "And what happened to this man after you treated him?"

"I don't know. He left in the middle of the night and I never saw him again." He sighed, remembering. "You reacted differently. Once the ceremony concluded, I sensed a stronger energy waiting to replace it."

"My spirit animal?"

He nodded. "Yes. You must think of this spirit's presence as a gift. It's up to you how to use its energy."

"May I ask—which animal is it? I saw several during my little trip through the light fantastic."

Zolin cocked his head, a puzzled look on his face. "The jaguar, of course."

"Just checking." She was inordinately relieved he hadn't said rabbit. An odd reaction for someone who didn't believe in the spirit world. Leine chalked it up to the residual effects of the ayahuasca.

"So, basically what you're saying is now I have the shadow of a jaguar on my soul?"

For the first time since she'd met him, Zolin smiled. "That would be an accurate assessment, yes."

"Just so we're clear."

A short time later, Nancy raced back to tell them she'd received a message from Lou.

"He's sending a helicopter." Out of breath, she leaned over and put her hands on her knees.

"Did you reach April?"

She nodded. "She was worried, but I told her you were going to be fine." She studied Leine. "You are going to be fine, right?"

"Of course." Leine started to get up, but Nancy stopped her.

"I told Lou you'd been wounded and needed help," she said. "They're going to fastrope down and airlift you out."

"I'm going to need to be outside when they get here."

"Then Zolin and I will help you." She sized Leine up. "We could carry her, couldn't we?"

"Yeah. That's not going to happen," Leine said, her annoyance obvious. "I can walk."

Nancy and Zolin exchanged looks.

Leine scowled. "I'll be damned if you two are going to carry me out of this cave. Hand me the AK."

Zolin gave her the rifle. Using it as a makeshift cane, she limped toward the tunnel, then stopped. The weakness she felt annoyed her, putting her in a seriously bad mood. *Mind over matter, Leine. If you don't mind, it doesn't matter.* Where the hell was this jaguar energy when she needed it?

She took a deep breath and let it go before she glanced at them over her shoulder. "Are you two coming or not?"

48

Austen Newell ended the call, took the SIM card out, and destroyed it before tossing it in the trash. The voice on the other end of the line had assured him that Herberto would no longer be a problem.

With that small piece of business taken care of, he wheeled over to the bar to make himself a celebratory drink. Martin's daughter, Nancy, was scheduled to come in that morning with important news.

He took his drink and rolled out onto the balcony, where he could see Central Park. He was too high up to hear much traffic, although he did kind of miss that. The pulse and beat of the city made him feel alive, which had been an epic shift in his mind-set. After he'd contracted the organism that caused his paralysis, the natural world had ceased to inspire him. He'd felt betrayed by the one thing he thought would always sustain him: nature.

His earpiece chimed. "Yes?"

"Mr. Newell, I have a Nancy Stokes here to see you."

"Send her up."

He rolled back into the office and stopped at his desk, where he pressed a button under the lip of the desktop, buzzing her in.

She walked through the door and set her purse on the chair, then removed her coat and gloves and draped them over the back.

"Thank you for seeing me," she began.

"Of course. I'm so sorry about your father. Martin was a good man."

She stared at him for a moment before she nodded. "Thank you."

Austen waved to a settee near the fireplace. "Sit down, please." He guided his chair so that he was directly across from her and clasped his hands in anticipation.

"You have information for me?"

Nancy sat on the settee. "I do." She waited a beat.

"And? It's good news, I hope."

She took a deep breath and let it go. "As you know, we found few recoverable artifacts, although I wouldn't have disturbed the sites we explored, regardless. We did find one thing."

"And that was?"

"The cure mentioned in the manuscript."

Austen's mood soared. He'd be able to walk again. Everything he'd done over the years had led to this one, shining moment. After hearing news of Dave's and Gunnar's deaths, he'd been plunged into despair, assuming the cure was lost.

He smiled. "That's fantastic news. Tell me more." She didn't look happy. The loss of her father must have hit her harder than she let on. A tinge of guilt fluttered in his belly. He ignored it.

What was done was done. Neither he nor Nancy could have foreseen the tragedies involved in their search for the lost city. If he was honest, had he been able to do things differently he probably wouldn't have.

Great discoveries sometimes required great sacrifice.

"In the manuscript, there is a brief mention of a blue and yellow frog."

Austen nodded. "I know of it." He'd practically memorized the conquistador's writings.

"It's known as the sinchi frog."

"Sinchi is the Inca word for strong health."

Nancy gave him a vague look. "Yes."

He gestured for her to continue.

She cleared her throat. "The sinchi frog is only found in a particular region of Peru."

"The Amazon?" Austen smiled encouragingly.

She nodded. "Yes. It's in the same family as the golden poison dart frog, many of which can be found throughout the region."

"And this frog is the cure?" He wished she would hurry up so that he could start the ball rolling to locate the frog. He'd have people send a specimen to his lab in Virginia so they could work around the clock to replicate the compound.

"According to the shaman we worked with, yes."

"But that's amazing news. Why so glum?" Austen's mood had gone from excited to ecstatic. Not only would this discovery add to his vast wealth, but he'd be able to pursue his love of adventure once again in the flesh.

She caught and held his gaze. "Austen. I'm so sorry. All signs point to the frog being extinct."

The words fell like an anvil between them. Stunned, Austen tried to spin what she'd just told him into something positive, but failed. "How do you know?"

"The Peruvian government confirmed they'd submitted the data listing it as extinct to the Ministry of Agriculture. There's been no trace of the sinchi frog for over seven years."

His mind raced. There had to be a way to locate at least one of the creatures. He couldn't have come so close just to have it ripped from his grasp. "Give me the coordinates. We'll blanket the area with a search party the likes of which has never been seen. We can find a specimen. I *know* we can."

"Austen." Nancy shook her head. "You can't. The area is an oil and timber concession leased to a Chinese firm."

Austen stopped cold. "Which Chinese firm?"

Nancy typed something into her phone. "The Shenyang Petrochemical Corporation."

The blood drained from Austen's face. It couldn't be. Seven years before, Austen Newell Enterprises, Inc. had brokered the concession between the Peruvian government and Shenyang Petrochemical. At the time, he'd been paid several million dollars for his services by the Chinese-owned company.

It wasn't enough.

"Austen, what's wrong?" Nancy rushed to his side. "Are you all right?"

Austen shook his head, despair hitting him like a two-ton slam to the gut.

He'd brokered away his life.

49

Los Angeles

Leine put the last of the silverware away. It was strange living in April's apartment without her there. With a sigh, she lassoed her wineglass and took a sip.

Santa had made one of her favorite dinners—*cochinita pibil* —to welcome her back from the Amazon.

"Thinking about April?" Santa asked, studying her over the rim of his glass.

She nodded. "I just hope she stays safe."

"I give her six months before she's back in LA."

"I don't know." She shook her head. "You didn't hear the conviction in her voice when she told me she was staying. She really wants to make a difference."

"That may be, but remember how she sounded when she told us she wanted to be a novelist? How long did that last?"

"A year."

"And now she wants to become a shaman? Shit, Leine. That's some intense stuff that takes *years* to master, and there's no guar- antee she'll be accepted if she does." He shrugged. "I hope she's finally found something she can stick with, but did she have to choose something that difficult?"

"Don't forget dangerous and not exactly in tune with the modern world. Where is she supposed to practice?"

Santa put his glass down and stepped closer to Leine. "Let's change the subject. Did you enjoy dinner?" His tone had dropped into seduction territory.

"It was definitely tasty." She held up her glass in a toast.

Santa smiled and pulled her to him. "I know what else is tasty." He leaned in to nuzzle her neck.

Leine gently pushed him away. "Again? This afternoon almost killed me," she chided. Given the intensity of their earlier lovemaking session, they'd obviously missed each other. But Leine needed time to herself. "How about a raincheck?"

Santa's intense gaze locked on hers, leaving her feeling like he'd stripped her soul bare. "No worries." He stepped back, breaking the connection, and picked up his glass. "So how's Nancy doing?"

"As well as can be expected, I guess. She applied to work for a non-governmental agency that works toward stopping the destruction of the rainforest."

"She quit the university?"

"Can you believe it? Gave up her position, her tenure, the works. Her role in Martin's death obviously did a number on her."

"As it should." Santa studied her. "There's someone else who had a number done on her. Something happened to you down there. You're calmer, more settled."

Leine shrugged. "I think I finally let go of some things."

"Does this 'letting go' have anything to do with the drugs that shaman gave you?"

"Maybe. I don't know. I need time to think."

"You're not going to make a habit of tripping out on

ayahuasca, are you? I mean, I get that it's the 'thing' to do in
SoCal, but it's still a psychedelic."

She smiled. "You know me better than that. Since when did I
ever intentionally do anything where I wasn't in control?"

It was Santa's turn to smile. "How silly of me." He drained
his glass and set it on the counter. "How's Lou doing?"

Leine sighed. Lou had taken the news of his brother's death
hard. "Devastated. Losing family is awful, especially with how
close they were. He'll get through it, probably by throwing
himself into work."

"Just like someone else I know." He gave her a long, slow
kiss. "See you around," he said, and left.

Leine walked over to the desk April had set up in a corner of
the living room and booted up her laptop. She entered her pass-
word and clicked on an encrypted file labeled *Pictures*.

The screen populated with dozens of gruesome photographs
of the trafficking scum she'd neutralized over the years.

She scanned the images on her self-described Kill Wall.
Interestingly, they no longer evoked the pain or rage she'd felt
when she'd captured and killed the guilty. She opened a utility
program that would scrub the pixels from a selected file, then
dragged the Kill Wall over and dropped it in. A moment later, a
message popped up on the screen:

Files permanently deleted.

Leine closed the laptop and shut off the living room lights
before heading into the bedroom. Exhausted, she shed her
clothes and slid into bed.

She didn't remember falling asleep.

ALSO BY D.V. BERKOM

ACKNOWLEDGMENTS

I have several people to thank for helping make this the best book possible: early readers Michelle and Brian Yelland, Jennifer Conner, Ali Mosa, and editors Ruth Ross and Laurie Boris - thank you for reading subsequent drafts and for all your great comments - this book would be a hot mess without your amazing input; to TSODA134 - the time and effort you've spent helping to make my books more realistic has been a godsend, especially in regard to weapons and operations. I'm eternally grateful that you made me take that damned Zumba class ;) to Bruno De La Mata and Dennis Hursh for reading an early draft and giving me great insight into Peru and the Amazon; to my awesome advance reader team—you guys outdid yourselves. Thank you, thank you, thank you.

And last, but definitely not least, to first reader and best friend Mark Lindstrom for his unwavering love and support, and so many kickass dinners. You're the best.

Writing a novel is never a solitary endeavor.

ABOUT THE AUTHOR

DV Berkom is the USA Today bestselling author of two action-packed thriller series featuring strong female leads: Leine Basso and Kate Jones. Her love of creating resilient, kick-ass women characters stems from a lifelong addiction to reading spy novels, mysteries, and thrillers, and longing to find the female equivalent within those pages.

After years of moving around the country and skipping off to locations that could have been movie sets, she wrote her first novel and was hooked. Over a dozen novels later, she now makes her home in the Pacific Northwest with her husband, Mark, and several imaginary characters who like to tell her what to do.

Her most recent books include *Shadow of the Jaguar*, *Dakota Burn*, *Absolution*, *Dark Return*, *The Last Deception*, *Vigilante Dead*, and *A Killing Truth*. Currently, she's hard at work on her next thriller.

***Go to dvberkom.com to join DV's exclusive Readers' List and be the first to know about new releases and subscriber-only offers.